ACKNOWLEDGEMENTS

Thank You:
God, for allowing me to create another project.
Leslie Swanson, for your continued support.
Sean G, my brother that God has given me.
My circle of friends for their support.

This joint is for the fellas and all the brothers out there with slashed tires, busted windshields and mad drama.

Big Ups to Dave Hollister, The Brat, Syleena Johnson, R. Kelly, Twista, Kanye West, Sean G, WGCI, V103, Power 92, Melanie Palmer, Nicole Logan, Farrah Ellison, Kelly Williams, Myrtle Rycraw Jackson, Wanda Smith, The Lowery Family, The Smith Family, My sisters, Lynette Smith {My big sis}, Pops, The guys on the block (Sangamon & Peoria), The Thomas family, Lisa Thomas, The Gandy family, The Allen Family, Donnell Jones, Terisa Griffen, Ahni, Tim Hardaway, Meechie and the Barbers at Imperial Kutz in Calumet City, Dixie's Kitchen in Lansing Illinois, Common, Sistah Souljah, Travis Hunter, Eric Jerome Dickey, E. Lynn Harris, Michael Baisden, Wahida Clark, Brenda Hampton, Carl Weber, Maxine Thompson, Drennon Jones, Nicole Logan, Alexia Le Day, Pistol Peete and Felicia Hurst, Black Pearl Books.

RIP-Grams (Ginger), Keith Jackson, Jeff Allen, Mark Groves

A Huge Hug and Kiss for all my readers. I am nothing without your support!

STILL CRAZY

← A Darrin Lowery Novel →

Black Pearl Books Publishing
WWW.BLACKPEARLBOOKS.COM

♦ CHAPTER ONE ♦
THE HOMECOMING

KEVIN ALLEN

They say that you can't go home again. In my case, I didn't want to, and perhaps, I never should have. I am here in intensive care at Mercy Hospital, and I may not make it because I let my dick get me into trouble. I stand 6, 3 and 240 pounds of solid muscle. With all the weight lifting that I do, I sometimes forget that I'm not invincible. Something as tiny as a bullet can help jog a brotha's memory back quick as hell. I'm losing blood fast as a team of white people wheel me from my room in the hospital, to the operating table.

As they move me as fast as they can down the hall, all I can seem to focus on are the lights overhead. They are almost bright enough to blind me, and with the fast motion to the operating room, the lights have a dizzying affect on my head. Being shot is already a pain in the butt. Being shot and dizzy, is just plain cruel. Someone should do something about that. My eyes were getting heavier and heavier, and I heard people yelling at me to stay awake. I wish I could help them, but I am just…so…damned…tired.

I woke up in a deep sweat. I looked around and checked myself for a bullet hole and there was none. I looked over at my wife who was still sleeping in bed with me. She was sound asleep. This was the third time this week that I had this dream and I couldn't figure out why. The drama with my ex-girlfriend is over. So why is it that I can't sleep? I got up to get a drink of water. I then went to the bathroom to splash water on my face. I sat on the toilet with my head in my hands wrought with guilt. I looked at my wife who was still in the bed, and I thanked God for her. She has been so understanding this year, and I feel so guilty for all the things I put her through recently. I feel so guilty that I may never have a peaceful night of sleep again, ever in life.

A FEW MONTH'S EARLIER…

I'm an author. A few months ago I began suffering from some serious writer's block. I had a major deadline coming up and nothing on paper. This was the last book to be written under my current contract. That means that I stand to make an even bigger deal with my own publishing house, or something ridiculously huge on the open market from competing publishing houses. That is, if I can get this last book completed. To not get it done means a breach of contract, the possibility of my getting sued, and rumors starting that I no longer have the edge needed to be one of the top African-American authors. Once that mess gets started, there goes my career, my house, and my luxury lifestyle. As the deadline approached, I began to doubt myself and my abilities. I also began to argue more with my wife, Tamara. We were already arguing a lot lately over bills, not enough quality time with one another, and not enough vacations together. Now we were arguing about my writers block and how getting over it is the most important thing going on for both of us right now.

Tamara is a teacher and gets the summers off. I don't have that luxury, which is something that I tell her over and over again when it comes to planning vacations and quality time. She hates my job at times, and most days, I envy hers. She hates the fact that I am always touring, always writing, and always working on marketing my books all year round. I have explained to her a million times that the book deal is not as luxurious as most people think. My first deal was for three books at 3.6 million dollars and a percentage of sales. I got the 3.6 million up front. After taxes, that left me with 2.2 million. A lot of people don't know it, but your marketing and production of your book comes out of the author's cut. To make matters worse, if your book doesn't sell, most of the money that is advanced to you has to be paid back. So I had to bust my ass and make sure that my first book sold enough, so I at least made the money that was given to me. I tour to keep us in the lifestyle that we have grown accustomed to.

I got my book deal shortly after I got married. When I got the deal, I spent $40,000 on a 2004 BMW Z4 roadster for myself. I bought Tamara a Cadillac Escalade that cost $55,000, and I bought us a six bedroom, four bathroom house in Somerton North Carolina. The house was 6000 square feet. It had ten foot ceilings, three staircases, wooden kitchen cabinets, granite countertops, stainless steel appliances, hardwood floors, a two story foyer, Pella windows, a three car garage with side entry, and a third floor that had a world of possibility. It was our dream home. The cost for our dream home was $689,000. That doesn't include electric, taxes, upkeep, maintenance and small things like food, clothes and recreation. In order to keep all this stuff, I needed to write. Not only did I need to write, I needed to write well.

Black folks are funny about their authors. One day we have their full support, the next day, we might not. That's the business. I've tried to tell Tamara everything that I do today counts toward our future. Writing is very touch and go. Times are hard. Some people aren't interested in reading anymore. Some people simply don't have the money to shell out to read a book. Hell, these days a paperback is what, $20. 00?

MEETING MY WIFE

I'm a Chicago guy. I was born and raised on the city's South Side. After I received my Master's degree in Psychology, I went to North Carolina to visit my good friend John Gandy. John had a slamming ass Blues Band, and was going to school to be a Chef. He had the summer off from school, so he and I decided to catch up on things and kick it up in the country. While there, I met this fine ass honey colored sister that later became my wife. I tell you, I was hooked on Tamara from the very first moment that I laid eyes on her.

They say you can never meet your soul mate in a bar or club. They are wrong. You can meet your soul mate anywhere if it's meant to be. My boy John was playing his heart out on the saxophone at the local watering hole, and from across the room I could see Tamara applauding him like she was his lady. My boy was seducing my future wife with his instrument, and I was admiring this vision of beauty from across the room.

Tamara stood five feet two inches tall. She had a body like Jada Pinkett Smith, with just a hint more breast than Jada has. Tamara has dark brown eyes, muscular calves, thighs like an Olympic skater, and short fade like Jada Pinkett wears. There are few sisters that can get away with that cut. Tamara could rock any style that she wanted and from any angle she would still be— breathtaking.

I needed a way to approach her, but was unsure about what I should say. In my home town of Chicago, I would approach her with confidence because Chicago sisters hate weak ass men, or men that seem unsure of themselves. Up here in the Carolinas, women were just the opposite. They equated confidence with arrogance. There was nothing that sisters from the Carolinas hated more than an arrogant ass black man from some big city. I ordered a Rum and Coke for myself and asked the bartender to give me a white zinfandel. I took the two drinks and began to make my way across the room. I ordered the wine because that's all sisters' seemed to drink in the Chi when they listened to Jazz or Blues.

"Hi. I noticed that you had no drink in hand, so I figured that I might bring you one"

"I don't drink"

"Oh. Really?"

"Yes, but thank you for the offer"

"My name is Kevin"

"I didn't ask"

Ouch. That hurt. I started to walk away. Persistence is the key. Kill her with kindness. This is what I thought to myself as I sat there looking crazy with two drinks in hand. I felt so self-conscious standing there. I was hoping to God that not too many people were watching me. Since I already had the drink, I gulped down the zinfandel and chased it with a swig of the Rum and Coke. I then placed the drink on the nearest table.

"So, I was wondering if I could have a few minutes of your time to get to know you a little better…"

"…Are you an alcoholic?"

"I'm sorry…what?"

"Do you have a problem with alcohol?"

"No of course not, why would you say that?"

"The way that you scarfed down that drink, I would think that you had problems with alcohol"

"Well, you said that you didn't want it"

"I didn't want it, but you could have maybe given it to someone else"

"I don't operate like that"

"Like what?"

"I don't try to buy one woman a drink and then move on to another after being turned down"

"Interesting"

"So how does a brother go about getting such a pretty sister like yourself to open up and talk to him?"

"I'm talking to you"

"Yeah, but you aren't giving me a chance to really get to know you" I said with a smile.

"That's not true. Your name is Kevin. You are obviously a city boy from either Chicago, Detroit, or New York. You are presumptuous, and you're an alcoholic" She smiled as she turned her back to me to listen to John play. John was now playing Your Love is King by Sade. I have to admit, my boy was doing it with this damned sax. I wished he would put it down and go back to playing the piano or something. Tamara was rocking back and forth to the music and her rhythmic movements were driving me mad. She had on this all black dress that looked just like the famous white dress that Marylyn Monroe wore when the wind blew it up. Tamara had on three inch heels, and I swear that she had the best looking legs that I have ever seen on a woman in my life. The dress was shorter than the law should allow, and her legs looked like they went on forever. I remember thinking to myself, "If the legs look this nice, I bet the sex is the bomb!" I was staring at her legs and I let out a smile that said I was willing to whatever it took to have a taste. I then heard someone clear their voice and when I looked up, Tamara was looking me dead in my mouth.

"Don't be looking at me like a three piece dinner!"

"I'm not"

"Yeah, you are"

"Well, I'm sorry baby. I just can't help myself. What can I say? You're stunning"

"Kevin, what makes you think that I'm here alone?"

"What makes you think that I care?"

I could feel that South-Side confidence welling up in my chest, and it was hard as hell to keep it under control. This girl was fine as hell and I wanted her. I didn't give a fuck if she was married, a nun, or was promised to a Saudi Arabian Prince. I was going to step to her and try to make her mine. She was going to be my lady even if I had to whip the ass of every country brother in this bar.

The first set was over. John stopped playing and was conversing with his band as they decided what they were going to play next. The Jukebox kicked in and overhead music began to play. Tina Turner's Private Dancer came on. I remember thinking to myself, "What the hell?"

"Did someone have an eighties flashback?" I joked.

Tamara didn't look like she appreciated the joke very much. Seeing my mistake, I decided to correct my mistake.

"Let's dance"

"Yeah, right"

I grabbed her little ass by the arm and brought her to me. She tried to resist, but when she felt the power in my arms, I guess she decided to go with the flow. I was all the way committed now. She was either going to find me charming or she was going to go the fuck off.

"I don't want to dance"

"Girl, come here!"

She cut me a look that said she was not accustomed to taking orders.

I pulled her to me. Her mouth might have said no, but her body was feeling me. As I pulled her up close to me, I held one of her hands in mine and kept the other around her waist like a gentleman. Back and forth we danced. She took in my Drakkar cologne and I took in her Red Door by Elizabeth Arden. The way that we danced, it was obvious that we both had previously taken lessons. She probably took dance at her mother's whim. I took dance because my football coaches said that it would help with my eye-hand-coordination.

I danced with Tamara close to me. I held her in that few minutes like she was mine and like I never had any intention of ever letting her go.

"You are pretty light on your feet"

"Not bad for an alcoholic from Chicago, Detroit or New York"

"So which is it? I mean, where are you from Kevin?"

"I'm from Chicago"

"The Windy City"

"That's right"

"So what do you think my boyfriend will say about your pulling me on the dance floor like this"

"I think—if he's smart, he will politely ask to cut in"

"And your response will be?"

"My response will be, I'm sorry partner, the lady is spoken for—she's with me now"

[laughing] "Oh, so you're just going to gangster me from my man?"

I held her even closer to me. I held her so close that she could feel both my heartbeat and my passion.

"Now that I have you in my arms—I'm never letting go"

I looked her deep in her eyes when I said it. She knew that I was serious. Perhaps the whole day and way that we met was corny. Perhaps to most folks it sounds silly. In that small moment in time, the moment that I looked her in her eyes I knew…I loved her.

We danced every song that was played during the break. I held her close, and by the third song, she held me back. By the fourth song, she smiled a smile that warmed my heart.

"I see that you met my wife's younger sister, Tamara" John said.

"Tamara? What a lovely name"

"Man, you danced with her all this time and you never asked the sister her name?"

"It doesn't matter"

Tamara smiled.

My last name is Allen.

Tamara smiled and said, "Why are you telling me?"

"Because one day you're going to take my last name"

I held her tight and smiled at her. She motioned for the bartender.

"Can I get some service over here?"

"I thought you didn't drink?"

"This is a special occasion"

The bartender walked up and asked, "What will you have?"

Tamara said, "White Zifandel"

I smiled to myself.

John pulled me away from Tamara to talk before the next set began.

"You know... she is here with someone else tonight"

"No shit? Wow"

"So what are you going to do about it?"

"I don't know. What should I do?"

"Maybe leave her your number and let her tell him goodbye"

"Naw, fuck that. Besides, if she is with someone, where is the nigga at?"

John smiled and pretended to take a sip of his drink.

"Her boyfriend is the brother in the red jacket in the corner that is mean-mugging your ass"

I turned and looked at him. It was hard as hell to not break out laughing.

"The brotha with the perm?"

"That's the one. Don't sleep on him. He is in the gym everyday and rumored to carry a piece. This ain't Chicago. This is the south. Let her deal with him. I'll catch up to you later and give her all your info"

"Man, fuck that. If I leave, she's going with me. In fact, that's the plan. When you finish your set, hit me on my cell"

"Still the same ol' G. hunh? A'ight, I will give you a call later. I got your back though if some shit jumps off"

John went back to finish his next set and when I looked up, Tamara was talking with her date. I can't call the brotha her man, because if he was, then he should have spoken up when I was all up on her. I was strapped, but I didn't want to start any shit down here. Besides, I just received my Master's degree. I was here to celebrate. The conversation between Tamara and this other cat looked like it was getting heated, so I figured that I would go and save my future wife from what was obviously a poor choice in men.

"Tamara, let's go for a drive" I said.

"Tamara, who is this nigga?"

"Now that's a word that I would be careful with. My name is Kevin. What's your name brotha?"

"That ain't none of your motha fuckin business!"

"Keith…stop" Tamara interrupted.

"Keith? I had a boy named Keith once. He died a few years back. He was cool as hell though. Anyway, listen partna, I'm sorry that this went down like this. She said that she was here with someone, but I didn't believe her"

"What do you mean you didn't believe her?"

"Well, I was talking to her, flirting with her, and no one stepped up, so I assumed she was alone and simply blowing me off"

"If she was blowing you off, you obviously didn't get the message"

"Naw, I didn't. Anyway, I didn't mean any disrespect, but she's leaving here with me. So why don't I buy you and your boys a round of drinks before we call it a night"

I might as well have been trying to teach deaf brothers to hear. This guy Keith was getting more and more upset, and his boys were clowning him. The louder he got, the calmer I became.

"Nigga, you got to be out of your goddamned mind if you think that you are leavin here with my lady"

"Keith, I'm not your lady. We went out a few times and things just aren't working and…"

Tamara was talking and I had to politely interrupt her.

"Look Bruh, rather than cause a scene and get embarrassed by either her or me, why don't you just call her tomorrow and you and she get some closure then…"

"Excuse me! I speak for my goddamned self, you are about to join his ass and be alone!"

I smiled, and stood quiet.

"I'm sorry sweetheart, my bad. Please…continue"

"Keith, we're done. I am walking Kevin here to his car and in a few minutes you and I will talk and get some closure tonight as to why we can't see each other anymore. I will be back in a few minutes. [turning to me] You—outside"

I followed Tamara outside, and she was fuming the entire way. While she was thinking about choice words for me, I was checking out her ass. She was bodied up so nice that I was thanking God for the opportunity. The more pissed she became, the harder she walked. The harder she walked, the more that ass bounced. She had a walk when she was mad that made people shudder in fear. She is only like 5'2", but that little fine motha-fucka can be a dynamo when she wants to be. I just met her and already I knew she was about to curse my ass out. It would be the first time that she fussed at me. Little did she know that there would be hundreds of times more that she might verbally tear my head off. I didn't mind one bit. That's how sexy my baby is. She turned around to let me have it, and I was all smiles.

"For starters Kevin, I'm a grown ass woman, are we clear?"

"Yes baby"

"I pay my own bills, I run my own life and if you see me beyond tonight, there need to be some ground-rules"

"Ground-rules, got it"

"You don't speak for me!"

"Got it"

"You don't run me, make decisions on my behalf, and you are not to interrupt me like that again"

"Got it. I was just trying to help you out and provide a diplomatic solution to the situation"

"No you weren't. You were trying to find an excuse to pull that nine millimeter out of your back. Either that or you were looking for a reason to start some shit. That tough guy shit, is not cute at all. Neither is your arrogance, or presumptions"

I was shocked. How did she know that I was strapped? She hadn't known me twenty minutes and she already understood my every move. That shit was turning me on.

"Anything else?" I asked.

"No, I guess that's it"

"Are you sure?"

"Yeah, I'm sure"

"Can I get a small peck on the lips to make up for our first fight?"

"A kiss? Are you crazy?"

"I think I'm crazy about you"

"That shit sounds corny"

I took her by the hand and tried to lead her to my car.

"Come on, let's go for a drive"

"Kevin I just met you. I'm not getting in the car with you"

"Then follow me to my hotel. I'm staying at the Hilton. We can have drinks in the lobby and talk"

"I said that I was going back in the bar"

"Fuck Him"

"What?"

"Fuck Him. Come on, kick it with me. You'll have more fun. Besides, you don't need to go backward and retread old ground. Let's move forward"

"You know, you talk a lotta shit"

"Yeah, yeah I do. So, how about it? Follow me to the Hilton"

Tamara looked at me like I was crazy and I gave her one of my million dollar smiles that showed every tooth in my head.

"Please? I promise I'll behave"

Tamara shot me a look that said that I was full of shit. Shortly after that though, she gave me a half a smile which later changed into a full smile. She shook her head as she headed to her car. She knew she would have a better time with me anyway.

Tamara jumped in her Chevy Cavalier, and followed my rental to the hotel where I was staying. We found two large lounge chairs in the lobby and I ordered pizza from a nearby pizza parlor. I ordered drinks from the bar, and we sat in the lobby and talked until the early hours of the morning. We talked about our goals, our dreams, and our values. I got to know her on a level that all couples should get to know one another. That was our first date—pizza at the Hilton. After that, we went on date after date after date, and the next thing that I knew we were married. For a long time, she was my muse. She was the only inspiration that I needed. I went back to Chicago only once, and that was to get my belongings. I decided to make the Carolinas my home. As far as I was concerned, wherever Tamara was, if I was there beside her, that was where I wanted to be.

Initially, we rented a small three bedroom ranch home. It wasn't much, but because we were in love, it was all that we needed. The book deal came right after we got married, so for a pair of newlyweds, we were right on track. I was beaming like a schoolboy when I got the book deal. Tamara didn't even know that I had been shopping for a book deal. I wanted to surprise her with a better life for us. I remember thinking to myself that I wanted to give her everything that her heart desired. Surprising Tamara with our new house gave me the greatest feeling on the inside. The way that I did it was slick as hell.

Tamara and I went on many dates when we were courting. We hit museums, the movies and traveled all over the state. One of our favorite pastimes though was to go house shopping in the more expensive parts of town. The house that we eventually moved in was one that Tamara had always liked. That is why moving into it was so special. The day I received the keys for the house, I came home to our three bedroom ranch, and asked her to go for a drive with me. She didn't know about the book deal yet. She thought that I was still teaching at the local city college. The day that I showed her the house, she was at home cooking her ass off. She was making some smothered chicken in gravy with onion, biscuits, rice and baking a cake. I begged her to go driving with me, and she was insistent that she needed to finish her cooking. I told her to leave the cooking and let's just be together.

I played things off like that day was like any other day. We stopped at the local ice cream parlor for ice cream, we picked up a few items from the grocery store, and then we did our usual ritual of looking at houses in the hills. One by one we drove by the huge houses in Somerton. We went through our normal dialogue. Each time we looked was like the first time. Only this time, I knew we were no longer wishing.

"There is a nice one"

"Oh, and that one is even nicer"

"Wow, Kevin, that one is my absolute favorite"

I pulled the car over.

"What are you doing?"

"Let's go look at it?"

"Kevin, no. If people see us lurking around here, they are gonna phone the police"

"Fuck Em, Let's just get a closer look"

Tamara cut me a look that said she was not going to feed into my bad behavior.

I gave her one of those million dollar smiles of mine.

She shook her head and got out of the car.

I brazenly walked up the walkway.

"Kevin what are you doing?" Tamara whispered.

"I just want to get a closer look and see how people like this are living"

I walked up to the front door and listened to it like a damned prowler.

"Kevin what the hell are you doing?" She whispered.

It was hard as hell for me not to break out laughing. I kept up my charade. I tried the door, which I purposely left unlocked earlier and pushed the door open.

"Kevin!" Tamara whispered loudly.

I walked in.

Tamara stayed outside.

"Kevin? Kevin!" she whispered loudly.

She loved me, but I guess she didn't love me enough to break the law.

I stuck my head out of the door and whispered loudly, "Babe, you gotta come see this!"

"No, Kevin you come out those people's house right now. Kevin? Kevin I'm not playin with you"

"Tamara, come see this"

"Kevin, no"

"I'm not leavin until you come see this" I said insistently.

Tamara tipped up to the door mad as hell and she peeked into the house. There on the floor were roses, wine, a picnic basket and a radio.

"What the hell?"

I handed Tamara a card.

She opened it up and that card only said two words.
WELCOME HOME.

Tamara was stunned.

She looked up at me with tears in her eyes.

"Is this?"

"This is our house babe"

Tamara gave me a look of joy. I gave her one of my award winning smiles. She stood there for a long time stunned. She seemed like she was frozen in place. I lit the fireplace, walked over to her and gave her a hug and a kiss and lead her to the space on the floor. We sat there on our living room floor, and we hugged in front of the fireplace. For a long while we didn't speak. We were both overjoyed. Our long life together was just beginning to get on track. We knew this would be one of many great accomplishments.

"Kevin, what about dinner?"

" I can eat it tomorrow"

"What about the ice cream in the car?"

"Bring it in the house and put it in the freezer"

"We have appliances?"

"We have appliances"

Tamara went and got the ice cream and put it in our refrigerator. She then decided to walk and take a quick tour of the house. I hadn't gotten the furniture yet because I figured she would want to decorate the house. She walked upstairs, downstairs, in the basement and all over the place. She ran in the backyard to get a look at where she would plant her flowers, and she opened every closet and every cabinet in the place. She was giddy like a schoolgirl. It was like watching a young girl decide on the many wonderful things that she could do with her Barbie Dream House. The only thing was, Tamara was not Barbie. After she saw every inch of the house, she was beaming with joy. She came back beside me and began telling me a million different ideas that she had for our house.

Tamara walked back in the kitchen and was telling me that she already wanted to change the color scheme. Her voice echoed from the kitchen. I stayed in the living room by the fireplace.

"I want to change the color to a bright white with a burnt orange trim. I am also thinking that I need one of those racks that suspend the pans in the air. For a kitchen like this we can't have just any cookware. I am going to have to save some money and get some Sabatier cookware. Now that I think about it, we will need new dishes too. Kevin? Baby are you listening to me?"

Tamara headed back to the living room where I was laying on the floor with two glasses of drink poured, naked as the day I was born. She looked at me with shock. I gave her one of my award winning smiles. She returned the smile before she spoke.

"You know, you are nasty"

"I know"

"Why do brothas do that?"

"Do what?"

"Just get naked for no reason, you know how you all do. One moment you're dressed, the next you all are naked as hell sporting a hard on. You should put that thing away, it's dangerous"

"Come here"

Tamara walked over to me with a seductive smile of her own. I stood up and offered her a sip from my glass. I then took her chin in my hand and gently pecked her on the lips. I placed both hands on her waist, and we danced to a rhythm all our own. As we danced, I kissed her eyelids. I then kissed her neck, her cheeks, and her forehead. She held onto me and although no music played, you would have sworn we were two teens and a school dance.

I cupped my wife's ass as I danced with her. I then slowly undid her apron and tossed it to the floor. I kissed her neck some more before pulling off her top. Tamara undid her bra as I kissed her collarbone, back up and down her neck, and beneath her earlobe. I sucked on her earlobe for a while and whispered sweet nothings in her ear.

"You are so beautiful"

I kissed her chest, then took her breasts in each hand, licked them, teased them and sucked them hard and soft before moving back to the nape of her neck.

"I'm such a lucky man. I love you Tamara. You hear me girl, I love you"

I kissed down the front of my woman's body. I kissed her stomach, her ribs, and the space between her breasts. I then kissed her deep on the mouth and slowly undid her pants. I peeled her blue jeans off of her to expose that big round apple-bottom of hers. I palmed her ass before giving it a gentle spank. I hit her ass in an upward motion and felt it do the wave as her backside jiggled.

"All this ass, what's a brotha to do?"

"It's yours to do whatever you want with it" She said seductively.

I laid her down on the floor by the fireplace and began to grind on top of her. I kissed her deeply as I felt the heat between her legs. Her pussy pulsated and my dick throbbed. Up and down and ever so slowly my body snaked up and down my wife's body. I teased her, kissed her and told her over and over again how beautiful and sexy she was. I kissed her collarbone and caressed her between her legs. She opened them and invited me to touch her more. I felt her become moist and I gently moved her panties to the side to expose her moist vagina. I kissed the tops of her breasts, ran wet circles around her nipples and fingered her clit skillfully.

Her breathing became rapid as I fingered her faster and faster. As I fingered her, I kissed down her body. I kissed her inner thigh and drove her mad with anticipation. I teased her with my tongue, kissing her everywhere but where she longed to be kissed. When I felt like she could no longer take my teasing her, I began to slowly tongue and lick her clit. My tongue danced around the tender piece of flesh. Tamara let out a a long sigh as I began to satisfy her orally.

As I licked her clit, I fingered her deeply, alternating paces. I fingered her fast and slow and fast again. Up and down her breasts heaved as I devoured her. Her nipples were erect, her eyes were closed with passion, and she was simply a vision of loveliness. After minutes of my teasing her, Tamara began to cum.

"Aw, shit…oh yeah…right there…aw shit…right there…yeah baby that's it. Aw damn, baby that's it…right there Kevin…Right…there!"

Tamara's body bucked. Her nipples were facing due north and her back arched deeply as she came on my tongue. Before she could gather her composure I rubbed the head of my penis against her pulsating clit. Tamara tried to back away. I held her steady. I teased her for seconds on end before entering her slowly. We both let out a satisfying moan. I then began to take slow even strokes inside of her. My muscles flexed hard as I began to stroke harder and harder from a push up position. Tamara put her legs on my shoulders giving me the angle I needed to go deeper inside of her. I stroked her fast and then slow. I began to kiss her neck again. I used one hand to rub the back of her head and the other to cup and squeeze her ass as I went deeper and deeper inside of her. Over and over again I stroked inside my wife. Minutes later, I came. As I climaxed, my wife rubbed the back of my head and we held one another until we drifted off to sleep.

That was three years ago. That was three stories ago. Now I was at a place in my career where I needed a new book like nobody's business. If I had another bestseller, and I was able to negotiate a major publishing deal, I wouldn't have to worry about money the rest of my life. If I didn't get over this slump that I was in, it means that I would have to either have to go back to school for my doctorate, or go back to teaching. I didn't want to do either. My ritual of complaining about my need to get this deal done was getting on my wife's nerves.

"Babe I've got to think of something. I've got to get this book deal done"

"Yeah you do, because you are worrying the hell out of me with your talking about it all the time. "

"If I don't get this thing done, we are going to be in the poorhouse"

"There is no such thing as the poorhouse"

"Wanna bet?"

"Kevin we'll be fine. I love this house, but I love you more. If we have to downsize, that's cool. If we have to go back to an apartment, it's cool. If we have to tighten our belts and you have to go back to teaching for a while…"

"…That shit is not cool. At least, it's not cool with me" I interjected.

Tamara seemed fine with the way things were and she seemed if she was cool with tightening our belts if we had to. I guess I was the one with the problem. I wasn't ready to give up anything. In fact, I knew what it meant to be poor. There was no way in hell that I was going back to that lifestyle. Tamara could see that I was stressed, so she walked over to me, kissed me on the cheek and began massaging my shoulders.

"Okay baby, I have an idea. I read your other two books and although they are both love stories, the core of each of them seems to stem around Chicago. There are all these wonderful references to Chicago and what the city has to offer as well as that lifestyle. Maybe you need to go back home again for a little inspiration"

I thought about it and smiled. I knew the city like the back of my hand. I never thought I would need to go back to Chicago, to write about Chicago, but Tamara was right. I needed to vibe off my city in order to put a new joint out there.

"Now ya see? That's why I married you. I love everything about you, even the way you think. Going back to the Chi is a good ass idea. So how much time can you get off from work? I was thinking we could …"

"...Whoa cowboy, I said you can go home to Chicago. I have work to do, lesson plans, and state-wide testing for my students. You need to go and get your mojo back"

Laughing I said, "Ain't nothing wrong with my mojo"

"That's not what I heard"

"Girl, quit playin, you know a brother be bringin the thunder"

"I have to admit, last night had a storm-cloud or two, and there was even a little lighting, but if there was thunder, it was the sound of your ass sleeping"

"Aw damn, did you have to cut a brother so deep?"

"Yeah, a sister had to pull your player card a little bit brotha"

"Well I ain't sleepy now"

"Bring it on Cletus, Bring it on"

"Girl, git yo butt on up them stairs"

"You ain't ready for this"

"Naw sister, you ain't ready for this, I'mma have your ass speaking about six different languages in a minute"

"As long as I am saying that I'm cumming, I don't give a damn what language it is"

Tamara and I went upstairs to the master bedroom and we made love over and over and over again (until I fell back asleep).

The next morning I made plans to return to Chicago. I told Tamara that I would be gone at least a month. She said that she would come and see me in three weeks after the state-wide diagnostic testing for her students had begun. I was a little put out that she could let me leave so easily. I guess either she was being supportive of me, or she was tired of hearing me bitch and complain about needing to get this next book out. I jumped on the first plane out of the Carolinas and headed back to my home town of Chicago.

♦ CHAPTER TWO ♦
THE WINDY CITY

Going back to Chicago was a good thing and a bad thing. It was good because I was home. It was bad because I left Chicago to get away from many things. I was happy to have my degree, and happy to be writing as a career. I was even happier that I had the courage to leave the city and make use of my skills elsewhere. The competition in Chicago is steep. The politics in the workplace are ridiculous, and the opportunities to get in trouble are triple that of what they are in the Carolinas.

I landed in Midway airport and the minute I stepped off the plane, I was reminded of how hard it was going to be to stay out of trouble while I was home. Midway

Airport is on the south side of town (the south-west side to be exact). That's my side of town. As soon as I stepped off the plane I saw sistas out there with "C" shaped asses, washboard abs, perky round breasts, and dressed to the nines. Sistas from the Chi knew how to dress and grab a brother's attention. Today was September first. The weather was not too hot and not too cold. The most common outfit on the streets for black women were leather boots or heels, form fitting jeans that accentuated their apple-bottoms, and t-shirts of all sorts of varieties, from Phat Farm to FUBU, to Sean John. Each style accentuated the roundness and firmness of each pair of bouncing breasts.

I shook my head as I looked at all the wonderful varieties of beautiful black women that got off the planes. Some had short hair (but perfectly styled), long hair, Halle Berry styles, dreads, bald, and they were all bodied up nicely. Then there were the many different flavors of women that walked by. There were chocolate sisters, caramel sisters, almond sisters, vanilla, mocha, and my favorite, coffee with just a hint of cream. Black women were doing it, and I loved to watch them do it. Sisters were coming and going to many different parts of the globe and they were out there making a difference. I love corporate black women. It had been awhile since I had seen sisters sporting thousand dollar suits, designer clothing from head to toe, and makeup that was flawless.

"Welcome Home" I thought to myself.

I was going to be staying with my family while I was here. I decided to pick up a rental rather than have my mother or sisters pick me up from the airport. I decided to stay with my family in the old hood because nine times out of ten, that is where my material is going to come from for my next joint.

Choosing a rental was a problem. I wanted an SUV, but in my old hood I know that whip would be okay for maybe three days before it would end up stolen. I didn't want to drive just anything though, so I was left with either flossin a nice whip, or keeping it conservative. Ultimately, I ended up getting a Grand Prix. It was fast, but it wasn't too flashy, so I felt that would be the wisest choice. I really wanted to get a Yukon Danali, but I will have to save that for my next trip…when I'm staying at a hotel downtown.

I jumped in the midsize car and headed to the crib where I grew up on 92nd street. I went south on Cicero to 79th street and headed east to Halsted. I could have taken a faster route to my old hood, but I wanted to take the scenic route and check out the bodies on the sistas on this nice ass late summer day. I drove slow down 79th street with the music blasting out of the speakers. I switched between commercials from Power 92, to V103, to WGCI listening to all the latest cuts. I was beaming at the thought of how hard Chicago artists were reppin' our city. Kanye West was bangin Jesus Walks on all the airways, R. Kelly's new joint just dropped Happy People, and from what I hear, all summer long people were bumpin Twista's joint, Kamikaze. I had all of their joints at home in the Carolina's, but I needed them again while I was back home. I made a mental note to stop at Best Buy this weekend to get a second copy and to look for new joints from Da Brat, Shawna and my boy Sean G.

Sisters in the hood were looking good as hell too. They weren't looking as sophisticated and fly as the corporate sisters, but they were doing their thing in the hood. As I drove to my family's crib and reached the Halsted strip, I saw nothing but round the way girls that had brothas beggin them for a small taste of their honey. There were sistas standing on corners with huge ghetto booties, listening to brothas who pulled over in cars try and shoot their best game at them. The brothers were clocking the sisters hard as hell. I forgot how brothas rolled in the hood. I saw so many Cadillac Trucks, Camry's, Lexus trucks and cars, BMW's and Mercedes that I thought I was at a car show. Each car had a boomin sound system, and each car was equipped with fly ass rims or spinners on them.

"Man, brothas are out here with their shit lookin tight, and I'm pushin this bullshit ass Grand Prix" That's what I thought to myself as I headed to my old hood. I hadn't been home 20 minutes and already that hood mentality was beginning to take affect on me. Kanye was right when he referenced how low black people's self esteem was at times.

I had money, and I was thinking to myself that I needed to show how much money I had by profiling in an expensive car. When my senses began to return to me, I thought to myself, "I don't need to be showing off. If anything, I need to try and be quiet about my shit" I got my head right and tried not to get caught up in how good Chicago sisters were looking. I sped down Halsted street ignoring all the fine ass women that I saw, and headed to my old neighborhood. I was there inside another twenty minutes.

Still Crazy

WELCOME BACK

I felt like Gabe Kaplan from *Welcome Back Kotter* as I drove down Sangamon Street pumpin WGCI from the speakers and looking at the block where I used to play football, basketball and get into the occasional fight coming up. As I reached the end of the block where my parents house was, I was stunned that my mother was out front waiting impatiently with my three aunts, my cousins, my sisters, their boyfriends, the parents of many of my childhood friends, and people that worked with all the many sets of people that were fans of my books.

"Aw shit" I thought to myself

I love all my people, and I love fans of my work, but this is not what I came home for. I slowed down to almost ten miles an hour as I approached my old home. My mother was looking impatiently at the car trying to see if it was indeed me that had pulled up to the house. I'm sure many people were expecting me to get out of a luxury car. If it was a short visit, I most likely would have. When I got out of the Grand Prix, everyone seemed to be surprised.

"There's my baby", my mother said.

"What's up big head?" My sister Joy said.

My cousins, and family members flooded me with a million questions as I grabbed my things out of the trunk.

"How long are you staying?", one cousin asked.

"Maybe a month"

"Why are you driving this car?" Another cousin asked me in a sharp tone.

"It was economical"

"So you're broke?" Another cousin queried.

"Yeah…Yeah I am. That's why I'm not staying at a hotel this trip"

"Damn man, sorry to hear it"

The suggestion that I was broke was a lie, but it was a good lie. By saying so, it would keep down the number of people asking me for money or asking me to join some multi-level marketing group.

As I walked into the house, there was my father and Reverend Turner sitting on the living room couch. My parents were deep into the church and they both listened attentively to the good Reverend whom I imagine was not here by coincidence.

"Ah, there he is. How are you Kevin? Please, come over here and sit with your father and I. We were just talking about something that might be of interest to you"

"I don't think so Reverend. It was a long flight and a long drive. I'm just here to catch up on some writing and kick it with my family. I don't plan on conducting any business while I'm here, or talking about any business"

"Kevin, don't be rude, come have a seat" My father said.

"Sorry Pops. Ma, can I speak to you for a minute?"

My mother looked equally upset that I didn't take the time to listen to the Reverend. She followed me into the kitchen where she had cookies baking, lasagna, chicken and a host of my favorite meals.

"Ma what are all these people doing here?"

"They want to see you"

"Ma, I didn't come home for all of this. I came home to write and get a break from my everyday lifestyle.

Coming home to people begging for money and looking for handouts is not my idea of a working vacation"

"Some people just want autographs"

"The autographs I can do. Advice on writing I can do. Questions about celebrities I can handle. One on one sessions where people ask me for money is going to make me go off"

"Kevin, I have listened to some of the ideas that people have and I think that you should entertain a few of them and…"

"No ma, I won't. Please ask anyone that was remotely thinking about asking me for money to leave. I am not giving out a dime"

"What about your tithes?"

"I pay that to the church I attend in Somerton"

"Why do you give that church money instead of the church that you were raised in?"

"Because that church teaches that tithes is not just ten percent of my bank account, but ten percent of my time and efforts. I can give by speaking to the youth at that church and not give one dime and the pastor doesn't say one word to me about my contribution. Here, ministers act like you can only get saved on consignment and like the true way to heaven is through the debit system. I'm not feeling Reverend Turner either. Can you especially send him home?"

I hadn't seen my mother in almost a year and a half. The reason for that is touring, working and trying to write can be demanding. I was frantic as hell that she cooked all this wonderful food for me, but I was mad as hell that she invited the free world to come and participate in what

I felt was "family time" I had three sisters, Joy who was 26, Meka who was 19, and Carla who was 14. I was going to get this book done while I was down here, but my sisters are who I really wanted to see. My mother went to ask the Reverend and other people in the house to leave. As she did, I sat at the dining room table and signed autographs of those people who brought copies of my books. I thanked each of them for their support and talked with each one long enough to let them know that their support means the world to me. I explained to each one of them, without them, there would be no me. I listened to what each one had to say in reference to why they loved or disliked my book, and I listened to their suggestions about character development for sequels (in the event that I ever write any).

I heard the Reverend say in a voice just above a whisper that he had no plans on leaving. He said that he needed to talk to me. He told my mother not to worry about my reaction. He said that he knew how to talk to people tactfully. Just saying so made the hair on my neck begin to stand. My sister Joy smiled because she could see that I was getting pissed. This is the reason why I limit the number of times that I visit home. The Reverend came in with a smile on his face.

"Kevin, we need to talk"

"What didn't you understand when I first came in the door?"

"Kevin, your last book was a best-seller. You are listed in this month's Ebony, Essence and XXL magazine as well as the SOURCE, and Today's Black Woman. You have money, and the Lord has put it on my heart to ask that you share part of what you have.

"Oh really?"

My sisters Carla and Meka walked in the door. They had just finished going shopping at Evergreen Plaza. They saw me and were all hugs and kisses. Carla, the baby sister, saw the look of pistivity on my face and was wondering what was the source of my ire.

"What's wrong Kevin?"

"Nothing sweetheart, everything is cool. I see that Ma hooked up some food, you ready to get your eat on?"

"Oh yeah, I'm glad you're home. One, I get to see you and kick it, and two, Ma goes all out of her way to cook when you come home. How long are you staying?"

"Maybe a month"

"A month? You know Ma is only cooking you this meal tonight right? Things will be back to normal around here tomorrow. Then you will have to go buy takeout if you're hungry"

We all laughed and smiled. The Reverend was still fixing his mouth to give me a sales pitch.

"Kevin, all I am saying is…"

"Reverend, I don't have the money that you think I have. My last joint was a best-seller, that's true. But I have a mortgage, cars, upkeep, a road manager, manager, and marketing that I have to do. That doesn't include traveling, taxes, car rentals, charities, and the tithes that I do pay. When it's all said and done, after I pay all my bills, I have nothing left but my spending money. That money is mine to whatever I want with"

"Don't you think that's a bit selfish?"

"Selfish? Selfish? Look Rev, I give to the church. I also give to charity. On top of that, I have a scholarship fund in my name set up for young black writers. I also do free workshops for young black writers every summer here at the McCormick Place. I am probably the least selfish person that you know. I give enough"

"Kevin, you can never give enough"

"I tell you what, I have given all that I plan on giving, so whatever you are selling, the answer is no"

"You would turn your back on your family, friends and home church?"

"Good Evening Reverend"

"Aren't you at least going to ask what I am asking for the money for?"

"I don't give a…"

"Kevin!" My mother interrupted.

A silence fell over the room. I let out a sigh knowing that I upset my mother. I didn't need to cause a scene, so I decided to be diplomatic about my response.

"You know what Rev, I'm going to be here a month. Can I spend at least 72 hours at home before you start in on me?"

"I'm sorry Kevin. I guess that's fair. My work isn't easy, but it's work that must be done"

"Yeah, it must be hard hittin' people up for money", I said sarcastically.

The Reverend scowled and said, "So will you stop by the church Saturday?"

Reluctantly, I agreed.

The Reverend thanked me and talked with my father for a while before leaving.

My father said, "Did you have to be so hard on him?"

"You would think with as hard as I was on him, he wouldn't want any money from me"

My mother said, "So what do you want to do now?"

"Let's eat"

My family and I prayed at the table and we sat up and got our eat on. My sisters each had to begin school in a week or so, and I was happy that we had at least a week to fellowship with one another. Joy asked me what I wanted to do next and I started barking orders to my sisters.

"Joy, you get the videos. Carla, you pop the popcorn, and Meka, you get the sleeping bags"

We all camped out in the living room and I listened to my sisters tell me everything that was going on in their lives. We talked about boys, career goals, what has been going on in the hood, what has been going on globally, Kobe Bryant, R. Kelly and what was going on in the world of Hip-Hop. Afterward, we watched The first season of Dave Chappelle's Chappelle Show" It was a great first night back home in Chicago.

THE NEXT DAY

I woke up and it was weird not being in my house in Somerton anymore. Being home almost made me feel like a kid again. To be honest, I kind of hated it. I looked outside to see if my rental was still parked out front, and surprisingly it was. My sister Carla wanted me to walk to the corner store with her to get some Cheetos and some pop. I looked at the clock on the wall and it said 11:00. Yep, I'm back in the hood. This is the only place where you can sleep until 11:00 and get up and still consider it to be morning. I jumped in the shower and came downstairs and drove my sister to the store and bought her everything that she wanted. She's 14 and I am seldom home, so I figured that I would spoil the hell out of her.

After she got a bag full of snacks, we headed to the Arab-owned sandwich shop. My sister got a corned beef sandwich and I got a pizza puff. I forgot how damned good those things were. Halfway home, I turned around and bought another one. When I came back out to the car the second time, there were about four older cats around my rental trying to holler at my baby sister.

"What the fuck is y'all niggas doing around my ride?"

They turned around to face me and they were all smiles when they saw who was speaking. I was pissed that brothers my age had the gall to try and holler at 14 year olds. Hell, I'm 28 so that would make half of them at least 30 to 32. The oldest cat, a guy named Mark, who we called Big Slim, spoke to me first.

"Kevin? Damn man how are you? This must be yo little sister, my bad. She hasn't been to the sandwich shop since you left"

"Yeah, I can see why"

"Aw man, don't be like that. I'm out here just like you are out here"

"I'm not trying to holler at teenagers"

"You would if you saw how they be dressin and dancin here in the hood. If I had known that was yo sister, I wouldn't have even tried to holler at her. Anyway man, how you doin?"

"I'm all right man, how are you doing?"

"Aw man, I'm straight. Just chillin. So what do you do for a living?"

"I was teaching for a while, now I am just kind of trying to find myself. So I came home"

"Yeah, that's right, I heard that you moved to California or something,"

"North Carolina"

Big Slim was called that because he was all of 6,4 when we were in grade school and he was rail thin. He stands 6, 6 now, and he looks exactly the way that he did in grade school. Big Slim could play the hell out of some basketball, straight up. This kid was so good, I know he could take Kobe off the dribble and dunk. This boy was certified NBA material, but he couldn't bring up his grades. Big Slim played ball like the rest of us up at Robichaux Park on 95th & Eggleston. People from all around the nation sometimes came to Robichaux to test their skills against Mark and the Neighborhood's best. Cats from the Pros came to play ball here as well as overseas players and semi-pro ball players. Big Slim got his hustle on by making all participants play for $10. 00 a game. This was just to play. The losing team in a 3 on 3, had to pay $20. 00 each to the winners. When it was hot outside, Slim got his hustle on. This brother was thirty something years old. He will be out there hustling ball until he is maybe forty five if no one kills him. This boy is one of the baddest cats out there in ball, and no one outside of the hood will ever know his name.

Big Slim was plugged into the rest of the hood and I thought that he might prove to be good writing material, so I asked him where would he be hanging out later. He said that he would be at the park all day getting his hustle on, after he got a 40 ounce of OE from somewhere. He said tonight he would be at the watering hole. I asked him what time and he said about 10:00. I told him that I would meet him there. I jumped in the Grand Prix with my sister and took off.

"So what do you want to do now?" I asked my little sister.

"Let's go shopping"

"Okay, let's go get Joy and Meka"

"Let's not"

"Carla, quit being selfish"

"Okay...I guess"

We went and picked up Meka. Joy had to work. She said that she would catch up to us later. I asked her if there anything that she wanted and she said no, she was straight.

Joy was studying to be a writer. Two writers in the family is not necessarily a good thing. Joy didn't want me spending a lot of money on her. She also had some jealousy going on. She was writing under a pseudonym to keep from riding my coattails. The problem was, she was unable, right now, to sell her writing samples. Because of the constant rejection, her self esteem regarding her writing career was low. I tried to tell her over and over again that it's not her writing that's the problem. The problem is that most of the major publishing houses are white owned and white run. They have no idea how to market African American books or to tell what's hot. At the Black magazines and publishing houses, the competition is too fierce because you have hundreds of thousands of submissions. I tried to encourage my sister as much as I could. Some days, my praises simply fell on deaf ears. Joy had to find her own way regarding her writing, and I had to let her.

I asked Meka if she wanted to go shopping and you should have seen the way that her face lit up with a smile.

"Hell yeah, and we need to get you some gear fast"

"Me, what's wrong with what I have on?"

"Bruh, look at what you have on for the hood"

She was right. I was rocking Hugo Vittelli Sandals, Braggi Slacks, a Hugo Boss linen top, a Platinum Wittenauer watch, a gold and platinum bracelet, and a wedding ring with five stones in it with 2 ½ carat weight. I had a one carat flawless earring in my left ear. After thinking about it, it was a bit much for where I was at.

THE PLAZA

I took my sisters to Evergreen Plaza where we broke out the plastic. I loved doing nice things for them. I thanked God everyday for the ability to do nice things for them. There was nothing worse than me being in the mall with a 19 year old and a 14 year old. Man, we went ballistic. I got them Baby Phat outfits, Sean John Outfits, G-Unit t-shirts, Tommy Hilfiger gear and I got them each half carat earrings for their ears. I let them decide on what I would wear while I was back home and they each picked out three warm ups. Some were Sean John and the others were Phat Farm. I Got a bunch of White Sox caps, Cubs caps, Bears caps and caps that had Chicago written on the brim. I needed these caps for North Carolina so I could still rep my city. By the time that my sisters and I left the plaza, I had spent close to six grand.

When I walked in the door to my mother's house with over eight bags of stuff, she shook her head with disapproval. I tried to get her to smile, but she wouldn't.

I found out why when I walked in the house. To my disapproval was the Reverend again. He seemed put out that I splurged so much money on my sisters.

"Kevin, I see you are back in a giving mood"

"Didn't I say see me this weekend?"

"I'm here to see your father and mother. I still plan to see you on Saturday"

"Yeah okay"

I helped my sisters with their bags and changed into a Sean John warm-up.

The Reverend yelled upstairs, "Do you feel guilty seeing me here today Kevin?"

I ignored him.

"The money that you spent today might have been put to better use had you been down at the church"

I was thinking to myself, "This MF doesn't give up does he?"

I came down in my sweat-suit looking fly as hell. I was rocking the suit and white on white Air Force Ones. I let out a sigh as I reached the bottom of the stairs.

"Let's go to the church to get this over with"

"I want to meet with you on Saturday. The deacons and the board will…"

"…I don't want to hear from the deacons and the board or anyone else. You and I need to go right now and you had better be able to give me your best pitch, Otherwise, the answer is no. That's how I do business. You obviously aren't going to give me any peace while I'm at home, so let's go before I jump on the next flight to North Carolina"

Reverend Turner was pissed at my insistence, but he knew that I was serious. This was his one and only shot with me.

"Okay Kevin, come on"

We got into the good reverend's car. His car was a Lexus Truck. It was the LX 470, Gold Edition. This bad boy was fully equipped, leather interior, a navigational system, sunroof, Jensen Speakers, ground affects, 20 disc CD changer, satellite radio, and a phone built into the dash. Just seeing this car while this fool asked me for money had my ass on ten! His license plate had the nerve to say BLESSED. The reverend pulled off and threw in the new spiritual joint by R. Kelly, He Saved Me. I liked that joint so I tried to vibe with it rather than start any shit with the Reverend. After the R. Kelly joint went off, he played Jesus Walks by Kanye West. Again, I tried to vibe with that, rather than trip with the Reverend. He then kept the music neutral by playing Far Away From Here by Kindred and the Family Soul. During the middle of this joint, he turned the music down and decided to ease his way into my head.

"Kevin, why don't you like me?"

"Do you really want to go there?"

"Yeah, I really need to know"

"Let's start with the fact that you are a beggin MF. Let's top that off with the fact that my parents are on a fixed income and they and my sisters have to live off just my father's pension, and my mother's part time gig. When I send them money, they give you ten percent of what I send. On top of that, they give you an offering. By the time they get through giving away money they have nothing left. That's why if I buy them a car, I just go and get the car. If they need money for anything, I tell them to simply give me the name of the creditor. I think you bleed people to death. It pisses me off to see you driving this fifty eight thousand dollar truck, knowing that I might have paid for it. Then, you have the nerve to try and make me feel guilty about the money that I spend on my goddamned family. This is my money, not yours nigga, mine. In the Carolinas, no one asks me for anything but my time. That is how I prefer it"

"You don't believe in giving back?"

"Giving back? Nigga please. I give. I sometimes give until it hurts. Most times, I give what can afford"

"Sometimes you have to give more than you can afford…"

"…Now you see, that is where you are wrong. Giving until it hurts isn't practical. It's just plain stupid. That's why our people sometimes can't get ahead. They tithe, they offer and they give what they don't have to begin with. They say you have to give 10% off the top to the Lord. Okay, I'm feeling that. But when you don't have shit to begin with, even God has to understand. My philosophy is simple, if you don't have it, don't give it! If in your heart you know you would give it if you had it, then yo, God knows your heart. I'm not worried about my parent's relationship with God. I'm not worried about my relationship with God. I'm worried about your influence and your relationship with my parents concerning God"

I was getting madder and madder by the minute. I left Chicago for many reasons. One of them was to keep from killing this MF. We had a pastor. We had a cool ass pastor named Mike Malone. Mike was a fifty something year old pastor that was from the streets. Mike might hit you up hard with the tithe or the offering, but you knew that Mike was going to take that money and someone whose lights got cut off would be cut back on. Someone whose family didn't know where their next meal was coming from was going to get fed. Mike also didn't drive a Lexus Truck. He drove a beat to shit 1985 Chevy celebrity. I was impressed with Reverend Malone. That was why one year I bought him a Ford F-150. I got him a red pickup truck and he used that truck to move people, to help people, to bring the kids toys, and to make a difference. Reverend Malone was the type of brother that you followed into battle. This brother was a leader. Like many of our leaders though, he was assassinated.

One day, a wanna be Gangsta named Leonard got mad at Reverend Malone because he gave sanctuary to a woman that once his ho. The woman came to Reverend Malone and said that she wanted to change her life. The woman's name was Mary. Reverend Mike preached to that woman. From what I hear, she found God that day. Leonard confronted Reverend Malone in the church. He tied the Rev up execution style and called him all types of names before shooting the Rev twice in the back of the head. Mary confronted Mike and he shot her at point blank range. Leonard tried to walk out like he was hard, like he was John Gotti. The minute people realized what had happened, homeless people, senior citizens, and even the hardest thug ass niggas in the hood jumped on his trifling ass and almost stomped him out of existence. Leonard spent nine months in ICU at County Hospital. Then he went to jail at County. A bunch of well hung brothers were waiting for his ass on the inside. Now and until the day he gets out of jail, Leonard will be somebody's bitch. Mary lived. She was shot at point blank range, and she lived. I guess when Reverend Mike saved her, he truly saved her and God put his hand on her life. Mary has been clean three years now.

Reverend Malone, however, is gone.

He was replaced with Reverend Turner, a forty year old pastor who preaches moving sermons, but who always has his damned hand out. My mother says that I don't like him because he's not Mike Malone. I don't like him, because if it were left up to him, my parents might be eating dog food in a few years if I don't monitor their spending.

"Look man, I work hard for my money. My father worked all his life for a small pension that comes out to $1100 dollars a month after taxes. If their house wasn't paid for, my parents would be struggling right now. My sister Joy's salary is what keeps them afloat. The money I give is supposed to be money for them to blow, not to give to you, the church, or anyone else. What I give them is so they can enjoy their lives together. For their anniversary, I sent them two tickets to the Cayman Islands. They donated them to the church. My father asked for three grand, I sent him ten, and he gave at least two to you…"

"God put it on his heart to…"

"…You put it on his heart. Don't lie on God, I'm betting that's got to be like a spiritual felony in heaven or something. All I am saying is you need to back the fuck off. Otherwise, I am coming after you"

"Is that a threat?"

"Yes"

We pulled into the church lot. I followed Reverend Turner in and on his desk were proposals. One proposal was addressed to me.

"This is a proposal to create a welfare to work program here in the community"

"Really?"

"We have a number of investors already lined up. Each one would donate a small amount of money to the initial startup costs until the grant comes in and…"

"…What's the bottom line?"

"I'm sorry?"

"The bottom line, how much is each partner to invest?"

"Well first I would like to tell you how the money is going to be spent and…"

"Save the pitch Padre, how much?"

"$20,000"

I looked at the other names on the list that were investing. Three were in the music industry and two others were writers like myself. All were Chicagoans.

"I'll send it to my lawyer. If he likes it and thinks it's a good idea, I'm in. There is one condition though"

"What is that?"

"You back off my family with these contributions that you keep asking for"

There was a long silence in the Church. After thirty seconds or so, Reverend Turner nodded his head.

I feel like I just paid for my parent's emancipation from the church. That shit didn't feel right.

"I'll take you home"

"Naw, that's okay, I'm straight"

JOY TO THE WORLD

My sister Joy didn't work too far from the Church so I decided to walk over and see how she was doing. I missed her earlier with the shopping, but I did get her a gift anyway. I got her a diamond tennis bracelet. She and I needed some quality time together other than eating popcorn and watching DVD's. I figured since I was over here, I would take her out to eat, plus she could drive me home.

I stopped into her job and was immediately stopped by her boss. Joy worked at Opal Publishing and her boss, co-workers and customers rushed me and asked for autographs and questions about my next project. I signed autographs and talked with all my sister's co-workers as I waited for her to finish the last of her paperwork. From there, she and I were going to Gino's East Pizza downtown.

"Mr. Allen can I have a few minutes of your time in my office?", her boss said.

"Sure, how can I help you?"

"I know that you are with another publishing company, but we are having an event at the McCormick Place next Wednesday. I would love to have you come and give a speech to the young authors that will be there. We are giving out a number of writing scholarships, and a lot of the people being awarded, mentioned you among their favorite authors"

I was a little apprehensive about giving a speech at my sister's job. I didn't want to contribute to our sibling rivalry. I looked in Joy's direction and she gave me a look that said it was okay. I agreed.

"We can't pay you much for the appearance Mr. Allen but..."

"...That's okay, I'll do it free of charge"

"Joy gave me a look that said, don't be crazy"

I smiled because I knew what she was thinking. I asked what the attire was and her boss told me that it was formal. I liked that. I hadn't been to a formal event in the city for a while. I said my goodbyes and Joy and I headed to the Honda Civic that I bought her a few years ago.

"So why did you really come home?", Joy asked.

"Are you tired of me already?"

"Of course not, it's great to see you. It's just been awhile since you were last here. When Ma told me that you would be staying here for at least a month, I figured something was wrong with your marriage. Is everything okay?"

"Everything is fine. I came home because I am out of material for my next book. I need to write another bestseller. This is my last book with my publisher and I am looking to either renegotiate a major publishing deal at my publishing house, or test the free market and sign with someone else. If the next book isn't really strong, I could lose a lot of money on the free market"

"Damn, so you are under some serious pressure"

"Yeah, I am"

"So what are you thinking about writing about?"

"Well I saw Big Slim earlier and..."

"...Big Slim? Kevin you aren't going to write about these idiots in the hood are you?"

"Yeah. I am. A lot of these brothers have some stories to tell"

"That's exploitation"

"No it's not"

"Yeah...it is"

Back and forth Joy and I had one of our famous debates. She told me that I didn't need to write about what was going on in the hood unless I was writing with the goal to affect change in the community. I explained to her if I didn't get this next book done, I was going to be living in the community again. She looked at me as if to suggest that she didn't want that, so we ended the debate with agreeing to disagree. She ended up saying that I should do whatever I need to do rather than come back home and live with them at age 28. We laughed and then went to dinner at Gino's East.

Joy and I ordered a deep dish with sausage, pepperoni, onion, green pepper and spinach. We laughed, joked and watched people, which is one of our favorite pastimes when we are downtown. We looked at people and tried to guess who was married, who was having an affair, who was gay, bi, trans and who looked like a crazed psychopath. Afterward, we ordered dessert to go, and we headed back south to the crib.

Joy dropped me off just in time for me to change into another warm-up and head out to the corner of 92nd and Peoria and hit the watering hole.

THE WATERING HOLE

The watering hole was not a club, it wasn't a bar, it was simply the corner of 92nd and Peoria. All the thugs, athletes and people in the hood that grew up in the hood,

Still Crazy

came to that corner sometimes and sat out and drank. The corner house belonged to an old man named Carl Wilson. Carl was a Vietnam veteran that didn't quite come back right from the war. The brother had flashbacks from time to time and the shit wasn't nothin nice. Carl wasn't crazy, per se, but he was a bit strange. He lived at home with his mother, at age 52. He never worked that anyone knows of, and he got a check every month from the government. We never saw him spend a lot of money. In fact, we never saw him in clothes that were not Army fatigues. Carl didn't fuck with anybody, and no body fucked with him. His mother never minded us drinking by her house on the corner. We didn't keep up much noise, and whenever she needed help with groceries, or moving furniture, she simply called whoever was on the corner to come over and help her out. When Carl would see a bunch of people outside drinking, many times he would come outside and join in. He was a cool ass older brother. Sometimes he would talk about the war. Sometimes he would talk about what it means to be a man. Most days, he talked about how sneaky white people were.

I walked up to that corner with a couple of forty ounce bottles of beer. One was Old English, another was Miller Genuine Draft, and the other two were Shlitz for the older brothers that were out there. I broke out with a bunch of cups. Brothers were out there drinking Boone's Farm, Wild Irish Rose, Night Train, and all the cheap drinks that brothers drink on corners across the nation. When I came with the OE, MGD and Shlitz, you would have sworn that I was giving out free passes to heaven.

"My man! Right on time!"

"Yo Kevin man, what have you been up to?"

"All right, My nigga, thanks for lookin out"

"We gon drink good tonight and get fuuuucccked up"

The thugs in the hood loved it when one of the ballers, athletes or regular Joes came to the corner to kick it. We generally brought better drinks and more of them because we knew how to show each other to a good time.

It had been a long time since I was last here drinking. The last time that I was here was when a girl named Sheena Clark got raped. Sheena was a fine caramel colored honey in the hood. She had a father who was a cop, but a cool as cop named Officer Clark. Officer Clark never fucked with anyone in the hood. When he got off work, he didn't give a damn what happened on the block, as long as no one disrespected his house. Well, his daughter, Sheena was fine as hell. Not only was she fine, but she was one of those braniac type girls. You know the ones, the ones that answer all the teacher's questions and the ones that were ready to even go as far as to argue points with the teachers. Sheena was one of those girls. Way back in grade school, it was obvious that she was going to be somebody.

Sheena was drop dead gorgeous. She had light brown eyes, a fat ass like her mother, Mrs. Clark and she was top heavy. Her titties were huge as hell in grammar school. I used to love seeing her run in gym, just to watch those bad boys bounce. Some of my best hardons came from watching Sheena. Guys in the hood used to talk about how they would tap that ass given the opportunity. Everyone used to talk that shit, but no one was actually going to tap—anything. Officer Clark had brothas in the hood so scared to look at his daughter that we figured

Still Crazy

once she got in high school, her prom date, would probably be her first date.

Sheena went to high school at Kenwood. She was smart as hell and that was a good move for her. The older she got, the more beautiful she became. The girl was proving to grow smarter and smarter as she got older, and her body? Man she had body out of this world. By the time she was off to college, everyone in the hood swore she had implants. Her breasts were so full, so round, and just too damned perfect. Either she had implants, or her dad and mother had some damn good genes.

Sheena didn't date much in college, and her prom date was her actual first date. She went to prom with this guy named Will Johnson. Will was one of those nerdy ass brothas that couldn't fight, couldn't play sports, but he was from the hood, and he was smart as hell, so no one messed with him—much. Officer Clark liked Will. He figured Will could take care of his daughter and he knew that Will was going to be someone. Will and Sheena both went to U of I downstate. They dated freely in college, and their relationship prospered. She was majoring in Pre-Law, and he was majoring in Dentistry. We used to clown Will and tease him about wanting to be a dentist. What nigga in the world wants to be a damned dentist? Will stated that is what he wanted to be, so brothas in the hood had to respect that shit.

One day Sheena was home from school on break. She and Will were supposed to sit down and talk with Officer Clark and tell him that they were engaged to be married. Both she and Will would be home for two weeks, but the time just never seemed right to tell Officer Clark about the planning of their nuptials. One day that week Sheena and her dog (an annoying little fucker named Pierre) went jogging through the hood. Sheena had on U of I shorts, a t-shirt and some white Nike track shoes. I remember seeing her that day and commenting on how those titties still bounced like they did in grade school, only now they were bigger. A lot of people saw her that day because one girl named Linda, commented as Sheena ran by, "those breasts can't be real" All throughout the hood, Sheena ran; her and her dog.

An hour later, the dog returned home, with blood all over him. Mr. Clark was watering his front lawn and many of us were sitting out on the corner, talking in front of our cars (those of us that drove). When Mrs. Clark saw the dog, the blood, and all the commotion that the dog was keeping up, she began screaming hysterically. Officer Clark came running down the street like a Drill Sergeant. He told all of us with cars to scour the neighborhood for his daughter. He had every athlete, student, thug and even a few homeless guys looking for his daughter. He jumped in his BMW and he and his wife looked hard for Sheena.

A homeless guy named Hank (We called him Cuda) flagged us down. He was tearful, and he pointed down the alley where he normally slept. A mob of us walked down the alley and there naked, and in shock, with her legs spread wide open in the alley, was Sheena. She was bloody, beaten and motionless. A few minutes later, Officer Clark came with his wife. They ran down the alley and screamed as they saw their daughter. No one had covered her up, because we were all in shock ourselves. I watched Officer Clark cover his daughter with a blanket and try to get her to recognize him. The look on Sheena's face was so lifeless.

Everyone respected Officer Clark. Everyone knew him to be the strongest of men when it came to his character. That day, he cried like an infant himself as he held his daughter and rocked her in his arms until the paramedics arrived. He, his wife, and Sheena who was still in shock, went to the local hospital.

We asked Henry who did this to Sheena, and he said that he didn't know. He said that he was going to lay down where he normally lays in the alley, and then—he saw her. He knew who she was. He said that he was so hurt that someone could do such a thing to such a precious little girl. Henry cried that day as if Sheena were his daughter.

That night we all drank. That night, when Will found out, he was hurt beyond words. He felt so helpless. The look on his face was one of total defeat. He wanted to be there at the Hospital, but he was not considered immediate family, so he ended up at the watering hole drinking with us. Two hours after that, we were joined at the watering hold by one more drinker…Officer Clark.

"You know, I have an idea who did this to my daughter" Officer Clark said as he took a swig of Old English.

There was a long silence on the corner as he spoke. Officer Clark was in the same clothes he had on earlier, a plain white t-shirt, jeans, and loafers.

"Who do you think did it?" Big Slim asked.

"Billy Wallace"

"Are you sure Officer Clark?" Big Slim asked.

"Detectives at my precinct told me that he was seen going in his house covered with blood and he looked as if he had been in a fight. That is what one of his neighbors said to 911 about three and a half hours ago. They say that I can't jump to conclusions. They say that his mother did not allow them to come in and they are trying to get a warrant for him now. Mrs. Wallace also hired a lawyer who is already saying that Billy can't be questioned because he is ill"

"That's bullshit", I said.

"Yes, Kevin, it is, but that's the law…and I can't do anything about the law, because I'm a police officer"

Officer Clark took a hit from a bottle of Night Train that we had been passing around (this was before we used cups and we simply passed forties and bottles to one another).

Big Slim said, "You can't do shit, but we can"

There was no reply from Officer Clark. He just took another hit off that Night Train.

Officer Clark began to walk to his house. He stopped after walking just three steps.

"You know, I hate what he did to my daughter, but I don't want him dead"

There was a long silence on the corner.

"If you had it your way, what would you like Mr. Clark?" Big Slim asked.

"I don't wish death on him. I just want him to wish that he was dead"

Again there was silence on the corner.

Officer Clark kept walking to his house.

Still Crazy

BILLY WALLACE

Billy Wallace was a crazy MF in the hood. What was worse, was that he was a new MF in the hood. The area where we all grew up was all one unit where one gang was predominant. This fool, was representing another faction from the first day that he arrived in our hood. He stood 6,6, He was all of 300 pounds, and he was built like an offensive lineman. Billy was crazy. He shot animals in the hood for no reason, he started shit with the brothas in the hood for no reason, and he had been arrested a number of times for assaulting his own mother whom he lived with. It took six police to get his big ass down one day when he went off on his mother for not making him breakfast. There was no way to describe him other than being a huge unruly MF. Big Slim led the charge. He took a hit from the last of the Night Train, lit a joint, and passed it around.

"I never liked that MF anyway"

Big slim led a mob of 20 of us over to Green Street where we headed to the Wallace household. I have to say, there is nothing worse than a mob of young men in their twenties.

One guy named Bobby D., knocked on the door to the Wallace house. It was about midnight when we went over there. Mrs. Wallace opened the door with straight attitude.

"What ya'll niggas want at my door?"

Bobby snatched the screen damn near off the hinges, and snatched Mrs. Wallace to the ground. He locked her hands behind her back, put his knee in her butt, and pinned her to the grass.

"Help! What are ya'll doin to me? Help! Somebody help me!"

She screamed loud as hell. Her big burly ass son came running downstairs. He sounded like a damned horse running on a cobblestone street.

I looked at Big Slim and said, "The police will be on their way"

Big Slim said, "We only need a few minutes"

One by one brothas ran up into the Wallace home. When Big Boy made it to the last step to run outside and see why his mother was screaming, Big Slim hit him in the face with a lamp. I tripped Billy to the floor. One by one, brothers in the hood stomped, kicked, punched and beat on Billy. We whipped his ass for old and new. He had bandages on his face where his mother tried to patch him up from his obvious fight with Sheena. He might have been 300 pounds, but Sheena I guess was in pretty good shape. Billy looked like he had been in the fight of his life. The stupid motherfucker was still in the same shirt that he had attacked Sheena in earlier.

His mother screamed out for Mercy.

"Please, ya'll please, my baby boy is sick! Ya'll hear me? He's sick, he has no control over what he does sometimes. Lawd have mercy on my boy. Ya'll let him go! I'mma press charges, I'mma identify all of ya'll to the police if you don't let him go! I'mma..."

CRACK!

Bobby hit Mrs. Wallace with an ugly right cross. He knocked her unconscious with one blow like some shit out of the movies. I was stunned and now angry.

"Bobby, what the fuck did you do?"

"The bitch wouldn't shut up"

Another brother named Raymond, that we called Ray-Ray, asked, "What do we do with Billy?"

Big Slim said, "Let's castrate his ass"

I was like, "Whoa, Whoa! Big Slim, no. Man we can't do no shit like that! I'm not trying to be party to a MF murder"

"We ain't gonna kill him Kev, we are just gonna cut him a bit"

"Slim man, naw. Man, don't do this shit"

"What if it were one of your sisters, Kev?"

That threw me off. I didn't know how I would react if his victim were Meka, Carla or Joy.

I threw my hands up and said, "Yo man, I won't say nothing to nobody, but I'm out. I'm goin home"

"See you at the watering hole tomorrow?"

"Yeah, if none of us are in jail or on the fucking news"

I went home that night.

Billy Wallace was not castrated, nor was he killed.

He will never walk again.

He's in a wheelchair for life, he had severe trauma to the head, and a punctured lung.

This was before he was sentenced to spend the next ten years in jail for raping Sheena.

We were each put on probation for the events that took place that night. I assumed that it was Big Slim that crippled Billy Wallace. I was wrong. The crippling blows came from Will, Sheena's fiancée. He showed up that night too. He wailed on Billy with a steel pipe until he couldn't raise his arms any more. Billy violated his woman. This was the woman that he planned on spending the rest of his life with. We never told the police that Will was there with us that night. We all got probation, and Big Slim got probation and racketeering. Big Slim went to jail, but he was out in four months. When he got out, we all drank again at the watering hole.

We seldom spoke to Officer Clark again after that night. Sheena, never fully recovered. She walks around the hood now, but she dresses all covered up. She still lives at home, she speaks to hardly anyone, and she is just so — withdrawn. She and Will never recovered either. It wasn't for lack of trying on Will's part. They tried therapy, pastoral counseling, and a host of other interventions, but Sheena never really came around. Will is a dentist now, with a fine ass Puerto Rican wife. He still stops by from time to time, and when he does, he brings a bunch of drinks to the watering hole. That was the last time that I was here on this corner.

Big Slim walked up with about nine cases of beer. He obviously stole them and no one of course, was going to complain.

"What's up Kevin?"

"Whad up Slim, how are you bruh?"

"I'm straight"

Big Slim brought me up to speed on everything in the hood. He told me who was now on crack, who was dead, who got married, and who got locked up. I was blown away by some of the stories that I heard about various people in the hood.

Still Crazy

VICKI HARRISON

While sitting on the corner drinking beer, I saw a figure head our way that looked like a woman. I couldn't see who it was because they were so far away, but whoever it was had a walk out of this world. The figure was switching so much, rather than say that she was switching from right to left, she was switching from east to west. The only problem with the person was that they were coming at us at an incredible speed even though they were walking. In a matter of seconds I could see why the person was walking so fast—it was a crackhead.

The woman was headed toward all of us at a high speed because that was how she walked. She obviously wanted something to drink, and I guess somebody here on the corner was her dealer.

"Anybody here need their dick sucked? I'll suck it good for $5.00"

I was thinking to myself, "Damn, what the hell. Can't we just drink in peace?"

Big Slim was like, "Naw bitch, get the hell away from here"

Big Slim kicked her square in her ass. All the other brothers out there started laughing.

One of the brothers, a short dark skinned brother named Hank, pulled out three dollars.

"You can do me for three dollars"

"Dammit Hank, I need five"

She must be $5.00 short for a rock.

Hank said, "Bitch I got three, now what you gon do?"

"Fuck you Hank!"

She told him fuck you, but she walked over to him, unzipped his pants and began giving him head right there on the corner.

"Are you out of your fuckin mind? Nobody wants to see that shit! Hank, at least go behind the car" I said.

"A'ight Kevin. I keep forgetting since you left the hood, you are like a young Martin Luther King and shit"

"Martin Luther hell, I'll beat yo ass! Take that shit over there"

Hank and the Hype went behind the nearest car and she did her thing for three dollars.

I asked Big Slim, "How do you even maintain a hard on with a hype? How can your dick stay hard with a bunch of hard legs around?"

Big Slim said, "Hank's right, you are like a Martin Luther King"

"Fuck You Slim"

We all sat there laughing. Big Slim went back to bringing me up to speed about what was going on in the hood, and before I knew it, Hank was done.

"Damn Hank, that quick?" I said.

"Fuck You Kevin"

The hype wiped her mouth picked up a beer, gargled with it, spat and guzzled the rest.

"I still need two dollars"

I was disgusted by her presence so I reached in my pocket and gave her a five.

"Thank you baby. Damn, you look familiar, what's yo name?"

"Kevin"

"Kevin Allen? Heeeeyyyyy Boo!"

I looked closely at her face and her sunkin eye sockets. The woman was rail thin like Kate Moss, and she stunk all to be damned. After looking carefully at her face, I was blown away at who she was.

"Vicki?"

"Yeah Boo"

"Damn"

She went to hug me and I kept her at arms distance. I looked at her with pity and as I did, she averted my eyes and began wringing her hands. She looked up at me again and I gave her a look that said I was brokenhearted by what I saw.

"Babygirl...what happened?"

There was a silence there on the corner. Vicki looked down at the ground like a scolded child. Then she looked up with anger and contempt.

"They will tell you about me I'm sure!"

With that she walked off. She walked off like a creature in the night. She used to be so damned pretty. Now she reminded me of Gollum in The Lord of the Rings.

I grabbed a beer and asked Big Slim what happened to Vicki. The story that he told me was awful.

To begin with, I have to explain how I knew Victoria Harrison. Vicki and I went to grade school at Washington. She was in eighth grade, and I was in seventh. Vicki looked like a young Halle Berry when she was in grade school. We used to take standardized tests in grade school. They were called the Iowa basic tests. When the grades all came back, we each used to compare the high scores. Our teachers would post many of the high scores. Vicki, was scoring on the twelfth grade level in eighth grade.

I used to have the biggest crush on Vicki. I used to beg, prod and try my best when I was younger to get her to go out with me. In grade school it was because she was not interested. In high school it was no, because she was older than me and college boys were sweating her. Fortunately for me, we went to two different colleges. In college, she met a basketball player at The State University. The ball player's name was John Akins. Akins was all-city, all state, and he was a hell of an athlete. Pro scouts were checking him out, European scouts were checking him out, and semi-pro teams.

Senior year, Akins blew out his knee. He tore his ACL. The minute that happened, his stock sunk. Vicki stood by him, married him, and moved him into her mother's house. He worked hard at rehabbing his knee, and she supported him and her mother. A few years later, Vicki's mother died. She took it hard, but she got through it. After that, she threw herself into her relationship with her man. Akins never was able to return to the athletic level that he once played. When it was obvious that he would never play pro ball, he became depressed. As a result of his depression, he began using crack.

Akins used crack, and one day brought some home for Vicki to try. She loved his dirty drawls, and because she loved him—she began smoking. Both of them began smoking and doing any and everything for money. One day, a year later, a city college coach saw Akins at a pickup game. Akins wasn't watching the game, he was trying to beg for money. The coach took Akins to a rehab center, cleaned him up, and helped him to kick the habit. The coach then made Akins sign a management contract, and got Akins a tryout overseas. The problem was Akins had to get to Europe on his own.

Vicki was still using crack. This pissed off Akins. Rather than help his wife as someone had helped him, he put Vicki out of her mother's house—the house that she grew up in. He then did some legal maneuvering, and sold Vicki's mother's home. He is now making $385,000 a year in Europe. His wife is here in the hood sucking dicks for five to ten dollars at a time. Big Slim brought me up to speed and I have to admit, I was kind of brokenhearted by the whole thing.

"Damn man, what else has gone on in the hood?"

"Mad shit's been happenin in the hood Kev, mad shit"

"What else has been going on?"

"Remember Cooley, Big Mike and Jonah?"

"Yeah"

"Well, them three niggas saw Set it Off one too many times. Instead of trying to rob banks, these fools tried to hit up an armored car"

"What happened to them?"

"Man, as soon as those fools jumped out on them armed security guards, they got full clips unloaded in they ass. All three of them fools is dead"

Big Slim gave me story after tragic story, and I made all types of mental notes. It seems that if I ever needed a story, all I needed to do was come home again.

Me and a bunch of the brothers in the hood drank and told lies well into the night. I called it a night at about

2:30. They of course stayed there until 6:00 AM. While the rest of the world was getting up to go to work, these cats were headed to bed. They will sleep until maybe 11 in the morning to 1 in the afternoon. Then they will back up and into shit. Big Slim of course would be at his office—the basketball court.

The next day, I got up and went to the park. As usual, there were a bunch of guys playing ball and there were a ton of challengers sitting in the grass waiting on Big Slim to show up so they could play against him. They were waiting around like they were waiting on a Rock Star to show up. About 12:30, Big Slim was seen off in the distance, finally headed to the court. I guess everyone is late for work from time to time, even thugs.

Big Slim showed up and looked as if he were hung over. I asked him was he okay, and he said that he was fine. He looked worn the hell out. Granted, we are not getting any younger, but I figured staying up all night and drinking during the day was like second nature to the brothas in the hood. I used to burn the candles at both ends myself, but that was years ago.

"Big Slim, are you sure you are okay?"

"Yeah Kev, I'm alright, watch me. You playin?"

"Naw, I'mma just check you out"

I hadn't played ball in years. I could play though. I was a guard in grade school, high school and college. I also played quarterback in college. I stand 6, 3 and I weigh a chiseled 240 pounds. The only reason I didn't play was because it had been so long, I was rusty and I didn't want to make a fool out of myself.

Big Slim chose a bunch of nobody's to be on his team and he began playing against the visitors from all

Still Crazy

over the state. A lot of the challengers talked shit, made threats and did a lot of swearing, but no one was ready for Big Slim on the court. Big Slim was clowning cats with amazing dunks, outside shots, inside shots and even a 360 degree dunk. Watching Big Slim play was a thing of beauty. He put in work on cats and picked up all types of cash doing so.

Around 2:00, a Cadillac truck pulled up. It was followed by a limo, and a fleet of other luxury trucks. A couple of pro ball players got out with an entire entourage.

"Aw shit" I heard Big Slim mumble.

Each one of the guys that showed up was famous. Each one was also known to be dirty a player, even in the pros. These guys didn't show up to gamble per se, they came to make a point. They were each dressed in their warm-up uniforms.

"Which one of you dirty uneducated niggas is the one they call Slim?" # 12 said.

"I'm the slimmest one out here, and it's not slim, It's Big Slim motha fucka, what ya'll Uncle Tom, pretty boy, sellout mothafuckas want?"

"We're here to play nigga! [throwing the ball at Big Slim] Check ball!"

Big Slim caught the ball and spat.

"Motha fucka, I don't play for free"

6 said, "I tell you what, you broke ass niggas pool all of your change together, we will double that shit, and then play for it; winner takes all"

Brothers from the hood started showing up at this point. They hated the fact that these brothers showed up talking shit. It didn't matter that they were pro ball players, they came to our hood disrespectful as hell. They had a few bodyguards with guns, and they had their hos, and one nigga figured that he would videotape their victory. They didn't know it, but had Slim just given the word, half the brothas in the park that day would have just shot and killed these motha fuckas. The problem with that is killing five or six pro athletes brings too much attention and heat to the hood.

"So what ya'll niggas gonna do? How much money ya'll got?"

"How much money can yo bitch ass cover?" Another voice said.

The other voice was that of a brother named Billy Brackens. We called him BB. He was the Kingpin of our hood, and he sold cocaine, heroine, weed and pharmacy drugs to people with Cancer, HIV and other diseases that had expensive ass prescriptions attached. BB was a regular pharmacy.

"We can cover anything you spoon fed niggas put out there"

#4 was from the hood, not our hood, but he grew up in the projects in Philadephia. He knew where this was going.

6 was smelling his piss and decided to get cocky and throw a high figure at us. I guess he figured that a high figure would mess us up psychologically and take us off our game.

"A hundred grand"

BB said, "Show me a hundred grand"

#6 said, "You show me a hundred grand"

BB gave his woman the keys to his truck pulled her to the side and talked with her for a few minutes.

"Okay, done. My girl will be back in a few with the cash. Now where is ya'll shit at?"

Some of the pro players started getting nervous. They walked off into some shit and now it was too late to un-ring the bell. A few minutes later, BB's truck came back with 100 large in a briefcase.

The pro players each had between ten and twenty grand on them. Their hundred grand was their spending money, all of their spending money. BB had his woman park his truck beside the pro player's entourage.

Big Slim looked a little pale for a dark-skinned brotha.

"You okay?" I asked him again.

"Yeah. Are you in? I can't play with just anyone against these niggas, and we are playing for two hundred grand"

"Three hundred grand. They are supposed to double the initial bet, and to answer your question, yeah I'm in"

I went to my car and switched into some shorts and a Magic Johnson throwback jersey. It had been years since I played, but I figured the shit is like riding a bike, once you start, it will all come back to you. Big Slim picked three more ball players from the hood, and we ran a five on five. If we won, two hundred grand went to BB, but we would each make 20 grand.

Big Slim took the ball and threw it at #6.

"Ball in bitch, let's go"

The game was to 32. Three pointers counted and there were no free throws for fouls. This was a game of street ball. The only one of the pro players that really knew street ball was #4 and I had his ass on lock. We traded baskets with the pros for the first 22 points. They scored and we scored. Each team was blown away by the other team's skills. Their center became so frustrated, that he elbowed our guy, Big Mark to the concrete, almost knocking him out. While Big Mark tried to shake the cobwebs out, Big Slim pulled the rest of us together and began to talk.

"First of all, if you get in trouble with the guy guarding you, get the ball to me. Each of you, pay attention to your man. #6 tends to play to his right, so you force his ass to the left. #4 does a double cross over whenever he is confronted, so when he hits the ball on the third bounce, steal the ball with your left hand. Their center is frustrated because he can't handle Mark's fade-away shot. So the first play will be Mark's fade-away, the second will be a steal by Kevin, then we force the other guard to the left, that's another steal and ya'll leave the rest to me.

Big Mark got up from his injury, we filled him in, and we went ahead to play—for three hundred thousand dollars.

I threw the ball in to Big Slim who did a cross over, spun and passed the ball back to me. I threw a behind the back pass to our other guard, who tossed the ball in to Big Mark. Mark did his textbook fade-away, and we were up 24-22. #6 tried to dribble fast to his right, and Big Slim forced him left. As soon as he did, I stole the ball and did a fast break layup to the hole. We were up 26-22. #4 got upset and took the ball immediately from his teammate. He tried that bullshit crossover of his and sure enough, on the third bounce, I tried to steal the ball with my left hand and I was gone. I did another layup and we were up 28-

22. I looked over at Big Slim who just winked at me. I thought to myself, "This brotha knows basketball like a doctor knows anatomy.

"Slim, you need to be coaching or something. I swear to God your talent is being wasted here on the court. You need to…"

"…Hold on there young Martin. We have a game to play"

Big Slim took, the ball and brought it directly to # 12, the fool that started all this shit to begin with. He was the same cat who hadn't scored a single point in this game. He was quiet as hell now.

"Check ball nigga"

Big Slim tossed the ball to #12. Instead of passing the ball, he tried to take Big Slim one on one. Slim picked his pocket, spun off him and did a reverse layup.

We were up 30-22 against pro players.

Slim took the ball again and pushed it right back in # 12's chest.

"Game point bitch"

12 threw the ball to #6. He tossed it to #4. He tossed it back to # 12 who thought he had a free layup. Big Slim blocked that shit off the backboard and I got the rebound. I pitched the ball to Slim who crossed over #12 who fell down. He then tossed the ball behind his back and shook off # 4. Big Slim tossed the ball back to me, I tossed it up in the air for an alley-oop, Slim did a 180, grabbed his dick with his left hand, and tip dunked it with the right.

The park erupted with cheers and applause.

Big Slim got nose to nose with #12.

"Get the fuck off my court"

"Not before givin me my money BB said"

Reluctantly, they gave us every dime that they owed.

I took the video footage from their guy. The ballers bodyguards walked up in the court like they were about to start some shit. As they walked up on the court, the doors to BB's truck opened up and ten more brothers got out heavily armed. They had M-16's, Glocks, Uzi's and Sawed off Shotties. That is what BB must have been talking to his lady about.

Now we had a situation.

BB said, "My money, please"

#12 said, "We need the video footage back"

I said, "Hell No"

#12 said, "Then we got a problem"

BB said, "No we don't. My niggas are going to shoot to kill. So you do what you want, just don't take all day"

I headed to my car.

"Hey, hey come back here!" # 12 yelled at me. I opened my trunk, changed my clothes, and switched tapes as I laid the tape into the trunk. I then came back to the court in the gear I had on when I first arrived. As I got back to the court, it appeared we were still at a standstill.

Big Slim said, "Kevin you are a college boy, any suggestions on how we deal with this?"

We all knew that we couldn't afford to kill pro athletes. They knew, if they attacked any one of us, this was going to end in bloodshed. We were all stumped.

Still Crazy

I said, "I got an idea, phone the police. Let them sort this shit out"

BB said, "Good idea. We might all go to jail, but they ass will be on TV tonight"

#12 said, "No! What will it take to get that tape back?"

I said, "The title to one of those trucks"

"What?"

"You heard me. You rich niggas gamble all the time and walk around talking shit about gambling for titles. So, sign the truck over"

They signed a truck over to me, I gave them the tape I had in my hand, and we all calmed down. They drove off immediately, and BB gave us each twenty large.

Big Slim asked, "So young Martin, why did you give them the tape? You know you are getting soft since you moved away"

I laughed at Big Slim.

"I switched tapes as I changed clothes by my car"

BB asked, "So what's on the tape that they have?"

"The alleged R. Kelly Sextape"

We all broke out laughing.

BB said, "Let's go mass produce these tapes, before they come back. We can send one to SportsCenter"

We all headed to BB's crib to relax. I went in my new truck.

I kicked it with the guys from the hood for a few hours and then went back to my parent's house to shower. I walked into a house that was smelling good as hell. My mother was making some lasagna again.

I showered, came down and kissed my mother on the cheek, and broke out my laptop. I had my story. I was going to call it, The Homecoming by Kevin Allen. I was firing away and hitting those keys like my life depended on it. My mother put a plate of lasagna beside me. By the time I got my first taste, it was cold. I ran off a hundred pages of good stuff during the first sitting. I forgot what it was like to be in the hood. I forgot about all the drama and real shit that sometimes goes on in the Chi. Basically, I forgot where I came from. This shit was funny. A week ago, I was in Italian shoes, $300.00

Slacks and shirts, and designer everything, white designer everything. People trip on Russell Simmons, P. Diddy and other black designers saying that their gear is too expensive. Compared to some of the white designers, Russell, Diddy and all the other designers are reasonably priced. Plus I'd rather that my money went to black designers. I see all the work that Russell and Diddy do in the community with their foundations, grants and other charity work. By buying black, I am actually giving back to the community.

Joy walked in from work and was happy to see that my mother made lasagna. She fixed herself a plate and sat beside me.

"Did you get a tuxedo yet?"

"A tuxedo? For what?"

"The formal event you agreed to speak at for free"

"Aw shoot, I'm sorry Joy, I forgot"

"Did you prepare a speech and an agenda for the workshop?"

"Naw kid, not yet"

"Kevin!"

"Joy, I got you. Trust me. I haven't missed a deadline yet"

"Okay Kevin, just remember this is my job"

" I got you. Do me a favor will ya, go upstairs and get me that Cartier box on my dresser. I got this bangin ass watch that I want you to see"

Joy went to get the box and handed it to me. I was still typing.

"Open it up" I said.

She opened it up and her faced lit up as she saw the diamond tennis bracelet inside.

"Kevin, you shouldn't have"

"Yeah, I probably shouldn't, but I did. I see you bustin your ass at your job and I see a lot of promise in your writing under your new penname. I admire that you want to find your own way, but I am still your brother. It brings me happiness to be able to do for you. Please accept it and know that I love you kid"

Joy hugged me. I hugged her back and went back to typing. I stayed up half the night working on my new book. When I finished the first hundred and fifty pages, I called my wife to ask her about her week and how the testing was going back at home. She said that she missed me, but she couldn't make it up to see me for at least two more weeks. We talked dirty to one another and said our I love you's.

"Baby, this was a great idea of yours. My coming home has helped me to find my muse"

"I'm just glad you aren't sitting around here moping anymore"

"Yeah, well I am working on something big. I can't stay away from Chicago as long as I did anymore. I need to visit home more often"

"You ain't messin' around with any of them fast ass city girls are you?"

"No baby, I'm not"

"You ain't back to gang-bangin and shit are you?"

"Naw, I'd have to be down here another month or so for that" I joked.

"No drive-by shootings? No Gangsta shit goin on there?"

"Naw baby, I mean damn this ain't L. A. it's not 1930 Chicago either. For the record also, Al Capone is dead" I said laughing.

"Don't act like people don't get shot in Chicago Kevin"

"Okay, people do get shot in Chicago, but if they do, they get shot because they did something"

"I'm scared to come down there"

"Baby, everything you heard about Chicago is hype. It's a beautiful, peaceful city. Nobody will fuck with you as long as you don't fuck with them"

"We'll see. I will see you in two weeks. I have to get my lesson plan together"

"Okay babe. I love you"

"I love you too"

I hung up the phone with a smile on my face. My sister Meka came downstairs.

"Where did you get the truck?"

Still Crazy

"You wouldn't believe me. Let me tell you about my day..."

♦ CHAPTER THREE ♦
LUST ON A 2-WAY STREET

KEVIN

That night I prepared a bomb ass speech, and even better agenda, and the next day, I got up and went to the Plaza to pick out a tuxedo. This was after I picked up the rental car from the park and took it back to the rental company. I was flossin in my new truck and lookin damned good if I do say so myself. I picked out a black and gold Sean John tuxedo with a pair of black Stacey Adams. I had the tuxedo tailored to fit, and I went and bought a Sean John watch to match. I then headed to Calumet City and got my hair cut by Big Meechie at Imperial Kutz. I went back to my mom's crib to work some more on my book. When I got there, Reverend Turner was there wondering if my lawyers had gone over the paperwork for his welfare to work program. They thought it was a good idea, but they thought my contribution should be no more than ten thousand. I wrote the Reverend a check for ten large and not a penny more. He looked dejected, but I didn't care. I then drove around to see if I could find Big Slim. I hadn't seen him in a while.

"Anyone seen Big Slim?" I asked as I pulled up to the park.

"Naw man, try up by the liquor store"

I went to the liquor store and there was no sign of him.

"Anyone seen Big Slim?"

One brotha said, "Yeah, he's workin"

I was thinking to myself, "You have got to be shittin me"

"Where?" I asked.

"In the alley of 94th and Emerald"

I drove over to 94th and Emerald and asked a brother if he had seen Big Slim.

"Yeah, he's workin in the alley"

I crept in the alley doing three miles an hour and I didn't see Slim anywhere. I honked the horn on the truck and yelled out.

"Hey Slim!"

Just then I saw him come to the side window of a house on my right side.

"What Nigga? Why you makin all that damned noise? Can't you see I'm workin?"

No this nigga ain't robbin somebody's crib and calling this shit work.

"Never mind, I will talk to ya later"

"A'ight"

I drove around front and there was Big Slim's two best friends, Bobby and Hank. Hank was eating an apple, and Bobby was giving directions to a bunch of young thugs on loading the stolen merchandise into a U-haul truck that they also stole. It looked like the brothas were actual movers. They each had on blue Dickie coveralls like they were professional movers.

"So explain this shit to me" I said.

"Young Martin, what's up man?" Hank said.

Bobby said, "Well basically, new people moved in, they didn't have any type of alarm or dog, and this is our little way of welcoming them to the hood"

Hank said, "Yeah, this will be a lesson on security measures and shit"

"Where are the owners?" I asked.

"They left all dressed up and shit. I guess they went to celebrate having a new home. I figure they will be gone for hours, Big Slim says with an operation like this, you only take what you can in twenty minutes time. He is in there picking and choosing what to take"

I shook my head with disbelief.

"Don't ya'll give a fuck about robbing people?"

Both of them said in unison, "Nope"

"How would you like it if someone did that shit to you?"

Hank said, "I got two rotweilers, an alarm and a Doberman. If a mothafucka steals anything out of my house, shit, he earned it"

I asked, "What about the fact that you all are moving shit out of the house rather than in it?"

Bobby said, "People are so dumb, they won't figure the shit out until tonight when this shit is on the news"

Again I shook my head in disbelief.

"I'll holler at ya'll ass later"

I went back to my mom's to type some more.

THAT WEEKEND

The night of the event for my sister's job, I was tight. I did my presentation at the publisher's office in Hugo Boss sandals, faded Levi Jeans, a bright white t-shirt, and a Cubs hat. Many of the students in the workshop were blown away at how down to earth I was. I talked to them about publishing, self publishing, marketing, and never giving up on their dreams of being a writer. There were twenty scholarship recipients, and there were another 30 students, or young people that were in the workshop as well. It made me feel proud to see so many young black people following their dream. It also made me thank God for his blessings when it dawned on me that many of these people were here because they wanted to see me. The workshop was a real success. Now I was ready to change into my tuxedo and kick it at the dance that they were having afterwards. Right now, I had to field some questions.

"If I haven't been able to sell my work, does that mean that I need to give up and my writing has no potential?"

"No, it means that you simply haven't sold anything yet. Maybe it's not your time, or maybe you haven't had enough exposure yet"

"What does it mean when publishers say that your work is not right for the market right now?"

"That one is tricky. Sometimes, it's self explanatory. In that I mean, romance sells, but urban drama is what's hot right now. Personally I think if your joint is hot, it will sell no matter what. So when people say that the market is not right at this time, I think it means that they aren't feeling you right now. I am assuming that you are talking about traditional publishers who are usually white. I'm not knocking white people, but they have no idea how to market our books"

One kid thought that I was being racial. "Mr. Allen isn't that a bit racist to say?"

I smiled to myself. There is always one.

"What's your name young brother?"

"Jerry Howard"

"Well, Mr. Howard, did you see the movie Love Jones?"

"Yeah"

"What did you think of it?"

"I thought it was hot"

"But most critics here in the Chi thought it was awful"

There were whispers among the workshop participants in agreement as I began again.

"Did you ever wonder why our movies get such bad reviews, and why even when they go to DVD, if they didn't get an Oscar or an Emmy, our movies traditionally sell less than the mainstream videos?

"No, I just figured that our movies bombed sometimes because they are so stereotypical. And in reference to the DVD's, I just figured that the stores made them affordable"

I laughed.

"Son, white America is not going to make anything affordable just for you or the community that you live in. Our movies are cheaper because that is how they are marketed. To mainstream consumers, our entertainment has less value. That, is a contradiction in itself because 80% of what is hot by way of entertainment, is what we produce. You would be surprised at how many of our books get changed into movies and how much Hollywood whitens up the lead characters, or simply adapts the story from a totally different perspective"

"A white perspective?"

"You said it, not me. Next question"

"Mr. Allen, why is the African-American section of bookstores so small if there are hundreds of thousands of us submitting works each year?"

"Because, just like everything else, they are only going to let a few of us in at a time. I believe that many traditional publishing houses know that we have stories that need to be told. I also think if they let us in publishing, they know we will become the dominant force, just like we do in everything else"

"So I should keep writing?"

"You all should keep writing. First of all, you should be writing because it is your passion, not because you are trying to get paid, although getting paid is nice. Next, you have to keep writing, keep plugging and believe that it's going to happen. Besides, there will be days once you are signed, that you will need those old stories, articles and screenplays; especially when you have a deadline to meet"

"Mr. Allen, do you ever suffer from writer's block?"

I smiled at the question. "Yes I do"

"How do you get through it?"

"I look for the thing that keeps me going. I look to my muse, and I generally get back on point"

"What is your muse? Is it your wife?"

"She can be quite motivating and captivating, but she is not my muse. My muse is the city of Chicago. That's why I'm home now. I am working on my next book"

I fielded some more questions and then closed the workshop. Afterward, I signed autographs and took some pictures with the kids. My sister Joy came in and applauded my efforts. She was already dressed for the event in a stunning dress by Kimora Simmons.

"You did a good job"

"Why thank you ma'am"

"Ready to change into your tuxedo?"

"Yep"

"The dressing room is down the hall on your left"

I changed into the tuxedo and I was looking good as hell if I do say so myself. I was looking like the MF Ebony Man of Chicago. I smiled a million dollar smile as I opened the door to the dressing room and took my sister's arm. We headed to the adjoining ballroom. I was blown away at the fact that they were playing House Music in the ballroom instead of Hip Hop, which is what I was expecting to hear.

"Joy, what's up with the House Music?"

"My boss asked me what was your favorite music, and I told them House Music. I know how your old ass be trying to recapture your youth and listen to all that post disco shit and do all those old dances"

I laughed my ass off. House Music was my weakness. As soon as I heard the hot beats from my days of hanging out at LaMirage, Mendel, Sauers, The Underground, The Music Factory and The Chick Rick House, I took off my jacket and started dancing. The DJ played White Horse, Let No Man Put Asunder, Love Sensation, Dr. Love and hot joints by Frankie Knuckles, Jamie Principal, Ron Hardy and the Hotmix 5. I danced so damned hard that I was sweating my butt off.

After a while, the DJ took me back a little further. He played some S. O. S Band, Laid Back, Roger & Zapp, and Heartbeat by Taana Gardner. I was truly tweakin when that joint came on. I broke out with all the old dances. I did the Wop, the Gigolo, the California Shake, the Robin Hood and then broke out into that cool stroll brothers do when they are tired. The DJ then played It's Time for the Percolator. I was blown away by the joints that the DJ was playing. Next I heard the lyrics to one of my favorite house joints.

Should I listen to what you say,

Or listen to what your folks say,

It's a tough decision to make.

I don't really want to lose you,

But I don't want your folks to,
Turn me over to the hands of the law.
I guess they think that, I'm not good enough for you.
I can tell the way they act, and their attitudes,
As the tears flow from my eyes,
I feel a hurt inside,
As I reach, reach out to you
Oh girl I'm so confused,
Oh, Oh I'm trapped, like a fool I'm in a cage and can't get out…

Man, I spun out and started dancing my ass off again. That was my joint back in the day. The DJ spun that joint, then went to washing machine, and then the House Music Anthem, Move Your Body. I tell you, everyone over 28 was jammin in the dance hall. Sisters kicked off those shoes and began dancing. All the adults were lost in the music. The young people were looking at us like we were crazy. They had no idea what house music was or what it meant to my generation. My sister broke out laughing.

"So what is it with you and this damned music?"

"House Music is more than music baby-girl. House is a way of life. It's a feeling down on the inside of you. It's taking everything great, everything soulful about our people, and putting it into one genre, one movement. You have old disco, and it can be house. Classic Hip Hop—can be house, any music that makes you smile or takes you back to a time when something special was happening in your life or in the lives of our people—that's house. It's hard to explain, but you can mix anything with house music. You can blend Marvin Gaye, hot beats, even Dr. King's speeches. Then, as the music plays, just allow it to take you wherever it is that you want to go. Hell, I have even heard Frankie Knuckles mix gospel in a lot of his joints.

Just then But For the Grace of God, started playing. The DJ went from that joint to a Mr. Fingers Remix, Michael Watford, and then started blending in some Hip Hop. That finally made the younger people happy.

"Now see, this is real music. Hip-Hop has House Music faded"

I laughed at my sister. "Hip-Hop is the house music of your generation. Just like House Music is still around and has grown considerably [House Music is now Global] so will Hip Hop."

The DJ played a joint by Jay-Z and Joy started dancing her butt off. It was obvious that music had a great influence in our family. Just as I lost my mind when the house music played, she snapped out as the Jay-Z joint went to LL's hot new joint Headsprung.

"Now see, this is true Hip-Hop" Joy said.

"I'm feeling you. Hip-Hop has come a long way since my day"

"Your day? I thought all you knew was house music when you were a teen?"

"Oh hell no. I rocked my early Hip-Hop also. If you go in the basement of the house right now, I got some Run-DMC, Doug E. Fresh, Slick Rick, Early LL stuff like My Radio and Rock Da Bells. I also have KRS-1, EPMD, Public Enemy, and a ton of stuff that opened the doors for rappers like Pac, Biggie, DMX, Nas and today's cats"

"You learn something new everyday" Joy said.

The DJ spun another hour or more of Hip-Hop and he tore it up. People young and old were wondering who was in the DJ booth spinning like that. To my surprise, he was not a he, but a she—my middle sister, Meka. This was her side hustle, and damn she was good at it. I saw her in the booth and she took a break to ask me what I thought. I hugged her and told her that she had mad skills and that she was doing a damned good job.

"I'm glad you like the way that I spin, because this is what I want to do with my life. I was hoping you could talk to Ma and Pops about me doing this as a career. If it came from you, that might soften the blow some"

"Meka, you want to be a DJ?"

"Not just a DJ. I mean I would like to maybe be a radio personality, but for the most part, I want to spin records"

I was blown away. I expected her to do something else with her life, only, I really wasn't sure what. Initially, I was turned off to the idea. Then I thought about all the people who told me that writing was also a fluke. Had I listened to that shit, there is no telling where I might be. Nope, my sister needed my support, and she was going to have it.

"I'll talk to Ma and Pops first thing tomorrow"

"Thanks Kevin"

I looked over at Joy.

"Did you know that she wanted to be a DJ?"

"You see I hired her"

"Good point"

"You gotta admit, the girl has skills"

"Yeah, she does"

SLOW JAMS

The lights in the hall went dim. They didn't go dark, just dim. Mcka, then threw on Adore by Prince. That is a timeless classic that puts everyone in the mood. I was just going to head to the refreshment table to get a drink when I heard a familiar sultry voice say, "Do you want to dance?"

YOLANDA CARTER

"Hello Yogi"

"Hello Kevin"

Just when I was truly enjoying being home in Chicago, the worst possible thing that could happen to me, just walked in the door. I never saw Yolanda arrive. Had I seen her first, I would have quietly tipped out of the door. Yolanda Carter or "Yogi" as I called her was my ex-fiancée. We dated for five years. We dated the latter part of high school and all of my undergrad. Yolanda was drop dead gorgeous. She stood five feet, six inches tall, and she had a honey brown complexion to her. She had shoulder length hair that was full of body. She has dark brown piercing eyes, juicy lips, a 36C chest, and an ass that was like something out of Nelly's video, tip drill.

Yolanda was dressed in a black form fitting dress that hugged the hell out of her ass and accentuated her curves. Her breasts were full in the delicate material and it looked as if she didn't have on a bra underneath the dress. There was a slit in the front that was so high, if a breeze came threw the door, her panties, if she was wearing any, would show. The V in the front of the dress came all the way down to her naval. She had on suede high inch heels and she was looking good enough to eat.

"You didn't answer my question, do you want to dance?"

I fingered my wedding ring and showed it to Yolanda as I said, "I don't think so Yolanda"

She smiled seductively, and she slowly walked away. Before departing across the room she said, "Chicken"

Almost as if on cue, my sister, Meka played One Woman Man by Dave Hollister. I looked up at the DJ booth and Meka was all smiles. She knew I got the message of her playing the Dave Hollister joint. I sang the chorus to myself as Dave Hollister's joint was blasting overhead.

Seeing you reminds me of, all the nights I used to beat it up, I would do it again but I can't. Cause everything is different now, I've finally settled down, and became a one woman man.

I began to wipe sweat from my brow, because I obviously dodged a bullet. My sister knew exactly who Yolanda was. All three of my sisters hated her ass. My sister Joy came over to see if everything was okay.

"You okay Kevin?"

"Yeah. What is Yolanda doing here?"

"Shit, I don't know. I'll ask the bitch to leave"

"No, No, No. I was just wondering why she was here"

"I imagine she paid her $25.00 like everyone else"

"So what affiliation does she have with writing?"

"She doesn't. She probably heard about the event on the radio and heard that you were one of the guest speakers. After hearing that you would be here, that probably prompted her to buy that hooker dress to get your attention"

"You think the dress is for me?"

"Hell yeah! I tell you, men are so stupid"

"Well, I'm cool. I'mma just sit here and have my drink"

"Why don't you call your wife?"

"What?" That snapped me back to reality.

"Call your wife. See bruh, I see what's happening here. You're having a moment of weakness because that bitch is here. What you need to do is call your old lady and either talk to her, or simply tell her that you love her. That's what you niggas should do when your dick starts talking to you and logic starts leaving your body. It's just like an alcoholic or a base head. When you get that Jones for a hit, you need to call your sponsor—your wife or girlfriend"

"That's almost crazy enough to work"

"That's what all men should do when they feel like they are going to stray"

I started to dial my wife. As I did, I surveyed the room to see where Yolanda was. She came in with another woman that was equally as beautiful as she was. Her girlfriend was a light skinned honey with hazel eyes and an ass just as big as Yolanda's. Yolanda's girlfriend walked in my direction to get a drink. I let my phone ring at home in Somerton. I was hoping that Tamara was home, but tonight she was in step-areobics. She wouldn't be home until much later. Just then, my eyes met with Yolanda's who mouthed the words

"I'm wet" from across the room. I tried to pretend that I didn't see her. I looked away while sipping my drink and then looked up again. This time she mouthed the words, "Come fuck me" She looked toward the dressing room where I had changed earlier. My heart started beating really fast and I became light headed. I hadn't danced in a while, but I could feel perspiration on my forehead. I let out a sigh and said a small prayer. "God, give me strength"

Like I said, Yolanda was my ex. Not only was she my ex, but she was the freakiest woman I had ever known. We both have some clinical issues that need to be resolved, that's how freaky we were. We were a tandem that would put the Red Shoe Diaries to shame. We fucked in public places, private places and did some shit that was off the charts back in the day. I was with Yolanda five years and I never, and I mean never, got tired of fucking her. When she mouthed the words I'm wet, I thought I was having a flashback. That was some shit that I started. Me and this broad had serious chemistry. When I saw her my dick automatically got hard. She also automatically got wet. I know, because I would check her pussy when we were out. I would call her on my cell phone and say, "Are you wet?" She would respond, "Yes baby"

I would say, "Do you want to fuck me?"

She would say, "Always"

I would say, "How bad do you want to fuck me?"

She would say, "So bad, that I have to finger myself throughout the day until I can come home to you and we cum together"

That was our script. We did this shit all day, everyday, and we fucked any and everywhere that we could. We did it all, vaginal, oral, anal, toys, domination, role-playing, you name it. I enjoyed the hell out of that pussy. I love my wife, but that pussy? That pussy is the most memorable pussy of my life.

Every guy has a woman in his past that was a straight up freak. Most guys have at least one woman in their past who was so freaky, even twenty years later, the thought of the woman will make them smile and make their dick pulse. More often than not, these women are not the man's wife or current love. Women that were true freaks were the best thing since sliced bread. Every man has one in his life. Mine was Yolanda Carter. Just like other men, the reason that I broke up with Yolanda is the same reason all men break up with a super freaky woman — the bitch is crazy.

Yolanda was no different. She was crazy. When some people say crazy, I know, you think maybe she had a temper or she was just the type to wild out on a brotha. Naw, you don't get it then. When I say crazy, I mean C-R-A-Z-Y.

The last time that I saw Yolanda she was being hospitalized. Yolanda was crazy like the sister in A Thin Line, or Like Glenn Close in Fatal Attraction. One day we got into an argument and I walked off from her ass. This broad jumped into her Chevy Baretta, and hit me with the fucking car. I never told anyone about that incident. I awoke in the hospital with fractured ribs. To help me with the pain, Yolanda would come to the hospital and gently give me head. That is the crazy shit that I am talking about. If Yolanda was on her cycle, she gave me head for at least an hour, almost as if to oblige me until she could give me the pussy. When we were in college, if I wanted sex, head or whatever, she would give it to me day and night without question. No matter how tired she would be, if my dick got hard, she felt it was her duty to get it back down. In bed, she was great. Outside of the bedroom, she was psychotic. She used to accuse me all the time of fooling around behind her back in undergrad. This was impossible, because she was always with me. She used to accuse me of plotting to leave her if I was away from her more than a few hours. I spent a good portion of our relationship trying to convince her that I wasn't. The night that we broke up, was because she saw me speaking to a woman at a bookstore. Mind you, I was there with her. When the woman walked to her car, Yolanda followed her, sprayed her with mace, kicked the shit out of her, and beat the woman even after she fell unconscious. Someone called the police as it was happening. Rather than get jail time, Yolanda went away for a while. Her parents and I both agreed that she was emotionally unstable. I quietly just walked out of her life.

That was my last major relationship before my wife. Now here she was again, looking good as hell. She blossomed from being a pretty girl, to a fine ass woman. Yolanda asked another man in the room to dance and he very quickly obliged her. I watched the two of them dance to a slow joint by Avant. The man's back was to me, and Yolanda's eyes once again met mine. She looked at me intently and seductively as she held on to the man that she was dancing with.

"She's pretty isn't she?" a woman's voice said.

I turned around and it was the woman that Yolanda came in with. She had her drink in hand and looked at me with a seductive smile.

"She's okay" I said.

"She misses you. All they way over here she commented on how special your relationship was"

"I'm sorry, my name is Kevin Allen, and you are?"

"Just call me Kitty"

Kitty was fine as hell. Her speaking to me out of the blue threw me off. I was curious as to what game Yolanda was now playing.

"So, Kitty, you are Yolanda's co-worker?" I asked as I began drinking my rum and coke.

"I'm Yolanda's on again off again lover"

I almost spit my drink out of my mouth.

"I'm sorry, what?"

"Her lover"

"So Yolanda is now lesbian?"

"No, she's strickly dickly"

"Then how…"

"She is my girlfriend. She's one of my closest friends. We mostly talk, shop and do girl stuff. We each have had men in our lives over the years and when they fuck up or break out hearts, we sometimes turn to each other for comfort"

My head was spinning now. Two fine ass black, women with fat asses and titties to die for were doing each other? Aw, shit. My shit was harder than quantum physics. I was thinking what every man in place would be thinking, How can I be down? My dick began to rise fast in my slacks. I had a really quick fantasy about a ménage a trios and when I came out of my trance, Yolanda was looking me dead in my mouth. She knew what I was thinking. I had to get out of here. I began to finger my wedding ring and it took a lot of restraint not to walk across the room and take Yolanda in my arms. I thought to myself, "I'm married. I am very fucking married. I love my woman, and I simply need to get the fuck out of here"

I smiled at Kitty and gulped the rest of my drink. I then headed toward the door.

"Nice meeting you Kitty, good luck with Yolanda"

I was proud of myself. I left.

THE 9705 CLUB

I was too wired to go home to my mother's house, so I headed to the 9705 bar on Halsted. That was my spot when I used to live in the hood. As soon as I walked in, the bartender, Adrienne gave me a warm smile.

"Hey, Kevin, how are you boo?"

"I'm fine Adrienne. How are you?"

"Baby, I'm blessed"

"When was the last time that you saw any of my old crew?"

"Oh baby they are in here all the time. I saw Derrick a few months ago, and I saw Jamie Kennedy just six weeks ago. You know Jamie has a son now that he was keeping secret from everyone including Mia"

"Damn, he is out there like that?"

"He was for a minute"

"See, Mia should have given that boy some babies"

"She just did. Jamie and Mia had twin girls"

"What about Loretta?"

"She had two terrible bouts with Cancer, but she is okay"

"And Derrick? Did he get with Rose or Stephanie?"

"Both. That girl, Rose went back to her husband, and that girl Stephanie is seeing someone new. Your boy, Derrick blew up after that. He needs to get his butt back in the gym"

Adrienne had the 411 on everything. She was a fine ass sister that every one of us men wanted, but none of us could have. She was a free spirit. She was also fine as hell. Did I say that already? Anyway, to keep my mind off Yolanda, I asked about other people that we both knew. Adrienne was a damned good listener. We went to grade school at Washington together, High School at Julian, and college at Columbia. She has a number of degrees, but rather than work in Corporate America, she works here at the 9705 Club.

"What are you having?"

"I'll take a seven and seven"

"No rum and coke?"

"Naw, I had that earlier. I think it's time that I went with something a little stronger"

"Woman problems?"

"Yeah, what else"

"I heard you got pussy whipped by some pretty ass country girl"

"How did you hear that all the way down here?"

Adrienne just gave a look that said, "Nigga please"

"How are Leon and David doing?"

Still Crazy

"Leon almost lost his damned license falling in love with one of his clients. He didn't get with her, but he came damned close. The ethics board suspended his shit until he completes therapy himself. David is looking for a new partner until Leon gets his shit together. He's now doing motivational speaking"

"Man, it sounds like it's been crazy around here. It seems that all the guys that I used to kick it with, have nothing but drama going on"

I threw back my seven and seven and asked Adrienne to hit me with another one.

"Instead of those seven and sevens, why don't you drink this?"

She put a reddish brown drink in front of me and I gulped it down. It was smooth and it had a strong kick to it.

"What was that?"

"Hennessey"

"Why are you giving me Hennessey?"

"You need to fuck with that Hen if you are going to deal with what just came through the door"

I turned around and walking through the door was Yolanda. All the men in the club were checking her out. I took in a deep breath and let it out slowly. I then tried to pretend as if I didn't see her at all.

Yolanda walked by me and went to the Jukebox to play some tunes. At 9705, the DJ didn't come every night. The nights that he wasn't there, you had to use the Jukebox. Yolanda walked by me and pulled a number of single bills out of her top and fed them into the player.

"I let out a gentle sigh"

Adrienne poured me another glass of Hennessey.

"Ain't that the crazy bitch that you used to deal with back in the day?"

"Yeah"

Adrienne poured herself a drink.

"That's the same bitch that hit yo ass with a car, ain't it?"

I drank my drink. I then said, "Yep"

Adrienne shook her head with disbelief and smiled to herself. She had another shot of Hen.

"Kevin, let me tell you what is about to happen. You are about to ask my advice about her, and I'mma tell you not to fuck with her. She is going to entice your ignorant ass and you are gonna probably end up hittin it, and then Kevin...that broad is going to make your life hell. Why is it that you and the other brothas can't just say no to pussy every now and then? Why do you all punish yourself so bad? What is it about you boys from Sangamon Street? What is it about that block?"

I smiled to myself. I drank my drink and I spoke to Adrienne.

"Adrienne, I'm gonna shock you. I'm going to tell her that I'm no longer interested and that I'm happily married. After that, I'm going to walk out of that door and go home and get some sleep. This will be the second time tonight that I will have declined her advances"

"Uh-huh, yeah, whatever. That broad is about to work your ass like a plantation.

I walked over to the Jukebox where Yolanda was standing. She was playing Baby Hold On to Me by Gerald Levert. She was looking good as hell.

"Yolanda what is it that you want?"

She walked up to me, placed her left hand around my neck, kissed me gently on the lips, and deftly grabbed my package with the other, slowly jagging me off.

"Us. I want us again. I want you again. I want this dick in my pussy. I then want it in my mouth and then in my ass. You know what the fuck I want. Do you know what an ATM is?"

"Automated Teller Machine?"

"Ass to Mouth"

I took in a deep breath as Yolanda's grip on my dick became harder, and she jagged me off just a little bit faster.

"Yolanda, I'm married"

"Fuck me Kevin"

"I'm happily married now"

"Fuck me Kevin"

"I have been married for a number of years"

"You haven't taken my hand off your dick. Baby let's not play this game. Take me somewhere and fuck me. Please?"

She began whimpering and moaning in my ear.

"Please fuck me baby, please?"

Women are some dirty mothafuckas. They are powerful as hell and they know that they have the power, and we men are so damned weak. I tell you, women should have to pass a certification exam to distribute pussy. Too many women abuse their power over us. Hell naw I didn't take her hand off my dick and hell yes I was giving in to her tricks. How many brothas out there can say no to a woman begging them for dick?

I grabbed both of Yolanda's hands and held them in front of me and tried to snap out of her trance.

"Yolanda, I'm going home"

"Fuck me Kevin"

"I gotta go"

"Fuck us Kevin"

There was another voice behind me. It was the voice of a woman. There were two more hands on my dick from behind me. That fucked me up at first because I had Yolanda's hands in my hands. I looked behind me and it was Kitty. I was at a loss for words. I looked at Kitty who winked. I then looked at Yolanda who smiled, and then together, the three of us headed to the door. I looked at Adrienne as I headed to the exit. She just shook her head and laughed quietly to herself as I left.

I was looking for my truck. Yolanda told me not to worry about the truck because she was going to drive her car.

"Leave the truck here. We will take my car"

"I'm not leaving this truck here, someone will take it. Where are we going?"

"That's up to you"

Yolanda began kissing Kitty and palmed her right breast. That got me going, so I headed to the nearest motel. I drove to the Halsted Arms, but it was too seedy. I then drove to the Duke Motel, but that was equally as bad. I didn't want to go downtown, but I didn't want to just go anywhere either. I headed over into Oak Lawn Illinois and hit the Deluxe Motel. I made sure to pay cash, and then I parked the truck in the lot and followed the two women to the hotel room. They were kissing and feeling on one another all the way to the room. Other men seeing me walk with them were jealous. It was written all over my face what was about to happen.

I had been approached by women offering to do a ménage before, but I never went through with it. In fact, since getting the book deal, I have never slept with any of the women that have come to my book-signings. I have hidden an explicit photo or two that I have been given in a shoebox under my bed, but that's about it. I love my wife, so I would never do anything like that.

I can't explain why this so different. I can't explain why I couldn't say no. I was doing fine until Yolanda brought Kitty into the picture. The thought of a ménage turned me on like a motha. We entered the room and Kitty jumped on the bed. She smiled seductively at me. Yolanda caressed my cheek as she walked by and then spoke.

"So how do you want to do this?"

"This is your show. I'm just a spectator" I said.

"A spectator for now," Yolanda said.

"Yeah, a spectator for now," I quipped.

Yolanda looked to the floor and then smiled to herself. She walked over to the clock radio and turned it to V103. Teddy Pendergrass was singing Turn off the lights. I thought to myself that V103 always had excellent timing. Yolanda slowly began to undress. As she undressed standing, Kitty began peeling her clothes off right there on the bed. She stripped one article at a time. Each time that Kitty took something off, she tossed the article of clothing at my feet. Kitty had on a white lacy bra and panty set. The set was nice as hell. It hugged her curvy hips and breasts like a second skin. Not to be outdone, Yolanda had on the exact same bra and panty set on in black. Both women stopped stripping once they made it to their underwear.

Kitty went to a seated position resting her upper body with her elbows. Yolanda walked up to the bed and stood over Kitty. Yolanda rubbed Kitty's breasts and as she did, Kitty let out a gentle sigh. Her chest began to heave up and down and slowly, Yolanda released the mounds of flesh. Kitty's breasts were nice. They were very nice because she paid for them. They stood up on their own, nipples pointing north. Yolanda leaned over and kissed Kitty gently, savoring her taste. She then began to tongue kiss her passionately. After a few minutes, Yolanda began licking Kitty's nipples and my own breathing was getting heavier and heavier.

Yolanda then peeled her own bra off exposing her breasts which were natural and almost as perky and as full as Kitty's. They were beautiful caramel breasts with dark chocolate nipples. As she took her bra off, I thought about how much fun I used to have with her tits. I used to love feeling them, sucking them, kneading them and fucking them. There was nothing better to me when she was on her period than grabbing a bottle of lotion, rubbing it into her soft heavy mounds, and then placing my dick between them. A lot of my boys hate titty fucking. They think it's just jagging off on a woman's chest. Fuck that. For me, titties are just—wonderful.

Yolanda eased Kitty all the way down on her back. She then straddled Kitty's face without taking off her panties. Kitty began eating out Yolanda, her sometimes lover. She licked Yogi's crotch with abandon. Yogi began to moan and grind her pelvis against Kitty's face. As she did, she tossed her head back and forth with passion. She was trying to get to that special place. Kitty was taking her there. As Kitty ate Yogi out, she pulled her panties to the side and began to finger herself until there was a froth between her legs.

It was hard as hell not top crawl up to the bed and begin eating Kitty out. I wanted to so bad, but even more, I wanted to see how far this show was going to go. Kitty ate Yogi passionately, and she fingered herself with a frenzy. The music changed to an old Luther Vandross joint. As Luther began singing Superstar, I pulled off my shirt and shoes. Kitty began moaning as she was close to cumming. Yogi grabbed Kitty's hands and stopped her. Yogi then leaned forward, peeled off the soaking wet panties, tossed them to me, and smiled. She then leaned all the way over in the 69 position, and began to eat Kitty out.

I held Kitty's panties in my hand. With my forefinger and thumb, I rubbed the panties back and forth in my hand. They were so wet. I was getting more and more turned on with each passing second. I smelled Kitty's scent, and was taken in by it. I wanted Kitty and Yolanda more than I wanted anything.

Yogi got up, walked over to where I was standing and smiled at me. She could see that I was excited, and that turned her on. She then turned her back to me showing me that music video ass of hers. She crawled on the bed, hiked her ass in the air, and went back to eating Kitty out. Kitty was back in a seated position, resting on her elbows and fondling her own breasts.

I sat in the chair that was in the room and watched Yogi lose herself in pleasing Kitty's love-box. With her ass hiked up the way that it was, I could see that her pussy was soaking wet. Her juices slowly ran down her thighs and her pussy lips were almost calling to me. Kitty's chest was heaving up and down and she closed her eyes as she got closer and closer to that special place that all women love. Yogi's ass slowly rocked back and forth as she tried to stick her tongue deeper and deeper inside of Kitty. As Kitty's moaning got louder and louder, I began to get undressed. I stripped down to my boxers and as I did, Kitty opened her eyes and smiled at me. Our eyes locked as she was closer and closer to cumming.

Kitty closed her eyes again and began to whimper. She was close, very close. The song on the radio now was Lifetime by Maxwell. As Kitty began to rock back and forth and moan louder, I entered Yogi from behind. Yogi stopped eating out Kitty long enough to let out a gasp. I entered her all the way in from the back and rested in her wet warmth as her ass consumed my entire being. Yogi went back to eating out Kitty, only now she was letting out primitive moans. Kitty was moaning, Yogi was moaning, and I was moaning as I pulled out of Yogi all the way to the tip, and slowly went all the way back in. My dick was sloppily wet with Yogi's juices. I grabbed her baby making hips and drove my way up inside her trying not to disturb the rhythm of her eating Kitty out.

Kitty began to tremble. Her legs were vibrating like a pager. Her moans became louder and louder and her chest was heaving up and down really fast. Her breaths became short and she began to whimper and squeal. She kept saying over and over again, "Yeah, yeah, yeah, oh baby yeah, right there, oh yeah, right…there…right…yeah…yeah…. yeah!" Kitty started squealing at the end like she was Minnie Ripperton at the end of Loving You. She came—hard. She tried to pull away from Yogi, but Yogi held onto her. That was when I started to really get my stroke on.

"Don't let her go anywhere. Eat that pussy Yogi!" I demanded.

Yogi increased her grip on Kitty who was screaming at this point with passion,

"Fuck! Oh…Fuck…Oh my God, ohmygod. Fuck…Oh…baby please stop…baby please stop…please…"

"Fuck that shit Yogi, eat that pussy. Eat that mutha fucka like there's no tomorrow. Handle that shit girl, you know what I like"

I smacked Yogi's ass. She loved that shit. I gave that ass a few more good slaps and then grabbed a fist full of her hair and started getting off some good long strokes, doggy style.

Again Kitty tried to get away. Each time she did, I smacked Yogi on the ass and directed her to keep going.

"Fuck that shit, hold her ass Yogi. Get that pussy. That's right, handle that shit. Do that shit girl, work her ass like you want me to work you. Eat that pussy like you want yours eaten. That's what I'm talking about [slap] get that ass!"

Kitty squealed and then pulled away from Yogi and turned on her side. She was in a fetal position weeping and breathing hard. She tried to get her composure, but it was obvious that she came harder than she ever had before. As she lay there on the bed, I began to switch up my pace. I fucked Yogi with long slow strokes, then with fast strokes, medium strokes and slow again.

"You miss this shit don't you?"

"Yes Kevin. Oh Yes Kevin, fill me up baby, fill me up"

I forced her head into the pillows and began to pound away from behind, this time with all slow, long and even stokes. The room was filled with the sound of my body slapping hard up against hers. Maxwell was off, and the radio station was now playing Adore by Prince. I almost lost myself in Yogi's warmth. I had to stop while I was deep in side her and rest to keep from cumming. As I did, my dick throbbed and pulsated while inside of her.

Kitty crawled over to us and positioned herself back into the 69 position, only now, she was beneath Yogi and licking her clit and my balls. She tea-bagged me as I pulsed inside Yogi. When I was satisfied that I was not going to cum, I began to take long even strokes again inside Yogi. I came all the way out and went all the way back in and with each stroke, Yogi's legs began to tremble. In the Air Tonight by Phil Collins was now on and between my strokes and Kitty eating her pussy, Yogi was no match for the two. Her legs began to tremble. She grabbed two fistfuls of sheets, and buried her face as she screamed as loud as she could into the pillows. As she came, I buckled at my knees myself as I almost came. Yogi went from having her ass hiked in the air to laying flat on her stomach. All the time, I was still inside her. I slowly pulled out of her and tried to rest. I laid on my back and then Kitty turned her attention to me.

Kitty began giving me head. Her licking Yogi's juices off my dick got me harder than Viagra and poppers. Up and down she licked my shaft clean and then massaged my balls as she tongue kissed and licked the tip. I grabbed a fist full of Kitty's hair and helped her to take as much of me as she could. Yogi crawled beside Kitty, and together, they both alternated giving me head. At first Kitty sucked, then Yogi sucked, and both tongue kissed each other with the head of my dick between the two of them. Yogi stuck a finger in my ass as she deep throated me. She gave me head until she was tired. Without missing a beat, Kitty took over as Yogi licked and tongued my balls. I wanted to fuck Kitty next, but my dick had other plans. The next thing I knew, I was cumming harder than I ever had before. I shot seed like a fountain. Kitty and Yogi savored every drop. They both licked and sucked me past climax until I thought I might pass out. All three of us came. For an hour afterward, we lay there in each other's arms.

I took a quick nap. I dreamed that I was being given head. When I opened my eyes, Kitty was there deep throating me. Up and down she sucked me back to life. I grabbed a fist full of her hair and helped her to give me head. Up and down I guided her up my shaft, down to my balls and back up to the tip again. When my dick was at it's hardest, I stopped kitty and pulled her up to me. I kissed her deeply on the mouth and tasted my own flavor. I palmed her ass while we tongue kissed.

I then turned over with Kitty on the bottom. I kissed behind her ear, the nape of her neck, her collarbone and slowly down her front. I licked her nipples and began to squeeze her artificial breasts. They felt good. Whoever did her boob job did a damned good job. I licked her nipples feverishly and began to slowly finger her as I kissed all over the front of her body.

I kissed her stomach all the way down to her special place. I fingered her faster and faster while licking the head of her clit. Over and over again Kitty began to moan. Her juices were wet like a teenage girl. I loved a soppy pussy. It was so inviting. Faster and faster I fingered her. Faster and faster I licked her clit. Her lower torso began to rock as she became beside herself with passion. I fingered her with one hand, licked her clit, and squeezed one of her breasts with the other. I tweaked her nipple between my thumb and index finger. Minutes later, she was cumming.

After she came, I fell backward on the bed, tired from exhaustion. When I looked up a few seconds later, Kitty was straddling me with her back to me. She rocked back and forth and I stared intently at her round and juicy ass. I looked at Kitty's ass and smacked it hard. She moaned as I did and she made her ass clap back and forth on my dick. It was so round and juicy, that I thought I was ready to bust another nut. Just like Yogi, Kitty's pussy was soppy wet. She rocked back and forth faster and faster and she brought her ass up high in the air and then all the way down as she tried to get long even strokes just as Yogi had taken earlier. I heard the sound of the shower and assumed that Yogi was in there bathing. I decided to take advantage of the one on one sex, and I tapped that ass on Kitty for twenty minutes. I came on her back and then laid back into the bed. Kitty then gave me head until I passed right back out and went to sleep.

"That shit was the bomb" I said as I drifted off to sleep.

THE NEXT MORNING

That morning I awoke at about noon. Check out was at 11:00, but I didn't care. When I awoke, Kitty and Yolanda were gone.

"Where the fuck did they go?"

I went back to sleep. It was 3:00 PM when I finally left the Deluxe Motel. I was relaxed as hell. After all that sleep, I was ready to get into some shit. I went to my truck and headed back to my mother's house.

I got back to my mother's house and my sisters were playing monopoly and eating snacks when I came in.

"Well, look what the cat drug in, where have you been?" Joy said.

I said, "Out kicking it"

Meka said, "With that tramp I'll bet"

I said, "Didn't you ask me for a favor? Be nice"

My mother came downstairs and chimed in, "So where did you spend the night last night?"

I was surprised that my moms was grilling me like she did when I lived at home.

I laughed before saying, "Excuse me, ladies, I'm a grown ass man"

My sisters all smiled at each other and laughed a bit as they said, "ooohhh he's grown"

My sister Joy gave me a wry smile as she spoke. "Well, Mr. Grown ass man, your wife is upstairs"

I turned a lighter shade of pale. Joy and Meka high fived each other and laughed their asses off.

"Man, stop playin. That shit is not funny"

My mother walked over to me and said, "They're serious. She came in late last night. She just missed you at the event. Apparently, you had just left"

"Aw shit"

My mother gave me a look that said I should be ashamed of whatever it was that I did last night. Then she spoke.

"I told her that you went to a party in Wisconsin with friends. I have been leaving messages on your cell phone since last night"

I kissed my mother on the cheek. "Good lookin out" I thought.

I let out a sigh of relief. I had no idea where my phone was though.

"You ought to be ashamed of yourself, having your mother lie for you" Joy said.

I was still blown away by the fact that Tamara was here. I was glad as hell that I showered before I left the hotel. I went upstairs to say hello to my wife. I took that nervous walk that brotha's take when they are guilty of some shit and trying to play it off.

♦ CHAPTER FOUR ♦
WHICH WAY IS UP?

I went upstairs into my old room and my wife was there looking through many of the things around the room. She picked up my football trophies, my artwork and an old journal of mine with all my poetry in it. She looked at the various knickknacks in the room and smiled to herself. She had only met my family once before today, and that was at our wedding. My family really enjoyed Tamara, but because we live in another state, I seldom had time to get home. I take that back...I never made the time to come home. I needed to take the time so that my family could get to know this wonderful woman in my life. Tamara was looking good as hell. I had only been away from my wife for nine days, but I missed the hell out of her.

Tamara had on boots, tight Levi jeans and a Baby Phat t-shirt. Her hair was cropped nice to her head and that ass...man that ass was looking good as hell.

"Hey you", I said as I walked up behind her and gave her a big bear hug. I was praying to God that Tamara didn't smell another woman on me. I know that shit is impossible, but women and their damned instincts scare the shit out of me. I kept thinking to myself, "Just act normal and everything will be cool"

"Kevin, where have you been?"

"Partying. Why didn't you call me and say that you were coming?"

"I've been calling you. I had to ask your mom to come and get me from the airport"

I reached around looking for my phone. I still had no idea where it was.

"Damn, I guess you're right babe. I have no idea where my phone is. I must have partied too hard"

"You better be careful while you are here on your little sabbatical. I don't want any of these fast ass city women tryin to turn your head"

"What are you talking about?"

"These women here in Chicago, they are just so...pretty. They all seem to be rude and competitive. Many of them dress like they are models out of a magazine"

"Damn baby, where were you at that you saw all these fine ass honeys? Shit, Maybe that's where I need to roll"

"After your mother picked me up, She and your sisters took me shopping at some place called The Water Tower"

"The Water Tower? Well hell yeah, they look that way, but that's not all there is to Chicago. You were downtown. Downtown is expensive. That is far from the norm as far as Chicago women go. Don't get me wrong, we have some fine ass women here. We have some serious business savvy women here, but few of them model"

"What about their attitudes?"

"Well babe, sisters here have attitude because they have to compete with black men, compete with white men, compete with each other, and then deal with brothas coming at them trying to run game all day. It's not like in the Carolinas. Here the dating game, Corporate America, and adversity hit you all at the same time. If the sisters here have an attitude, chances are, they are justified"

"Justified or not, some of the looks I got from these women were scornful"

"That's because you're so damn fine and they're jealous"

I moved in to steal a kiss and nuzzle on her neck. Tamara instinctively grabbed for my package. I backed up some and played it off.

"Hey babe, don't forget we are in my mother's house"

"I'm just touching it"

I laughed a little as I held her in my arms.

"Yeah but doing it here makes me feel dirty, like I am being sneaky"

I came up with that story quick. The truth of the matter was that my dick was sore from all the fucking that I did last night and this morning.

"But you are sneaky" She said.

"You're right, I am"

I began kissing my wife and I cuffed that big round ass of hers. Sore dick or not, I couldn't change my routine. I gently hugged her and got a nice slow grind on in my room like I did when I was a teenager.

"So, any stories to tell me about you and teenage Chicago girls in this room?"

"Nah, nothing much to tell. I slept here and that was about it"

"No sexual escapades?"

"Nothing worth mentioning"

"So you were a good boy"

"Something like that"

"So when did the bad boy stuff that you do begin?"

"I don't think I started acting out until I got in college"

Inside I was smiling. I did plenty of dirt in that room. I lost my virginity there, had my first ménage a trois there, and even slept with one of my mother's friends, Ms. Patterson, right there on this single bed. Hell, I am still surprised that the bed is still here. I used to joke when I was younger and tell my boys that my bed needed hydraulics or shocks on it from all the ass I used to get.

My sister Joy walked into the room with a look on her face that said she didn't want to disturb me.

"Kevin you got a minute?"

"Yeah Joy, what's up?"

"Reverend Turner is downstairs. He wants to speak with you"

"Aw shit"

"Kevin don't talk that way" Tamara interrupted.

"Babe you don't understand, this MF has been getting on my nerves"

"Don't call the preacher a MF. He's a man of the cloth"

"The cloth must be made out of Egyptian Silk. He's always got his hand out"

"Kevin, be nice"

I let out a sigh. "Okay, let's see what he wants"

SINNERS AND SAINTS

I walked downstairs and there was the good Reverend waiting patiently to speak to me. He had on his "I need some more money" clothes on. I greeted him with a half smile as I came down the stairs.

"Reverend" I said sarcastically.

"Kevin, how are you?"

"I'm okay as long as this isn't a solicitation for more money"

"Kevin!" My wife interjected.

"Well Kevin, I talked with the board, and they wanted me to talk to you once more about the other half of the donation that we need from you"

"What donation Kevin?"

"The Reverend is working on a welfare to work program and he asked me to invest. I talked with Mark, our attorney, who stated that I should only invest ten grand in the program"

"Reverend, how much more do you need?"

"Well, I need another fifty thousand. I am asking Kevin for another ten"

My wife had that look like she was going to pull her checkbook out and pay the other ten thousand. She began fumbling through her purse and reaching for her checkbook. I could see the Reverend getting almost excited. That is, until my wife saw the look of disproval on my face. I then spoke to my wife in a matter-of-fact-type-tone.

"Mark suggested that we invest no more than ten thousand"

"Mark is generally so conservative and…"

She looked at me and saw that I was still against the idea of her making the payment.

"Baby, I'm sorry. You think we should take Mark's advice?"

"I do"

"Reverend, I'm sorry. I guess ten thousand will have to be enough"

That is why I married this woman. No drama. If I say no, that is enough for her (As long as I am being reasonable).

"That's okay dear. What did you say your name was?"

"I'm sorry, where are my manners? My name is Tamara Allen"

"Nice to meet you Tamara. I hope that I can convince you to visit the church and our program. In fact, I am leaving now. Maybe you and Kevin could stop by for a few minutes and meet some of the participants in our program. Right now they are working on the program for a benefit that we are having in a few weeks. I hope I can convince you two to stop by that day as well"

"That sounds wonderful" My wife said. "Kevin can I see the church?"

"I was going to show you the city and take you out to dinner now that you are here"

"Can we stop at the church first?"

Knowing Tamara's weakness for wanting to help people and especially the homeless, I caved in. "Okay, but we are only staying fifteen minutes"

"Okay" She said.

Reverend Turner began to say, "Fifteen minutes is hardly enough…"

I cut him a look that said I was ready to hurt him if he continued on. I kept telling myself in my head this is why I never come home.

I jumped in my truck and Tamara and I followed the Reverend back to the church.

"Whose truck is this?"

"It's mine"

"You bought another truck?"

"I didn't buy another truck. I kind of appropriated this one"

"Why are you dressed like you are half your age?"

I had on a Sean John warm up. I thought I was looking rather fly myself.

"This is a Sean John warm-up. You don't like it?"

"Not for going out to dinner later. It seems too laid back"

"Baby this is Chicago, no one gives a fuck what we are wearing I mean shit…"

"…What's with all the swearing?"

I was thrown off by her question, but I knew what she meant. I hadn't been home three weeks yet, and I was already in full Chi-town mode. My hat was cocked to the left, I was in a white warm-up, brand new white on white air force ones, ice in my ear and ice around my neck.

"My bad babe, being back home just…well…hey, I'm home this is how I am"

"Uh-huh, well while you are around me can we go back to the man that I married rather than this alternate personality. You seem so…different"

"My bad babe, so what do you want to eat?"

"We can decide on what to eat later. Why don't you tell me why you are so rude to that preacher?"

I let out a sigh and while we followed the good reverend, I filled my wife in on why I hated Reverend Jackass.

We pulled up a few minutes later into the church lot. Now that my wife knew this man was bleeding my parents for cash, her affect with the good Reverend changed. She was cordial and polite, but the purse strings were now tied tight. The reverend walked us around the church, showed us his office, and then made the mistake of showing us the plasma screen TV in his office in the church. Tamara cut me a look that said, "Do you see this shit?" I cut her a look back that said, "I told you"

We walked into the west wing of the church where there were beds set up, a washer and dryer, donations and a 32 inch TV that a bunch of women were watching. These were the homeless women and the women that were going to be in the welfare to work program. I was thinking to myself that the reverend could get the other ten grand that he needed by selling the plasma TV and his expensive ass truck.

The Reverend asked one of the women where was the Deputy Director of the program. One of the girls said that the Deputy Director was in one of the inner offices counseling one of the other women. The Reverend told me and my wife that he just wanted us to meet the Deputy Director before we left because the Deputy Director is who did most of the preliminary planning and secured the other donations. Reverend Turner knocked on the door and then opened it.

"I'm sorry, there are two people that I just wanted you to meet really quickly"

My heart practically stopped as Yolanda walked out of the office. She was dressed in a navy blue business suit. I swallowed hard as I saw her. I felt light headed and my knees felt like they might buckle from underneath me. She extended her hand first to my wife and then to me.

"Hi, I'm Yolanda Carter"

"Hello, I'm Tamara Allen"

"And your name sir?"

"Kevin. Kevin Allen"

"Kevin Allen the author?"

"Um…yeah, that's me"

"You write all those erotic stories and urban tales right?"

"Yeah, I uh…do"

I had to try and keep my cool but it was hard as hell. Tamara could see that I was acting weird, but she couldn't quite place her finger on why.

"Well I know that you probably have no time today, but I was wondering, there is one young girl in our program who is an avid fan of yours. If you signed her book, I think that would just make her day"

"Oh…Okay. Yeah, Yeah I'll sign it. Why don't you get the book now? I'll sign it, and then we'll leave. My wife and I are on our way to dinner"

"Dinner, really? Where do you guys have reservations?"

"We don't. I figured I would just take her to the Webber Grill and from there show her the rest of the city"

"Tamara where are you from? Are you from Tennessee or Mississippi?"

"I'm from North Carolina"

"Oh, that it explains it"

"Explains what?"

"The southern drawl"

"The what?"

"The southern drawl, the way you hold syllables. There is a twang in your voice. It makes you sound country and uneducated. I'm sure that's not the case, but it's how it's sometimes perceived up North"

"Excuse me?"

"Oh I wasn't trying to offend you. I'm sorry if I did"

Still Crazy

I was praying in my head. "Please God, don't let Yolanda start with these head games. Tamara will kick the shit out of Yolanda's ass and then kill my ass" I looked at the Reverend and motioned for him to say something.

"Ms. Carter didn't mean it the way it sounded Ms. Carter, please excuse our ways" The Reverend said.

Tamara's eyes tightened and she tried to read whether Yolanda was being catty or genuine. Yolanda smiled a smile that seemed sincere before she spoke.

"Ms. Allen I am so sorry. Please, forgive me"

"That's okay…I guess" Tamara said.

"It seems that I put my foot in my mouth. I'm so embarrassed. Let me get that book Mr. Allen"

"She's something else" Tamara said.

"Once again, I apologize" The Reverend said.

I let out a deep breath as I thought about my next move. Yolanda works here with the Reverend? Great. That is all the fuck I need. She must have gotten up out of bed this morning in order to come here and be at work on time.

"Kevin are you okay?" Tamara asked.

"Yeah babe, I haven't had much sleep. You know how crazy I get with no sleep. You decide on what you want to eat yet?"

"I thought we were going to this Webber Grill Place"

"Yeah, that's right. My bad"

Fuck! Fuck! Fuuuuuccccccckkkk! I'm tweakin. If I don't get my shit together and fast, I am going to lose my wife over some stupid shit. Be cool, be cool, be…cooooool. I let out a heavy sigh.

"Mr. Allen, I would like you to meet one of your biggest fans. This is Katherine Grace. We call her Kitty"

No way. No fucking way! This is what I thought to myself as I damn near passed out.

"Hello Mr. Allen. It's nice to meet you. I am a huge fan,"

"Thank you"

I took the book from her and began to sign it. I signed it as I sign most books, "Thanks for your support, Kevin Allen"

"Kitty is one of our special participants. She has a job modeling part time and she attends school at Kennedy King College. We are very proud of her. She is very accomplished for a 19 year old"

"Nineteen? You look so much older than nineteen"

"Kevin, that's not polite to say" My wife said.

"I'm sorry babe. You're right. Where are my manners? What I meant to say is that you look very mature"

"I'll be twenty next week"

"We're proud of her" The Reverend said.

"Oh-kay. Well, I'm hungry. Babe, let's go. It was nice meeting both of you"

I grabbed my wife so fast, that I damn near left skid marks.

I thought to myself, "I don't know what this bitch is on, but one thing is obvious… Yolanda is still crazy"

A NIGHT ON THE TOWN

It was hard as hell to keep my mind focused on my wife and not give away what had gone on for the last 24 hours. While my wife and I sat and had a wonderful meal at the Webber Grill, she told me about her students, and I wondered what was next with Yolanda. A lot of things were going through my head including the fact that I slept with a 19 year old girl. A few years younger and well, you know. I then thought about the fact that Yolanda is having a lesbian or bi-sexual relationship with a much younger woman. A woman that should be receiving guidance and care from her; instead, she is receiving sexual favors. That alone was unethical. I started to tell the Reverend, but I figured that would only add fuel to the fire. There was no sense in exposing Yolanda. She obviously gave me a pass. Maybe she was going to be cool about this. Our affair was just that — an affair.

I decided that I needed to show my wife to a good time and get my mind off Yolanda.

"So what do you want to do next?" I asked her.

"What is there to do?"

"Anything"

"Anything?"

"Anything. You name it, Chicago has it"

"I think I want to hear some Blues"

"You ain't said nothing but a word"

I took Tamara to the North Side. We hit beautiful Lake Shore Drive at about 45 miles per hour, and took in the city's skyline. There was a nice eastern breeze coming off the lake, and the breeze was gentle and intoxicating.

Off in the distance, you could see the Ferris Wheel at Navy Pier. It was lit up like a bright star on a dark canvas. I got off at Fullerton, drove through Lincoln Park, and drove pass DePaul University.

I banked a right on Halsted street and watched Tamara's eyes light up as she saw Blues Alley for the first time.

"Wow, all these are Blues Clubs?"

"No, only a few are. You have B. L. U. E. S. , Blue Chicago and Kingston's Mines. They are all Blues Joints. Then you have The Wild Hare which has Raggae, and a host of other spots. If we go just a little west of here, we can go to the Green Mill, The Green Dolphin, and hit all the Broadway spots. Which do you want to try?"

"What do you recommend?"

"I say we try them all"

"Okay"

We started with B. L. U. E. S., where we listened to my guy Pistol Pete, play the hell out of his guitar. Pete played as he always does, like he was possessed by Jimi Hendrick's and Prince. Tamara was blown away by Pete's skills as he seduced her with his guitar. From there we went to the Wild Hare where we danced to some reggae. Tamara was blown away when I told her that the very spot that we were dancing in, was where Nia Long and Larenz Tate danced in her favorite movie Love Jones. We danced to about four songs. While we were there we drank a few Kamikazes, and hit a joint that was being passed around.

I then took her to my favorite spot, which is Kingston's Mines. My guy Charlie Love was the emcee, and he introduced a bunch of good acts that played the hell out of some down home blues.

"I can't believe that the Blues here are so good"

"Are you kidding? The Blues originated from Chicago"

"Chicago? The blues originated from the south. What do city boys know about the blues?"

"Are you kidding me? The earliest blues recording was in 1920. Do you know what Chicago was like in 1920?"

"The blues were being sang way before 1920. They were sung in the south, deep in the south, probably in Mississippi and they were probably sang by some people who were either slaves or descendants of slaves"

"We are all descendants of slaves, and songs sang by slaves are Negro spirituals. There is a difference between the moaning that the slaves did and the moaning that black people in the Chi did back in the day"

"I can't believe that you are trying to give Chicago credit for creating the blues. Negro spirituals or not, the origin of the blues came from those slave songs. Can't you hear that?"

"There is a difference between singing from the heart because you are hurting and you need to be emancipated, as opposed to moaning because you are broke. Now when you are broke, that's a different kind of hurt. I'm talking about the type of hurt where there is no relief in sight. I'm talking about being hurt way down in your soul. I'm talking about being poor, when you got mouths to feed; So poor that you are livin on faith, so poor that you put water on the stove, season that water and have your home smelling like food, but you have no meat. I'm talking about communicating with God on whole new level"

"Kevin, you're crazy"

"I'mma show you how crazy I am"

I drove back south on Wabash Avenue, and took my wife to a special place, Buddy Guy's Legends. That left an impression on her ass about Chicago and the blues. On the walls of Legends were photos of everyone from the Rolling Stones to Eric Clapton to Buddy Guy himself. There were photos of Big Time Sarah, Bessie Smith, T-Bone Walker, and one of my favorites, BB King.

We listened to a number of acts that played, and together, we drank, smoked, kissed and allowed ourselves to be taken away by the music. It was almost 5:00 in the morning when we finally decided to call it a night. We held hands and strolled back to my truck arguing about where the blues originated. Tamara was from the country, so she insists that the blues began there, and being from the Chi, I had to rep my city. We must have had too much to drink because we did not hear someone walking up behind us. With my peripheral vision, I saw a large figure walk up on my wife's right side.

I snatched Tamara to my left with my left hand, tripped the figure walking up on us with my foot, and smacked him to the pavement as he was going down with my right hand. I released Tamara, used my left hand to grab the man in his throat and held up my right hand ready to pummel him to death if need be. This happened in a span of two seconds. I scared the shit out of Tamara and myself. My adrenaline was now flowing and I sobered the fuck up quick.

"What the fuck are you doing son? What the fuck is your problem walking up on me and my lady like that? Speak up motha fucka!"

"I just wanted some spare change, I'm sorry. I asked as you walked by but I guess you didn't hear me"

It was a homeless man. He was about 60.

"Where the fuck did you come from?"

He pointed in the middle of a patch of crabgrass, garbage and broken glass. Sure enough, there was a buggy and a box with what looked like his belongings among the trash. The man was dirty, white and soiled. He was so disheveled, that I hadn't noticed him. He blended in well with the trash.

"Man, I'm sorry dude. Here"

I felt so bad that I gave him a fifty spot.

"Thank You"

Tamara was looking at me like I was crazy. I took her by the arm and headed to my truck which was still a block or two away.

"You know, the young lady is right" He shouted.

"I'm sorry?" I said.

"The blues, they originated in the south, on the plantations. It was the music that was first sang by African slaves. They sang to relieve their oppression. They sang chants from their native Africa, made up rhymes about their lives, and sang songs about one day being free. Because they were not allowed to learn how to read or write, their songs, their voice and their struggle, was recorded through song. Those songs, evolved into the blues. Those blues, evolved into today's Jazz, Rock and Roll, R & B and what is now, Hip-Hop"

The white boy fucked me up with the history lesson.

"No offense, but how the fuck do you know all this"

"I used to teach history"

"You were a high school teacher?"

"I taught at The University of Chicago"

"Damn! How the fuck did you get here?"

"That's a long story"

Tamara said, "We've got time"

    We sat up and listened to a perfect stranger tell us how he met the love of his life in his wife. He met her in college and from the first moment that he saw her, he knew that she was the one for him. He married her as quickly as he could, and kept her all to himself. She completed him. She made him want more of himself, just so that he could please her. She was his life. She was his everything. For twenty years, they were married. For twenty years, not a day went by that they missed telling one another, "I love you" Together they had seen Greece, Paris, Zaire, the U. K. , South America and Alaska. Everywhere she was—he wanted to be. He loved her with all that was within him. He loved her more than life itself.

    He came home one day to find the love of his life unconscious on the floor of their kitchen. She had been preparing his dinner because it was her turn to cook. She too was an educator. She too taught at the university level. When he saw her on that floor, something on the inside of him hurt in depths that he didn't know existed.

    He took her to the hospital. As it turns out, she had Cancer. The man's wife was named Mary. The man's name was Ruben. Together they fought the Cancer.

Together, they lost. Mary received treatment after treatment but to no avail. A year later, after second and third mortgages, overtime, second jobs and a lot of prayer, Mary's life was taken by this disease, this horrible meticulous, and malicious disease. Cancer took Ruben's wife from him one day at a time, one piece at a time.

Ruben was a devout Catholic. Suicide was not an option because if he took his own life, he would never see his beloved Mary again in heaven. So he tried to live without her. He tried to live with his broken heart. And then, the bills came. Ruben told us that to be perfectly honest, without Mary, he didn't give a fuck about anything in life. For him, life was having Mary as his bride. His heart ached for her. His soul yearned to be reunited with her. Everything else, was secondary. He says that he found some peace in being homeless. He finds some joy every now and then in his fellow man. His life unfortunately, has no direction.

"Do you miss teaching?" Tamara asked.

"You know what? I do"

"Well, rather than be here until you are reunited with your wife, couldn't you maybe teach as you once did, as she once did, until the time comes for you to be with her again?"

"I don't know if it's in me anymore"

"Can you maybe give it a try?"

"Who would hire me to teach?"

"I don't know. Kevin?"

My wife gave me a look that she sometimes gives me when there is a problem and she wants me to fix it. She gave me a look that said that it would mean the world to her if I did.

"Babe, what do you want me to do?"

"Fix it"

"How?"

"Just do it"

I thought about my wife's wants. I thought about Ruben's dilemma. I then shot Tamara one of my million dollar smiles.

"The University of Chicago, huh?"

"Yep"

"Does it matter who you teach?"

"No, I guess not. After all, I am just giving it a try remember?

"Come with us"

I winked at Tamara. She smiled back at me. It was now 6:30 in the morning and neither of us had slept.

I took Ruben to a 24 hour Walmart in Calumet City Illinois, which is about 15 minutes outside of Chicago. I bought him a few pair of khakis, shirts, shoes and ties. I got him a watch, a razor, toiletries and towels. I then took him to breakfast at IHOP and the three of us got our eat on. After we were each full, I picked up my cell and dialed a number.

"Yeah, it's Kevin. I need to meet with you now. Right now! Yeah. I don't care what time it is. I need a favor. Okay, I will see you in a few minutes"

Tamara said, "Who was that?"

"You'll see"

Fifteen minutes later, we were back at the Church. Reverend Turner was in the parking lot looking rather disheveled himself.

"Kevin what is this about?"

"Do you want our relationship to improve?"

"Yeah, I do, I guess"

"Then do me a solid. Help this man"

"Who is he?"

"He's the new teacher / mentor for your welfare to work program"

"Kevin it's going to take a special person to teach these women. It will take someone with some serious credentials, many of these women have clinical issues and..."

"...He used to teach at U of C"

"Are you kidding me?"

"Nope"

The Reverend looked at Ruben and then looked back at me with disbelief.

"Well I guess God does move in mysterious ways"

"So you will take care of him?"

"Of course I will"

"A'ight. Peace"

"Will you be coming to service today?"

"Service? What service?"

"Today is Sunday"

"Nah, not today Reverend. I'm going home to get some sleep"

"We'll try Reverend" Tamara said

"Okay. Well I hope to see you all later"

"Yeah, right. Peace Ruben, it was nice meeting you"

"It was an honor meeting the two of you" He said.

I jumped in my truck and turned on WGCI to listen to some morning gospel. Tamara was looking at me a little crazy.

"What?" I said.

"One, I can't believe that you almost beat up that man and two, I can't believe that you are so conditioned to overlook the homeless. I can't believe you didn't see him"

"Did you see him?"

"Yeah, of course"

"Why didn't you say something?"

"I don't know. I thought you saw him. It looked like you did. As he was walking up I was already wondering how you could so casually overlook him. I mean, it doesn't say a lot for us as people to just overlook the disadvantaged"

"Look babe, there are thousands of homeless people here in the Chi. I can't help them all and I can't give money to everyone that I see"

"But Kevin look how much money we waste"

"Tamara, I earned that money and it's mine to do whatever I want with, including waste it"

"But that sounds so…bad"

"It does, doesn't it? I don't know babe, maybe I need to see a financial planner when I get back home or after the next deal is negotiated. In the meanwhile, we did help a man today. That felt good"

"Yes it did"

Tamara leaned over and kissed me.

"Where do we go from here?"

"The Chicago Hilton and Towers"

"Good, I could use the rest before I head back home"

"Home? Already?"

"Yes Kevin, I have a ton of work to do. Besides, Chicago is nice, it's just not…me"

I let out a sigh that said I was disappointed, and I was. In the same token, I needed to tie up some loose ends and get my ass back home — to Somerton.

"So how is the new book coming?" Tamara asked.

"I'm on page 210. It's good as hell and it will be finished within the next two weeks"

"What is it called?"

"The Homecoming"

"That's original"

"Be nice"

We checked into the Hilton, took a hot shower, and went to bed. We slept for what was left of the morning and part of the afternoon.

FEEL LIKE MAKIN LOVE

When I awoke there was a vision of Ebony loveliness in front of me. I heard the sounds of The Best of After Seven and there in front of me was my wife in a nice red teddy.

"You all rested up?"

"Yes I am. Where did you get the teddy?"

"The gift shop"

"Damn, the Hilton has a shop with lingerie? They got any sex toys?"

"It's not the Treasure Chest Kevin, it's more of a boutique"

"I'll have to remember that the next time that we travel"

"So, you think you can handle all this?"

Tamara spun slowly around so I could get a look at those hips, those tits and that ass. I felt my package stiffen as I began to lick my lips.

"Girl, you know you got a nice ass"

"Is that all you see when you see me?"

"It's not all that I see. It's the first thing that I see" I said jokingly.

"Well, you didn't marry me for my ass"

"Nah, the ass was a bonus. I married you because of your eyes, and that smile and the fact that every time I see you, I can't help but to notice how stunning you are"

Tamara smiled a school-girl smile.

She crawled up into the bed with me, tossed the covers aside and straddled her thick thighs on either side of me. I used both hands to palm her juicy bottom.

"Do you mean the stuff you be saying to me, or are Chicago guys just good at talking shit?"

"Well, Chicago guys do have game, but I mean every word that I say to you. You are my everything. I love you. I want you to one day have my child"

Tamara leaned forward and let me taste her tongue as we kissed. I held my wife's ample ass and ran my hands up and down her backside. I loved to palm her ass, but I also loved the hook in the small of her back, just before the point where her butt begins to curve. I caressed her backside as our tongues danced to After 7. I placed one hand on my wife's ass and the other on her neck, rubbing the back of her head feeling the soft waves in her short hair. I held her face in my hand as I kissed her cheeks, her eyelids, sucked her earlobes, and planted soft wet kisses on her neck. Tamara let out a gentle sigh as I kissed further down and kissed her collarbone. She began to grind slowly on top of me and I could feel the heat between her legs. Ever so slowly she began to grind on top of me, ever so slowly, I began to grind back. I was already naked and my dick was pulsating hard. I wanted to be inside of her, but I wanted to tease her also. Nothing in this world is more beautiful than a woman's face when she is cumming and when she is being pleased.

Tamara reached between her legs and undid the crotch of the teddy. She then laid more flat on top of me kissing me deeply on the mouth. She reached between my legs and moved my dick to my stomach. She then positioned herself so that her vaginal lips were on either side of my dick and she began grinding again, rubbing her warm moist pussy up and down my shaft. She placed both hands on my shoulders and rested her body on her elbows. She began rocking back and forth like I was a tree that she was trying to scale. Her mouth opened with anticipation of soon cumming. She began grinding in circular motions and I guided her up and down my dick by holding on firm to her ass. I began kissing her neck again and made her sit up some so I could free her breasts from the delicate material. I pulled the bra piece to the side to expose my wife's gumdrop nipples. They were a dark crayola brown and they were erect and demanding my attention. Gently I sucked and bit each nipple. I ran small circles around both breasts as I began to knead them.

Tamara was wet and now my dick was wet with her juices. Her eyes were closed as she began to pick up pace, grinding against me with unrivaled passion. Her grinding was so good that my breathing was rapid. She was jagging me off with her pussy and it took a lot of discipline to keep me from cumming. She then sat all the way up and began to grind harder, as if she were riding a horse naked. I began to buck with passion myself as I held on to her ass. She balanced herself by placing one hand on my thigh and the other on my stomach as she bucked even faster now. Her swollen clit rubbed against my shaft and we were both now lost in one another's juices.

"Aw shit…that's it…don't move…yeah…Aw yeah…Yeah…Fuck…right…there…. right…. eeeuuuuuuuupppp…. . yeah…oh…oh…yeah…yeahhhh. She squealed so loud that for a second I thought she was calling her sorority sisters. She came right there on top of me and then rolled over on her back. She massaged her breasts and fingered them to distract herself from the pleasure between her legs. I dove in face first to begin to devour her swollen clit which was still pulsating.

"Uh-un, No Kevin…No…stop…baby please…no…aw shit…no…Oh baby…Aw shit…

Tamara's breasts were heaving up and down and she tried her best to stop me from eating her out. She almost jumped out of bed to get away from me.

"Kevin, that's dirty. Are you trying to kill me?"

"Now you know you love that shit"

Tamara smiled at me.

"Okay, I'm gonna go jump in the shower now, peace!"

"Hey, you can't leave me here like this!" I said smiling.

"Here like what?"

Tamara walked over to me and smiled at my rock hard dick that was looking like a mini diving board. She took my dick in her hand and slowly began jagging me off.

"So what's all this?"

"You know what this is"

"So I take it you want some southern hospitality then"

I smiled at my wife. "You know it"

"Think you can handle all this?"

"Yeah, I think I can handle this" I smacked her on one of her butt cheeks.

"Okay then sailor, let's see"

Tamara peeled off the teddy and laid on the bed flat on her back. She then kicked both legs in the air, stuck one finger on her mouth and used the other hand to finger herself. That shit turned me on like a MF. She then grabbed both her ankles while her legs were spread, and teased me.

"Well, here it is"

I climbed on top of my wife and entered her from the missionary position, then to full push up position. I slowly eased into her wet warmth. I wasn't ready for the wet gush at the end as I entered her.

"Damn baby you're wet"

"You like that shit Kevin?"

"I love this shit"

"Then say that shit"

"Damn I love this pussy"

"Whose dick is this?"

"It's your dick"

"Whose dick?"

"Your dick, baby. Tamara, damn this shit is good"

"Say that shit Kevin"

"Damn baby your pussy is so good"

I started stoking my wife over and over again. I came all the way out to the tip and hammered all the way back in. Soon, the only sounds that could be heard in the room were the sounds of our bodies slamming against one another. After 7 had gone off and I was still making love to my wife.

Tamara got up and then turned over on all fours. Her juices had run down her thighs and we were both glistening with sweat. She rocked back and forth on the bed making her ass clap. That shit liked to have driven me mad. I entered her from behind and she let out a satisfying moan.

"Aw shit, right there Kevin, right there"

I grabbed onto her hips and began to take slow even strokes. I then stroked fast and then slow and then fast again. Again our bodies slammed against one another. I reached forward and cupped my wife's breasts and squoze them as I fucked her hard from behind. The room was filled with the clapping sounds of our bodies and the primitive moans that we were letting out.

"Aw shit Kevin, this dick is good"

"Tamara this pussy is so juicy"

"Take this pussy Kevin, take that shit, take ... that ... shit"

"Aw shit baby ... aw ... shit ... baby ... aw ... damn ... fuck ... yeah ... right ..."

"... right there, ooohhh yeah, oohh yeah ... yeah ... yeah ..."

My wife and I came at the same time right there in the Hilton and as we came, we both trembled and kissed and held each other until our tremors subsided. We then went back to sleep in one another's arms.

A few hours later, we got up and talked about our dreams and what was next for us as a couple. This was one of our favorite things to do. We also talked about where we would vacation once this next book was complete. I was thinking about the Cayman Islands. Tamara said that she wanted to visit Italy. We talked for a few hours. I then drove my wife to Midway Airport and we said our goodbyes.

"Can't you stay a few more days?"

"No Kevin I have to get back. Can't you come home?"

"I have a few more loose ends to tie up. I shouldn't be here too much longer though"

"Promise?"

"I promise"

We kissed and said goodbye. Tamara went home

I headed back to the old neighborhood. It was Sunday and I know that my mother cooked a ton of food. I was going to get my eat on, finish this book, say bye to everyone in the hood and get back home to my wife.

◆ CHAPTER FIVE ◆
THINKIN BOUT MY EX

TAMARA

    I enjoyed being in Chicago. It is a beautiful town with a world of things to do. I didn't do the one thing that I came to Chicago to do, which was to tell Kevin that I cheated on him while he was away. I prayed, I cried, and I wrestled with the truth the whole time that I was in Chicago. When I first saw Kevin in his old room at his mother's house, I just wanted to collapse in his arms and confess everything. Then he walked up to me and placed me in his arms where I have always felt secure. I just couldn't bring myself to tell him. Now I have no idea what I should do or if there is even any hope for our relationship. I love Kevin. I love him with all my heart. The thing is, I am riddled with guilt over what I did the night before I came home to Chicago.

TREADING OLD GROUND

After my Friday Aerobics class, I went to the grocery store to pick up some chicken breasts, sage, and wine. I figured while I was grading papers I would pamper myself a little and have something to drink while taking a nice hot sit bath in the Jacuzzi. I was looking a wreck. I sweated out my hair, and I was sore as hell from the workout that the trainer put us through. Our instructor, Andre, was in rare form that day and he worked the shit out of us. I was thumbing through the latest issue of Black Issues Review Magazine, when I heard a voice from behind me.

"Damn baby, aerobics really agrees with you"

I was thinking oh great, just what I need, yet another ignorant ass man approaching me. I turned around and was shocked at what I saw. It was Keith, minus the Jeri Curl, and looking good as hell. He had a woman with him that looked like Alicia Keys. She was prettier than me, but not as fit.

"Keith? Wow, I mean hello. You lost the perm in your hair I see"

"Yeah, well, I thought it was time to get caught up with the rest of the world"

"It agrees with you. When did you start wearing suits?"

"Shortly after we broke up"

"Really? Why is that?"

"Because he needed to be cleaned up a little if he was going to be walking around in public with me", his lady friend interrupted.

"I'm sorry, where are my manners…"

"Yeah Keith, where are your manners? I'm Wendy, Keith's fiancée"

"I'm Tamara. I'm sorry Wendy, I didn't mean any disrespect. I have to tell you girl, you do good work"

That eased the tension a little. I could tell that girlfriend was damn near ready to fight. Keith was looking a hell of a lot better, but I was not looking to steal him or anything.

Wendy saw that I was harmless and turned her frown in to a half of a smile.

"Well you know how it is. One woman's trash is another woman's treasure. Since you treated Keith like trash, I guess he is in good hands now"

"What's that supposed to mean?"

"Exactly what you think it means. You had a good man and you blew it! So now you have to accept your decision"

I know this bitch ain't trippin over Keith's crusty ass. Granted, he is looking better. I mean damn, he has this Morris Chestnut thing going on right now, but that does not change the fact that I left his ass because he was trifling. Girlfriend needs to be checked.

"Look Wendy, I don't know what Keith told you, but he was a lousy man when I was with him. You might have cleaned him up some, but it's what is underneath the surface that I had the problem with. You just happen to have good timing. You apparently came along just when Keith decided to grow the hell up. In our relationship I was the one being taken for granted. You have him now and trust me, I wish you the best of luck with him"

"Damn Tamara was it that bad?" Keith chimed in.

"It was bad Keith. It wasn't all bad, but it was bad enough"

Wendy said, "It must have been bad for you to play him like you did"

"What the hell are you talking about?"

"Did you leave him for a man that you met in a bar?"

"Yes, but…"

"…Did you clown him in front of all his friends?"

"Well yes, but…"

"…Did you tell him to wait for you and never returned?"

"Yeah I did all that, but the man I left him for is now my husband"

"Do you think that makes it better? He waited at that bar all night for you. He drank himself stupid and spent the entire night trying to figure out how he was going to win you back from the New Yorker that you took off with"

"Chicagoan"

"What?"

"Kevin is from Chicago"

"Whatever. Well I met him a few months after you dumped him. I made him cut his hair and start going to the barber. I made him dress like he had some sense, I and have been in his corner since you left him"

"So, what? What do you want, a medal?"

"No, I want you to get out of my man's face"

"Look bitch, you can have his trifling ass. And as you can see, he started speaking to me first. Don't get it twisted"

"Nah, don't you get twisted up in here"

"Ladies please"

"Shut the fuck up Keith!" Wendy and I both said at the same time.

I had to get myself together. I started to go there with Wendy, but I was still sore and I didn't want to have to break my foot off in her ass. I said a small prayer and put my items on the checkout belt.

"You know what, girl I'm sorry. I'm sorry that your man spoke to me and I am sorry that I stir up something in you that causes your insecurities to surface. You and Mr. Man here have a nice day. Keith, the look agrees with you and it looks like you found a woman that you truly deserve"

"That's right, he has"

My sarcasm was lost on Keith's woman. I grabbed my groceries and headed out of the store to my car.

I went home and showered instead of taking that hot bath that I wanted. I threw on my bathrobe, poured myself a drink, sliced some apples and began grading my papers and creating a new lesson plan for my kids. I called Kevin, but his phone went right to voicemail. I figured he was working hard on his new book. I hope he gets a major deal. I am thinking about leaving the school where I teach and go to culinary school. That has always been a dream of mine. The only problem is culinary school costs money, lots of money.

It took me three hours to grade all the papers that I had and to create a lesson plan. I began turning down lights to get ready for bed, when there was a knock at my door. I tied my robe tight and walked into the foyer. I then peeked through the peephole and there in his suit was Keith with flowers in hand. I opened the door with a look of confusion on my face.

"Keith? What the hell are you doing here?"

"I was hoping that I could talk with you"

"Are you crazy? This is my home. This is my home that I share with my husband"

"I thought he was in Chicago"

"How would you know that he is in Chicago?"

"It was on BET. He was just speaking at some benefit for young writers"

"Regardless to where my husband is, why would you disrespect him like this and come to our house?"

"Disrespect? If anyone was disrespected, it was me. Besides, I came here to talk to you, not fight with him"

"Keith, go home"

"Come have ice cream with me"

"No, I'm a married woman"

"Tamara please, it's just ice cream, damn"

"No Keith, I don't think so"

"Then I will have to just keep coming here until either you say yes, or Mr. Chicago, makes me stop coming around"

"You don't want to get into it with my husband"

"Naw baby, your husband don't want to get into it with me"

"Kevin will whip your ass"

"I ain't scared of him"

"I didn't say that you were scared of him. I said he will whip your ass if he finds out you are trying to push up on me"

"Well then, let's make sure he never finds out. I just want ice cream"

"I am not traveling around town with you. It will look like we are on a date. Besides Keith, don't you have a woman? Where is that low budget Alicia Keys that you were with at the store?"

"She's at home"

"So you all live together?"

"Yeah, for six months now"

"I see"

"Are you jealous?"

"No"

"Not even a little?"

"Not even a little. Keith, what do you want?"

"I just wanted to tell you that I miss you. I wanted you to know that I now know that I had a great thing when you were in my life. If you give me a chance, I will make it all up to you. If you just say the word, I will leave Wendy and we can start all over again"

"And what do you propose that I do with my husband?"

"Divorce him, marry me"

"You have got to be out of your mind"

"What is it about this nigga that makes him so special? Is it because he has money?"

"He didn't have money when I met him"

"Then what is it?"

"He loves me, I love him, and he is the type of man that I can build something with"

"And me?"

"You are someone that I once cared about, but that time is gone"

Keith had this look on his face like I broke up with him all over again. He headed toward the door again. Before leaving, he turned around and handed me the flowers. They were a bouquet of red roses.

"These are for you"

"I can't accept them"

"Please?"

I figured I would just throw the damned things away after he left. I took the flowers from him and gave him a half smile.

"Thank you Keith"

He leaned in to give me a hug. I gave him a half of a hug whereas he gave me a full one. His arms felt muscular and familiar. I don't know how or why, but that half hug turned into a full hug. The next thing that I knew, Keith's hand was on my ass.

"Keith, don't I…"

He nuzzled under my neck and planted soft wet kisses there. One hand was on my ass while the other took my chin and he kissed me ever so softly on the lips. He then kissed the nape of my neck, my collarbone, and ran his tongue up the front of my neck and gently sucked on my earlobe. Apparently his new girl taught him a trick or two with his tongue. It took him a quick second to open my robe and in one motion grab my right breast firmly and suckle it, squeeze it, tease it and run tiny circles around it at an incredible speed. My mouth protested, but my body became weak and started to give in.

"Let me taste you"

"No Keith, No"

"Let me taste you, I bet you taste good. You just got out of the shower, you're ready to be devoured, please baby let me taste you just one more time"

"I'm married"

"No one has to know"

Keith stuck his finger between my legs and I was embarrassed to say that I was soppy wet. Keith took my hand in his and guided my hand to his rock hard dick. He has seven inches of rock hard dick dying to get into my wet spot. He began fingering my clit right there in the foyer of my house. I let out a sigh as his finger began to pick up speed. I closed my eyes for a second, and when I opened them again, I focused on a photo of Kevin and me at the beach. There were photos all over our house of us together in various places around the world. These were places that we traveled together. These were photos that were taken of the two of us — in love.

"Keith, stop!"

"You don't mean that baby..."

SLAP!

"No! I do mean it. I'm sorry that things went this far. You are out of order—we—are out of order. This is the house that I share with my husband. Take your flowers and get out of my house"

I closed my robe. I felt like shit. I felt like such a whore.

"Keith, if you ever come here again, I will have you arrested"

"Tamara this is fucked up"

"Get out"

"One minute it's all good, the next minute it's not. This must be what Kobe went through"

"I believe that Kobe is innocent. We are the ones that are guilty. Now get out!"

"So what are you going to tell hubby?"

"If I tell him, I am telling him everything, beginning with how you came over here with flowers"

I pushed Keith out of the door and slammed it shut. I didn't sleep with him, but I did cheat on my husband. For that, I felt like shit.

I slid down the doorway and tried to get myself together. I decided to go visit Kevin in Chicago. I needed to be with my man. First, I need to go upstairs and masturbate. Right or wrong, Keith got me horny as hell.

SOLO LOVE

I turned on the house alarm and finished cutting off most of the lights in the house. I then lit scented candles around the house. I poured myself a glass of wine and used Kevin's remote to turn on the house speakers. I played Jill Scott's new album, Beautifully Human. I grabbed some watermelon scented body lotion from my night stand and I placed it next to me on the bed. I pulled out the special ivory box that I keep by the nightstand. I pulled out a small dildo, my pocket rocket, and a joint of Jamaican Red Weed.

I lit the joint, took a sip of wine, and then took one long hard hit of the joint. Jill was signifying about the man in her life and there I was laying in my bed talking about, "Gon girl, you tell him!" I poured a small amount of lotion in my hands and began to rub the lotion all over my body. I began with my breasts. I will be starting my period soon, so they are a little sore, but they are also firm and plump and full. I rubbed my hands on my breasts and pretended they were man's hands. Kevin always liked my ass, but he had a special thing for my breasts as well. I envisioned him taking them in both hands and running tiny circles around them with his tongue. I imagined that he was kissing them, teasing them, sucking them and gently biting them.

I kept one hand on my breast as the other stole away to my special place. I'm not Afraid by Jill Scott was now playing and as she sang, I let go of my inhibition and began to explore my body…to explore my own sexuality. I ran deliberate circles around my swollen clit and imagined that Kevin was done with my breasts and slowly kissing down my stomach, then my ribs, my thighs, and then back up to my neck. His breath was so warm, his mouth so wet, so…inviting. He kissed down my stomach and up again to my breasts. They heaved up and down with passion showing him that I was pleased. My nipples darkened, they became erect and they began to ache, but it was a good ache, a longing, a sexual urge that could not be denied. My man then turned me over on my stomach and began to kiss the back of my neck. From there he kissed my back, my round firm ass, the small of my back, my thighs, and my calves.

I began to become moist as I pictured him planting hundreds of wet passionate kisses all over my backside. My body shuddered with anticipation as I wanted desperately to feel his tongue in that place, my special place. I turned over myself as I continued with my fantasy. Jill Scott was singing The Fact is I Need You and I was on all fours reaching back and fingering myself feverishly. I needed my man right now. Damn, I wish he were really here. I pictured that he touched me there, as he did I let out a satisfying moan letting him know that his touch was more than welcome.

He fingers me while devouring me from behind. He licks my clit like a hot sticky dessert. He enters a second finger in my now wet pussy, and I begin to moan louder and louder as he increases his pace with both his fingers and his tongue. In and out he fingers me, occasionally taking his free hand and smacking my ass hard to distract me from cumming. For an eternity he teases me, pleases me and devours me with passion. My breathing became rapid, my pulse sped up, I arched my back farther in the air and my legs began to tremble as I came. My juices ran slowly down my thighs as my fingers continued to do their magic. My pussy throbbed and I became short of breath as the waves of orgasm passed through my body. I collapsed on the bed in my own juices. I reached up to take another hit of the joint. I took a quick hit and put the rest out. I then took a sip of wine and then ran a bubble bath in the Jacuzzi to wash away my sin and my guilt. I then spoke to myself.

"I'll go to Chicago and tell Kevin the truth...after I get some dick. Damn that sounds so wrong"

Naturally, I got to Chicago and chickened out.

KEVIN

I went to the park the next day to shoot some ball. I was almost finished with my new book and my agent was bugging the hell out of me on my cell phone. My agent's name is Kelly Connell. We were in a heated discussion on the cell phone.

"Kevin, can I at least have what you have written so far?"

"Nope, I will wait until I see you"

"When will that be? I didn't plan on seeing you for a few months at the BEA in Chicago"

"You will be seeing me in a few weeks"

"A few weeks? You are coming to New York?"

"Oh hell yeah. This new joint is hot. I am already thinking about a sequel in my head. I am coming to New York and before I go back home, I will either have re-signed with Universe or I am off to the highest bidder"

"If you give me what you have so far, I can advance the readings to the radio stations and begin your marketing blitz"

"Sorry Kelly, you are going to have to be patient"

"How much do you want me to ask for?"

"I don't know. What are all the other authors making?"

"I don't know. You know how hush hush everyone is about how much they make"

"Then I suggest that you get on the phone with the agents of Eric Jerome Dickey, E. Lynn Harris, Travis Hunter and Darrin Lowery and get me something comparable to what they get for multi-book deals"

"Kevin, you have been writing for some time. How many more books do you think you have left in you?"

"Enough to put my great grandchildren in college"

"But you have no kids"

"Exactly"

I hung up the phone. This next deal was going to be the thing that put me on easy street. I smiled to myself as I thought about the fact that the hood was about to save my life and my career. I walked up the brothas in the hood wondering where Big Slim was.

"Hey whaddup fellas, where is Big Slim?"

"Nobody knows. Ain't no body seen him in a while"

"Damn, for real? Is he locked up in county?"

"Nah, a bunch of brothas just got out of county last night, none of them seen him"

"Deep, well, I'm sure he will turn up. Ya'll niggas ready to play some ball?"

"Yeah, that's peace. Let's go"

I shot ball with the brothas and played three games. The next thing that I knew, the park was getting crowded with spectators. With Big Slim not here, every brotha in the hood was now vying for the top spot. Cats were out there doing cross-over dribbles, backwards dunks and trying their best to make Robichaux Park look like an And 1 tournament. I got a couple of fabulous dunks in and embarrassed a few people myself. No matter what I did or anyone else though, it wasn't the same out there without Big Slim. You can't just take his throne in the hood, you have to de-throne him. It's like Rick Flair said, "To be the man, you have to beat the man"

I played another three games and was beginning to sweat like a slave out there on the asphalt court. That was the other thing that I loved about the hood. In our hood, when we played ball for a long time and it looked like we were worn out, women that lived nearby brought us food, water and liquor. For a lot of them, they did it to feel needed. For many others, they did it to try and catch a man. Even if they knew that man was no good. Many of the women that grew up here are still here. Many of them are still at home with mom, if mom is alive. Others are on welfare and others still just have fucked up logic. Many are living the urban fairytale, being broke and being proud of being broke as long as they are together. This is why many of them brought us food and drink. Other women that showed up just wanted to be fucked.

I loved pussy from the hood. Many of the sisters here had asses and bodies that would put a video model to shame. Sisters in my hood could out dance, out fuck and out suck anyone on TV. When it came to pussy, and I mean some bomb ass pussy, my hood was the spot. There were honeys out there with their stomachs out, titties out and flawless makeup. I don't care where you are from, ain't nothing like a round the way girl. A couple of sisters offered me some sandwiches and drinks. Many of them were all smiles. Some of them actually read books and knew who I was. They also knew to keep that shit to themselves. I didn't want cats in the hood to know that I had any type of money. I would hate to have to bust a cap in someone I grew up with because they tried to raise up and steal from me.

Many of the sisters from the hood were checking me out. I was checking them out as well. The brothers referred to these women as the hood rats, but they knew damn well that these women were the staples in the community that kept shit running. There was this one fine ass younger sister checking me out. She was about 19 years old and she had the prettiest brown eyes. She was bodied up tight, and she had juicy suckable lips. I saw her and licked my lips as I saw her ass which was apple-bottomed like a motha fucka.

"So what's up? Your name is Kevin, right?"

[smiling] "Yeah, that's me. What's your name Ma?"

[in a really sexy voice] "Well, my name, is Lolita. My nickname is La-La"

"Well, La-La, thanks for the food love"

"After you finish with the food, do you want some dessert?"

"Nah Ma, thank you though. I got a girl. I'm not tryin to get in any more trouble"

"Your girl ain't gotta know"

She walked up to me and right there began reaching for my shit which was hard as hell. I smiled and copped a feel of that ass, which by the way, felt good as hell. But I wasn't tryin to cheat anymore on Tamara than I already have. That shit with Yolanda blew my mind. Speaking of Yolanda..."

"...Bitch, you heard him, HE'S GOTTA A MOTHAFUCKIN WOMAN!"

Yolanda had walked up fast as hell. I hadn't even seen her ass. She grabbed the young honey by her long brown hair and slammed the teen to the concrete and began kicking the shit out of her. I grabbed Yolanda and snatched her away from La-La.

"Yogi what the hell are you doing? What the fuck is up with you!"

"I'll kill that bitch!"

"You ain't gonna do shit. Where the fuck did you come from?"

"I came to see you. I didn't expect to see some young bitch all up in your face"

"What? Girl get yo ass over there by my truck and chill the fuck out!"

Just like old times. I had totally forgotten that Yogi and I weren't a couple. For a minute, I actually thought we were back in the relationship that we started all those years ago.

I walked over to La-La and helped the young girl up. She had a knot on the back of her head and a bruise on her cheek, but otherwise, she was okay.

"You okay babygirl?"

"Yeah, I'm okay"

"I'm sorry about that shit"

"That's okay. You could have told me that your woman was right there"

"First of all, she ain't my woman. She's an ex. Second of all, I didn't see her. The bitch is a little touched in the head. Had I seen her, there is no way that I would have let her do that shit to you"

"Well, I'm okay. I can't believe she ain't even your woman and she's trippin like that"

"You know how some broads can be"

"Can you come see me later?"

"Are you serious?"

"Yeah, I mean, you said she wasn't your lady"

"I also said that I had a girl too, remember?"

"I was just thinking that this was the least you could do. I mean, can you just maybe stop by for a few minutes later? Please?"

"Later like when?"

"10:00"

I let out a sigh as I helped her to the park bench. I looked at the girl's pretty lips, brown eyes, and some baby makin hips that were out of this world. I figured what the fuck. I decided that I would finish my book tonight, maybe tap that ass, use protection, and then head to the crib to be with my wife. It would be at least a year before I would come back to Chicago.

"A'ight ma. I'll come by about 10:00. Where do you live?"

"at 9332"

"Where are your parents?"

"I don't have any"

"How did you get the house?"

"It used to be my grandmother's"

"Deep. Well, look, I'll see you later"

"Promise?"

"Yeah, I promise"

DEALING WITH PSYCHO

"What the fuck is up with you?"

"Me? What the fuck is up with you?"

"Yolanda, why are you here?"

"I told you, I came to see you"

"For what?"

"To see if we could talk or maybe even re-kindle what we used to have"

"First of all, I am still pissed at that stunt you pulled with the 19 year old at the shelter. Second, I have a wife"

"Having a wife didn't stop you from letting that young girl feel on your dick just then"

"Maybe not, but that's not your motha fuckin business"

"Tell me that you don't want to still hit this. Look at me"

I checked her out and I have to admit, she was looking good as hell. Yolanda had on some knee high white leather boots that laced up the front, white stretch pants that hugged the shit out of her hips and ass, a red thong on underneath, a white mini t-shirt that said babygirl across the front and no bra. Her breasts were perfect in the tight cotton material and her nipples were erect. She was dressed like a ho, but she was the nicest looking ho I have seen in a long time.

"Yogi, I can't fuck with you anymore"

"You want to. Your mouth may say no, but your eyes are saying yes"

"Yolanda, I…"

"You want to fuck me again, I know you do. You want to feel my warmth, my mouth, my ass; you want to stick your dick in every hole, don't even try and front"

Damn, see this is why I left Chicago in the first place. I stayed in trouble when it came to pussy, Especially good pussy. Shit, I'm married. I can't keep doing this shit. I need to see a therapist.

"Let's talk in the truck"

"The truck, why?"

"Because I got my titties and shit all out for you and I am dressed like a hood rat to impress you and you obviously don't appreciate it. Besides, I don't want everyone in my business"

We went inside the truck to talk.

"Yolanda what do you want from me?"

"I want us together again"

"That's not going to happen"

"That's not fair Kevin. We never really broke up to begin with. You left me while I was hospitalized"

"That's not true. You had a nervous breakdown or whatever, and your parents and I talked and they thought it was best that we no longer see each other. You do remember hitting me with a car because you were mad at me don't you?"

"I remember that. I'm sorry for that. I worked through those issues in therapy. I'm all better now"

"So much better that you were willing to have a ménage a trois?"

"That is bullshit! You know I was just trying to please you. You know sex with me is off the chain and that I am a sexually free being. Tell me you didn't like that shit!"

She had a point.

"You fucking men! We cook for you, clean for you and do everything to be your goddamn fantasy and give you what you want, only to be cheated on, stepped on and mistreated because the truth of the matter is, you are all selfish as hell and none of you seem to know what the fuck it is that you want!"

Again, she had a good point. We sat in silence for a few minutes.

"I love my wife"

"You have a weird way of showing it"

"No matter what you say or do, I still love my wife"

"Uh-huh, whatever"

"I'm gonna drive you to your car and then I'm going home"

"Fine"

I took her to her car and then I pulled off. I headed to the crib to finish my book, shower, and go back home to Somerton. When I got to my mother's house, I didn't even shower. I began typing the ending of my book right then and there at my laptop. I had already been playing with the ending in my head. It was now time to write it. I hammered away at the keys as my sisters came in from shopping.

"Damn bruh, you smell like a wet puppy"

"I was playing ball earlier"

"So, what, typing couldn't wait until after a shower?"

"Nope"

"Writers, Oh well. We're all going out to eat. Do you want anything?"

"Just to be left alone"

"Well excuse us"

"I'm sorry Joy, I'm just trying to finish this book and then I think I am going to head back to the crib in Somerton"

"So no goodbye dinner? No last time around the table? When will you be back?"

"Christmas, I promise"

"You said that last year"

"I mean it this year"

We both began laughing. My sisters, and parents headed toward the minivan that I got them. They were headed to Applebees and then to the show.

YOLANDA

I was not done speaking with Kevin and he needed to know that I was still hurting over our relationship. I loved him. I always loved him. I even loved him when I "went away"

The reason that I went away is because my father had been molesting me since I hit puberty. For a long time, it was "our little secret" It stopped being our secret when I realized that it was wrong and when I started having feelings for boys my own age. I was traumatized by the whole thing. I could never tell my father no, and because he meant the world to me, I gave in to him. I felt like shit on the inside. I felt like I betrayed my mother. For years it went on, and every day of those years there was never a day that went by that I didn't think about killing myself. I told my mother what happened during my relationship with Kevin. It was my mother that sent me away.

Still Crazy

I used to write letters to Kevin while I was in the hospital. I clung to him and he was my hope while I was detained in a 3 ½ by 5 room. No one seemed to care about the breakdown that I was having. No one, until Dr. David Allen began treating me. David was a friend of Kevin's. He was an older guy that lived in David's old neighborhood. He was a very smart and insightful man that helped put me back together. When he learned of the molestation, he helped me sort things out, he helped me to cry, to get rid of the guilt and finally, to see my father put in jail.

It was months after that when I was finally released. All the time that David was treating me, he never told Kevin. I thought that he was kind for that. When I was finally released, I looked for Kevin, but he had gone away to school and was doing a lot of freelance writing and speaking. My mother thought that it was best that I let Kevin live his life while I worked on piecing mine back together. He pursued his writing and I went to college to get a B. A. in Human Service Administration. I never stopped loving him. I never stopped caring for him. I have a hard time understanding why he can't still feel the same for me. We never gave our love a chance. He doesn't know it, but I would give the world to him if I could.

I was on my way home when I decided that we were not through with our discussion. I need to speak with him for just a few more minutes. He has a wife right now and I will respect that, but only if he hears me out. I wouldn't mind being his other woman. I think if I can just get my foot in the door, Kevin will see who is the better choice and leave her for me. Besides, she may be pretty and all, but she is just some country bumpkin. I'm his high school and college sweetheart.

When I got to Kevin's house, his whole family minus him was getting into a mini-van leaving on some sort of outing. I reached into the back seat and threw on my white Baby Phat Jacket. His sisters and mother already hated me, so I figured it made no sense to get out of the car looking like a hoochie, so as they were piling in the van, I got out and caught Kevin's mother before she locked the side door.

"Hello Mrs. Allen, is Kevin Home?"

"Hello...Yolanda? Yolanda what are you doing here?"

"I just wanted to talk to Kevin really quick. I just saw him a while ago at the basketball court and he said it was okay for me to stop by"

"Oh did he?"

"Please Mrs. Allen, Please accept my apologies for what happened years ago between Kevin and I..."

"...You are a confused young woman. You hit him with a car. Do you remember that? Do you know how much pain and suffering you put this family through? I don't want you in my home and I..."

"I was molested"

"What?"

"There is a long version that explains why I acted the way that I did and then there is the short version. The short version is that I was in love with your son and at the same time my father was molesting me. He had been molesting me since I was 12. Psychologically, I was pretty messed up. My acting out was a cry for help that no one heard—not even my mother. Kevin and I are not getting back together or anything Mrs. Allen. We saw each other the other night at the event, and today we had a civil conversation. I'm the Director of the homeless program that Reverend Turner is putting together. I'm here on both personal and private business. I just need to talk to Kevin for ten minutes"

There was some shame and confusion on the face of Kevin's mother. After a few seconds, she stepped to the side and let me in the house.

"Yolanda, I'm sorry to hear about your father"

"It's okay. I forgive him. I'm just hoping one day that people will forgive me"

"Consider today a step in that direction. Again, I'm sorry. He's in the kitchen typing at his laptop. He is leaving for the Carolinas again in the morning"

"Thank you"

I went in the house that I was once welcome and familiar with. The Allen Family Household was spacious now that their son paid to have an addition put on. I looked at the laptop which was still on, and I called out Kevin's name.

"Kevin? Kevin are you here?"

There was no answer. I walked to the stairway and listened for him. The house was quiet except for the distinct sound of the shower. He was upstairs washing up. I didn't want to disturb him, so I sat at the table at his laptop.

"So, what do we have here?"

I started reading the story that he wrote and I have to admit, from the first few pages alone, it was masterfully written. There were some extra diskettes there on the table so I copied his story so I could read it to myself later. I slipped the diskette in my pocketbook and helped myself to some kool aid and chicken. A few minutes later, the shower water was off and I could hear walking overhead. I assumed that Kevin was getting dressed. I stayed downstairs another twenty minutes waiting on him. When he didn't come down, I decided to go up.

KEVIN

I was tired as hell. I finished the new joint, called my agent, told her that I would be seeing her in New York in two weeks and hung up the phone. I then called Tamara and told her that I was catching a flight tomorrow and coming home. I couldn't wait to get home and celebrate with my wife. Chicago life was wearing me out and I needed to get back to the country where things are peaceful. I took a nice hot shower, lotioned up afterward, and took my ass to bed to get a quick nap.

I dreamed that I was back home. I dreamed that my new book deal was worth like forty million dollars. I dreamed that Tamara and I popped open a bottle of Champagne and were taking it to the head as we laughed, hugged and celebrated financial freedom. I pictured kissing my wife's beautiful lips. I pictured caressing her and dancing with her and telling her how much I loved her as Maxwell played in the background. I dreamed that we held each other tight on a bearskin rug. We kissed in front of the fireplace and slowly began to become enmeshed in one another's arms as our passion for each other took us away.

I kissed her lips and then down the front of her neck. I slowly peeled off her top and began to fondle her nipples with my hands. As I played with her breasts, she reached between my legs and grabbed my package. She kissed me deep on the mouth as she began jagging me off. I threw my head back with pleasure as her hand felt so good. It almost felt as good as her mouth. The sensation was warm and inviting. She played with my balls with one hand and continued to masturbate me with the other. Damn, she felt good. I don't think I have ever felt this good from getting jagged off before. I mean damn this shit feels good, It feels so…good…so…damned…good…aw…shit…Tamara baby stop…wait…I don't want to cum like this…Tamara, baby…baby…please. I opened my eyes to look down at her and…"

"What the fuck? Yolanda? What the fuck are you doing? What…stop…Yolanda…Yogi…"

I don't know how, but Yolanda was in my old bedroom in my house and she was deep throating the hell out of me. I went to stop her and she batted away my hand. She then took my hand in hers and placed my other hand in her hair. I knew what time this was. She wanted me to make her give me head. That shit used to turn me on back in the day. I grabbed a fist full of hair and I worked her like old road. I ran her up and down my shaft and the only thing that could be heard in the house was her slurping sounds. On and on she went until I exploded in her mouth. I had to cover my face up with a pillow to muffle my screams. She licked me past climax. My ribs and shit were showing and the head was so good, that afterward, I trembled like a fish out of water. I rolled over into the fetal position and damn near put my thumb in my mouth and went to sleep.

"Yolanda, what are you doing here?"

"Your welcome"

I let out a sigh.

"I didn't ask you for the blowjob"

"You didn't stop me either"

"What man in America would have? Look the games and shit have to stop. I'm going home tomorrow"

"So I heard"

"Where did you…"

"Your mother told me"

"That's another thing, how did you get past my sisters and my mother? They hate your ass"

"I told your mother what happened that pushed me over the edge. I'm sure she is telling yours sisters now"

That brought a silence over the room. I never asked what triggered her breakdown. I sat up on the bed and listened to her as tears began to well up in her eyes. She told me how her father molested her. She told me that she didn't know how to tell me, or how to tell anyone for that matter. She explained that the reason she used to get mad jealous and act crazy as hell, was because she had no appropriate models to pattern after. Her parents barely spoke to her or each other. The three of them just seemed to be occupying the same space and staying out of one another's way. On and on she spoke about what she went through. She even told me that the doctor that helped to get her shit together was a friend of mine named David Allen. David, or Crip as I knew him, now had a private practice with another friend of mine named Leon

Alexander. Leon just got through some drama of his own recently and from what I heard from Adrienne, the bartender, he is getting some needed therapy. It seemed like everyone was crazy these days or in serious need of counseling.

Yolanda poured her heart out to me and as she did, I got dressed. I went downstairs and she followed. At the end of her telling me everything, I hugged her and tried to make things plain for her.

"So you see, we never really gave our relationship a chance. Now that I am all better, I just thought that maybe we could start over again"

I let out a heavy sigh this time.

"Yolanda…I'm married!"

"We could sit your wife down and explain things to her. I don't mind sharing my story with her. I just figured we would all shit down like adults and together we could explain to her that we were together first and that we owe it to one another to at least give our relationship a shot. Then, if it doesn't work out, for whatever reason, if she isn't seeing anyone, you will consider getting back with her later"

Yolanda was fine. I mean she was fine as hell. The pussy was the bomb, but is was obvious that she was still very mixed up psychologically.

"Yolanda…Yogi…do you hear yourself? Do you hear how you sound?"

"What's wrong?"

"What's wrong? What's wrong? You're fucking tweakin, that's what's wrong! I can't go tell my fucking wife that she and I have to take a timeout or breakup because my ex wants a legitimate shot at hooking up. That shit sounds crazy as hell!"

"Don't call me crazy"

"What?"

"Don't call me crazy"

"I didn't fucking call you crazy. I said the shit walking out of your mouth is crazy. Are you on any meds or anything?"

"No, I'm not!"

"Are you still in treatment?"

"No"

"Maybe you need to go back. No offense Yolanda, but you are trippin—hard"

She began to cry. Tears were flowing hard down her face and she was crying.

"Kevin, please"

"Yolanda, no. I'm sorry about what happened to you. I'm sorry that things didn't work out between us. Sweetheart, what you want…I can't give you"

"Kevin, I love you"

"I love you too Yogi, but I'm not in love with you"

"You love my pussy though"

I didn't respond. She gathered her things and I walked her to her car. I then hugged her and told her that I would pay the other ten grand that the Reverend wanted. She asked would I come to the opening of the welfare to work program and I told her that I would think about it. She hugged me one more time and then got in her car and drove off.

"Damn, that was a head trip. Aw shit, it's almost 10:00"

LA-LA

I headed east on 93rd street and headed back to the young honey's crib. I pulled up at 10:01. I got out, knocked on the door and was pleasantly surprised at how she came to the door. La-La had on a white teddy from Victoria's Secret and the whole thing was covered at the ends in lace. I don't know what it is about white lace on a black woman's body, but that shit turned me on.

"You're late"

"But I'm here" I said smoothly.

I walked in and the shortie began turning off lights, lighting candles and she cut on Me, Myself and I by Beyonce. I sat down on the couch in the living room where she already had a beer waiting for me. As Beyonce sang, La-La began to dance for me. I watched like a deer caught in a trance as the young girl moved seductively to Beyonce's voice. When the song went off, she kissed me on the lips. A new joint by Kanye West came on, and the sister started gyrating her hips and did a dance that the young folk called twirkin. The shit looked a little wild at first, but with the size of her ass and the teddy that she had on, I was feeling her. The CD went back to slow cuts again. This time there was a joint by Alicia Keys that came on. As Alicia sang, La-La slowly began peeling off the teddy.

"I take it you like Alicia Keys" I said.

"Yeah, I do. It's good music for sucking dick"

"Really?"

"Really"

La-La crawled over to me after she was completely naked and hiked her ass in the air as she leaned forward on all fours to give me head. She tried desperately to deep throat me, but that wasn't working. Her mouth felt good, but because she was young, she needed to work on her skills.

"You aren't as good at this as you pretend to be" I said.

"Be patient with me, I'm tryin to learn"

"So why me La-La, why not any of the other brothas in the hood?"

"Because unlike the other brothas, you will at least appreciate what I am trying to do"

To a degree she was right. A lot of the brothers called the sisters in the hood hos, rats, bitches and all other types of names. Me, I treated them decent. I at least acted like I had some home training. I threw my head back and closed my eyes as La-La began working her magic on my dick. Pretty soon all that could be heard in the living room was her slurping sounds. I was just about to let go in her mouth when I heard the sound of glass breaking.

"What the fuck?"

GOING UP IN SMOKE

When I looked up, there was fire everywhere in the front room. Apparently someone threw a Molotov Cocktail in to the window, but at an angle so the fire went right in front of the door. I heard glass breaking again and smoke started billowing in from the rear of the house as well. La-La screamed and began to cry like a little girl.

"What's happening! The house is on fire! What do we do! Oh my God, What do we do! Help! Somebody help us! Help!"

"Relax! Don't Panic, where is your phone?"

"I don't have a phone!"

Goddamned welfare bitches. This is what I thought to myself. My cell was in the truck.

"Do you have an extinguisher?"

"A what?"

"An extinguisher, a fucking fire extinguisher!"

"No!"

Fucking figures. It's hot than a mothafucka up in here and now I can't fucking breathe.

"Get down. Stay close to the floor!"

The front windows were barred. That was so niggas like Big Slim couldn't just come in whenever they felt like it. I was ready to panic my damned self. This girl inherited her family's home and the living room had old ass curtains, old ass newspapers laying around and old ass playboy magazines. Everything in the mothafucka was flammable.

La-La was still screaming. I can't blame her. I was ready to scream a little my goddamned self. Being from the hood and also a military veteran taught me one thing about a crisis, don't panic. Panicking won't do shit except contribute to the negative. I grabbed La-La by the arm and crawled to the bathroom. I then closed the door, ran the shower and the sink, wet the towels, and stuffed them into the cracks in the door. Together we both yelled for help out of the bathroom window which was also barred.

The Chicago Fire Department got there in about four minutes. Four minutes might seem quick, but in a house that is on fire, four minutes is a goddamned eternity! La-La started screaming again and I could no longer calm her down. I put in a quick ass prayer to God. I mean, I was talking to God so fast in my head, only he could have understood what it was that I was saying.

Yo God, It's Kevin. Man I don't wanna die like this. Not like this Lord. A fire? I mean I know I been fucking up lately but fire? Jesus, if you help a nigga out of this I swear I'll be cool. A nigga will pay his tithes and a nigga will give you the glory, JC please.

Just then, the door opened up and a fire fighter came in. He and a crew doused us with water as they lead us out of the smoking home. When we got to the street, the air was so good that it was orgasmic. The firefighters and paramedics gave us both oxygen and tried to sort out what happened. A crowd began to gather and everyone from the hood was checking us out.

"Damn, that nigga Kevin almost ended up a fuckin bacon crisp"

"Damn dawg, you a'ight?"

"La-La are you okay?"

"Damn, what about La-La's house?"

Damn, what about La-La's house? I bet she has no insurance and I am also betting that even if she did, nothing covers arson. She began to cry as the only place that she could ever call home, was now up in flames.

"Come on. I will take you to a shelter" I told her.

"A shelter? A shelter? I can't go live in no damned shelter! I'm gonna live in my house!"

"Ma'am, this building can no longer be lived in, I'm sorry" A firefighter said.

"No! Noooooo!"

She started kicking and screaming and having a nervous breakdown. I felt so sorry for her.

I gave her the keys and the title to the truck that I had. It wasn't much, but it was a start. I also gave her a check for $5,000. It wasn't much but it too was a start. I never paid for the truck so I wasn't really going to miss the money. The five grand was a drop in the bucket also. It just felt like I paid five grand for a blowjob which in my mind was five grand too much.

I had one of the brothers drive me back to my mother's crib and I had my sister Joy call me a cab. I had my fill of being home in the Chi. I needed to get south. I had the cab take me to the east side of town where I went to see Yolanda's mother, Claudette. I hated that bitch. I hated her from the first day that we met. I needed some answers though, because I swear, if I don't leave Chicago within the next few hours, I'm gonna catch a case for killing Yolanda. I know it had to be her that tossed the Molotov Cocktail in La-La's house. Now that girl's life is ruined.

I rang the bell to the elaborate home and waited for an answer. It was late at night but not yet midnight. I rang the bell some more until a few minutes later, Claudette answered the door.

"Kevin?"

"Hello Claudette, can I talk to you?"

"What about?"

"Yolanda"

"What about Yolanda?"

"I think she tried to kill me tonight"

I told Claudette everything that happened up until the fire. I asked her if she knew where Yolanda was, and she said no. I asked her how did she want to handle this and she almost seemed as if she didn't care what I did.

"I don't know what to say Kevin, you all are grown. What do you want from me?"

"I don't know Claudette, I was hoping to get some answers, or at the very least some support. Your daughter is causing me mad drama"

"But you slept with her"

"Yeah, I did but…"

"You slept with a woman that you knew to be unbalanced"

"Yeah, I did, but she told me she was better"

"Didn't she hit you with a damn car?"

"No one knows that better than you do Claudette"

"Actually, there is one person that knows better than me…you. So you knew my daughter had problems years ago, by her account she is better, so you took that to mean that you could fuck her, use her and send her off on the deep end and now you want my help. You are a fucking joke!"

"Me? You are the one that was too naïve to know that your husband was fucking your little girl! Or maybe you did no but you were too fucking scared or ashamed to do anything about it"

SLAP!

"Get out of my house!"

I deserved to be hit. I crossed the line. I let out a sigh and headed back out front to my cab. I looked back at the house, and Claudette slammed the door and shut off all the lights.

"Where to now my friend?" The Iraqi Cab Driver asked.

"The police station. I have a crime to report"

I went to the police station to report what happened at La-La's house. I told the police that I suspected Yolanda of tossing the Cocktail into the house. The police told me if I had no proof and there were no prints on the bottle itself, there was nothing that they could do. I started to go and get an order of protection. Then I decided that the answer was simple, I needed to go home.

"Where to now my friend?" The Cabbie asked.

"Take me to Midway"

I went to the airport and jumped on the first flight home.

♦ CHAPTER SIX ♦
TOO COMFORTABLE, TOO QUICK

KEVIN

I was so happy to be home. I had a cab drop me off in front of my crib and I jumped out quickly to tell Tamara that I was home. Upon seeing me she jumped on me like I had been gone a year or more off to war.

"Baby, you're home. Damn it's good to see you"

"It's good to see you too baby, what's up?"

"What's up? For starters, a sister is horny. After I get some, I'll tell you about my day"

"Sounds like a plan to me"

We didn't mix words. Although we had just made love the other night, it was like we were both starving for one another. I took my wife in my arms and kissed her deeply on the mouth while palming that ass. I tried to guide her upstairs to the bedroom, but she decided to break me off right there in the living room. We were all over each other like teenagers right after a school dance. I couldn't wait to taste her and I knew that she couldn't wait to be tasted. I kissed down her front, pulled off these tight ass grey sweatshorts that she had on, and buried my face in between her legs.

Tamara let out a satisfying moan as I ran circles around her clit and occasionally penetrated her with my tongue. In just a matter of minutes she was soaking wet. I then stuck two fingers in her and she let a satisfying moan. I fingered her, licked her and talked shit to her as I did my love play with my tongue.

"You like that?"

"Yes baby, I love that shit"

"You want this dick?"

"Oh baby, I do"

"You're going to have to earn it. You are going to have to cum really hard for me"

"No problem there baby, No problem…there…aw…shit"

I began licking her feverishly. I licked her clit fast, then slow, and then fast again. I then sucked her clit like a tiny penis and worked my way around the little rosebud until it was swollen and throbbing. I heard Tamara's breathing become more rapid. I knew she was almost there. Over and over again I licked her special place. I fingered her slowly, but I licked her fast. The two paces quickly brought her to the brink. Pretty soon afterward, she was screaming that she was cumming.

I let her come all on my fingers and my tongue. Tamara fought desperately to try and get away from me as I continued to lick her past climax. Her whole body shook with quakes when I finally let her go.

I smiled a sinister grin as I began taking off my pants. Tamara knelt right there in front of the couch and began rubbing my balls and occasionally stuck one in her mouth. She licked my balls for minutes on end and finally licked up to the tip and took my package into her warmth. Her mouth was so warm, so wet, and so perfect. I let out a moan as she began to deep throat me. Up and down my shaft she licked until my legs went numb. Just when I thought I could take no more, she mounted me with her back to me.

She slid up and down my pole and her juices flowed so hard that my dick was glistening with her fluids. I loved her pussy. It was a perfect fit. On top of loving her pussy, I loved the way that her ass looked as she went up and down on my dick.

"You like that shit Kevin?"

"I love that shit baby"

"Then say something"

"I love that shit baby"

"Show me, smack that ass"

I slapped her on her ass.

"Again, hit that motha fucka, show me what you workin with"

I hit that mothafucka just a bit harder.

"Aw shit, that's it baby. That's it, hit that shit, you all up in my shit. Damn you know I like that shit, you know I love that shit. Kevin, baby, damn!"

Oh, I was tearing that mother fucka up now. I was slapping that ass, thrusting hard up inside her and fucking her all she was worth. I then stood up, moved her onto the couch doggy style, grabbed her by her waist and started pounding that pussy. The shit was so good and so wet, that juices were damn near splashing out of her. Her shit was so good that I couldn't take my time and hit the pussy right tonight. She came, I was about to come my damned self. I hit that shit at a real god pace until I came so hard that I hurt my damned neck and back.

"Awwwwww Shiiiiiittttt! Fuck! Yeah! Damn! Aw, Aw, Aw…shiiiiiiittttt!"

Tamara then stopped playing fair and started backing that ass up on my dick. I could barely stand, barely speak, and my knees felt like they were about to buckle. Tamara started rocking that ass back up on me and started fucking me. She backed that ass up on a brother and had her shit clapping on my dick.

"Uh-huh, yeah nigga, you wasn't ready for this shit now was you? Uh-huh, you bout ready to scream ain't ya? Whose dick is that? I can't hear you nigga, whose dick is that?"

"Damn baby, you're gonna kill me…"

"…Shut the fuck up, answer me, whose dick is that?"

"It's your dick baby, it's yours, aw shit, Tamara stop"

"Say it's juicy"

"It's Juicy baby"

"Say it's the best that you ever had"

"Aw baby, it's the best, it's the best, it's…. Awwwww Shhhhiiiittttt!"

I came again. I came hard. I came so hard that my damned head hurt. No this motha fucka didn't make me come twice. I swear if we weren't already married, I would be driving this bitch somewhere and marry her ass all over again. I had a damned Charlie Horse in my stomach, that's how hard I came. I collapsed on top of her kissing her back and the back of her neck. As I did, she began grinding that soft juicy ass up against me.

"Tamara stop moving baby, damn. I can't take that shit"

She smiled a seductive smile.

"Okay baby"

I pulled out of her and went to sleep right there on the couch. She said I was smiling the whole time that I was out.

I slept a few hours and then got up the next morning looking for my wife. She left me a note saying that she had gone to aerobics. She fixed me breakfast which was on a plate on the stove. I got up ate a bit and decided that I needed to go running my damned self. Aerobics was making that pussy better as Tamara got older. I needed to get my ass in peak condition if I was going to kick it with her. I made it a habit to run every morning now so I could keep up with my wife.

Another two weeks passed and Tamara and I had sex everyday since I had been back home. I don't know what point she or I were trying to prove, but we had this animal chemistry thing going on for the first two weeks that I was back. I guess absence does make the heart grow fonder. Tamara and I slept with one another until we were both spent. During my third week of being home is when it was time for me to leave again. I was headed to New York to talk with my publisher.

"New York? How long are you going to be gone this time?" Tamara asked.

"A week tops. You know, you could always come with me"

"Kevin I have a class to teach"

Letting out a sigh I said, "I know baby, but I need to talk with the suits at the publishers to see where they are at in regard to my re-signing"

"I thought you wanted to go to a new publisher anyway?"

"Naw, not really. I have been with my publisher forever. I just want enough money where we don't have to worry about anything anymore. Besides, with the money that I am bringing in and will be bringing in, I was thinking that maybe you would quit your job"

"What? Oh, hell no"

"Why not?"

"Baby I love you, but there is no way in hell I could be around you twenty four seven"

"What kind of shit is that to say?"

"I don't mean anything by it, but baby we still need to live our own lives. You make enough money now for me to stay home, but that's not what I want. I teach because I love to teach"

"Okay. I understand. It's just that you are always preaching about more quality time"

"Yeah, and I plan to have that time, when we are both on vacation or when we are missing one another"

"Gotcha"

"Well, take it easy in New York. Bring me back a Coach Purse or two"

"I will"

THE BIG APPLE

A week later, I was in New York. It's crowded as hell there and very expensive. I hated New York because it was the one place that no one gave a damn about who I was or who I thought I was. I got celebrity treatment and mad props in every city that I have been in except NY. Most places I went, people were like "Hey, it's Kevin Allen" Here it was like "Yeah okay nigga, so what?" New Yorkers were funny to me. They were Chicagoans with a lot more attitude. I was hoping that my publisher wasn't going to take a New York attitude with me during these negotiations. I also didn't want them to throw me out on my Chicago ass.

I met my agent at the publisher's office and soon afterward, I was faced with the Board of Directors who were trying to hide that they were beaming about the new book. The CEO spoke to me first.

"Kevin, we like the book. We think that just like the others, it will be a best-seller. You have our complete confidence. So why did you ask for this meeting today?"

"Well, a few years back you all gave me a wonderful opportunity and got behind me in my writing endeavors.

I have made a decent living for myself and my family and for that, I would like to say thank you"

They each smiled and nodded in agreement.

"But, as you know, we are at the end of my contract. I have made you guys a lot of money. I think now, before my next book hits the shelves, we need to re-negotiate a new book deal. I'm giving you the first crack at me. If you guys make me a solid offer, one that is not the highest, but respectable compared to other African-American authors, I will stay with this publishing house and we can continue the relationship that we started a while back"

"And if we choose to wait until your contract expires?"

"Then, I'm on the market again and my talents will serve the highest bidder"

The CEO gave a slight smile at how brash I was.

"Kevin, I'm sorry. At this point, we want to wait before re-working your deal"

"What? Why?"

"Well to be honest with you, African American books are hard to market and hard to move"

"You mean to say because you know nothing about the African-American culture, you aren't sure how to market our books" I said rather sternly.

"Yes, I guess that's a fair assessment. In addition to that, since 9/11, people haven't been buying books like they used to. With this genre already being a questionable market..."

"...A questionable market? African American books and entertainment is if anything, an untapped market"

"That may be true, but as you eloquently pointed out, we don't know how to tap that market. Your contract is up in two months. We will join the bidding war to re-sign you, but we are not ready to sign you just yet"

I was speechless. Fucking New Yorkers, they don't give a damn about anyone. The CEO could see that I was stunned and tried to offer me some support.

"Kevin, your next book will be out soon. We are going to market the hell out of it, run commercials, magazine ads and put at least a half-million in the promotion. If sales move as projected, you will make somewhere in the area of five million on this project before taxes. That's a lot of money"

"If I make five million, that means that you have made thirty million"

"That's the business we're in"

"It seems like you are giving me the business"

"Kevin, I don't understand you. Just a few years ago you were living in the hood. You are living a comfortable lifestyle that many African Americans can only dream about. Isn't that enough?"

"It's never enough. What if I want to give back some? What if I want to own my own publishing company, or my own magazine?"

"All I am saying Kevin, is not now. Again, I'm sorry"

They each got up and left. I was there with my agent looking stupid as hell. I then got a phone call from Tamara who was crying.

"Baby, Tamara what's wrong?"

"You need to come home. There's been a fire"

THE LONGEST FLIGHT OF MY LIFE

I took a cab back to the airport and my heart was racing as I tried desperately to get to JFK. There seems to be no rushing in New York. I yelled at the cabbie to get me to the airport and he seemed to be oblivious to my ranting.

"I hate New York. There are too many motha fuckas here"

"Don't say nuthin about New York. You don't like it here, keep it to ya self. Otherwise, you get outta my cab"

"What? Nigga fuck you (even though the guy was Arabian or something) you better drive this motha fuckin cab and do yo motha fuckin job!"

The cabbie and I exchanged pleasantries as he drove through traffic. Initially he pulled over saying that he was going to make me get out.

"You get out of my cab"

"Man, if I get out of this cab, I'mma beat that ass for old and new"

"Then you will go to jail"

"Maybe so, but your ass will still be in intensive care by the time the police get here. Now try me if you want to. In Chicago, we shoot cabbies for talkin shit. Get yo ass in the car and drive bitch, or I'mma catch a case in this motha fucka"

"Fuck You!"

He cursed the whole way, but he got back in the cab and damn near drove on the curb to get me to JFK. I guess he wanted me out of his cab fast.

An hour later, I was at the airport. I raced through the airport like OJ used to do in those Hertz commercials.

I then jumped on the first flight back to the crib. It took a few hours. That few hours seemed like forever.

When I got home, my house had been burned badly. Just seeing it had me heartbroken. This was our house, our dream house, the one we used to drive by and look at. It took us years to get it the way that we wanted it. Just a few weeks ago, we made love all through the house like we did when we were newly weds. Tamara had been staying at her mother's since the fire. She and an investigator met me at the house. Tamara pulled up in her Truck and when she saw me, she just started crying. She collapsed in my arms.

"Kevin, our house…it's gone"

"It's okay baby, we will re-build. We have insurance"

The investigator said, "I'm not sure that insurance covers arson"

"Arson?" I said.

"Yeah. Someone threw a Molotov Cocktail through your window. That is what set the blaze. Had your wife been home or been sleep, she might not be here today"

I could feel the hairs on the back of my neck stand. My heart began racing and I swear I saw Jesus off in the distance trying to calm me down.

"Mr. Allen, do you have any enemies?"

"No, not that I am aware of"

"Do you know who might have done this?"

"No, not a clue. Wait a minute, there is this guy Keith, her ex. You might want to talk with him"

I figured I might as well kill two birds with one stone. I see that MF occasionally in town and he is always looking at me sideways, like he is trying to size me up or something. I'm tired of that nigga eyeballin me. Besides, I could use the diversion.

"Kevin what are you going to do?"

"I want you to go stay at your sisters' or your mother's house. I will be back in a few weeks. In the meantime, try to work with the insurance company. If we can't use the insurance, then we will have to just pay for everything all over again. Where is my car?"

"It's at my mother's house. Where are you going?"

"I have some business to take care of"

"What kind of business? Shouldn't you be here helping me with all this and…"

"Goddammit Tamara, handle this shit! I married a partner, a very capable woman! Quit acting helpless and handle this shit! Quit asking me questions also! When I say business, I mean just that—business!"

"Kevin, don't you yell at me! What has gotten into you?"

"I'm tired of being questioned all the time. I am tired of the third fucking degree! Can you just handle this shit?"

The inspector said, "I'm gonna go. My office will be in touch. You all obviously have a lot to discuss"

The investigator left. Tamara walked into our home, which was salvageable, but it was going to be expensive as hell to fix. She looked at me as if I had hit her. I guess my words hit hard. She looked back at me in pain as she walked in our home. I followed behind her.

"Tamara, baby, I'm sorry" I walked up behind her and hugged her.

She turned around and slapped the shit out of me.

"Don't you ever talk to me that way again. The next time that you do, I walk!"

The hit stung, but she was right.

I hugged her and pulled her close to me. "Okay babe, okay"

We held each other in the middle of the house; a place we once called our home.

"I have to go" I said as I headed toward the door.

"Why?" she said flatly.

I really did hate the fucking questions. One, because I was wrong to be leaving her in the first place. Two, because I hated explaining myself all the damned time. It was childish and worrisome, even when I wasn't doing dirt.

I let out a long sigh.

"Things in New York didn't go as well as I planned"

I told her how things went and explained to her that I was not any richer coming home. I told her that I was headed to Chicago to promote my new book which was due to be released in three short weeks. I also told her that I needed to meet with competing publishing houses and let them know that I am on the market.

"So I guess I shouldn't tell you that we're broke huh?"

"What?"

"Our joint account has a hundred grand in it, that's all"

"What?"

I was stunned. I did spend entirely too much money. I called my accountant on my cell.

"What the hell is up with my finances?"

"I was just about to ask you the same thing, why have you been spending so much money lately?"

"It's mine to spend. Am I really broke?"

"Liquid cash you have 100K in the bank. With investments, you are worth another million, but if we liquidate everything, after taxes, fees, penalties and interest, you can only cash that into about $450,000. But if you do that, you will have nothing once that's gone. You and Tamara can't make a hundred grand stretch until the release of your next book?"

"Shit, it looks like we are going to have to. Look man, you track my stats, how much is my next royalty?"

"You have another 85 grand coming in a month and a half"

"I hate it that royalties are only issued every three months"

"Hey, that's the business my friend. Spend it sparingly. When you get this next big check or an advance, you need to spend it more wisely"

"No, when I get out of hand, you need to call me"

I hung up the phone.

"We are going to have to tighten our belts some. Tamara, I need you to work with the insurance company and I will tell my agent to ask the publisher for an advance to float us awhile. They should give is a half million"

I hugged my wife and kissed her. I told her that everything was going to be okay. Next, I called my agent and had her ask for an advance. I was told that a half million would be deposited in my account within 72 hours. I then caught a flight back to Chicago.

♦ CHAPTER SEVEN ♦
SWEET HOME CHICAGO

KEVIN

I got back to the city and checked into a small Motel out in the south suburbs. I threw on some sweats and some all white kicks and I rented a Chevy Cavalier. It was a small car, but it was okay. I used to drive one before I blew up as an author, and I think it's about time that I started leading a sensible lifestyle again. I put on my driving gloves and headed out the door to my room. I didn't want anyone to know that I was home. I especially wanted to surprise Yolanda.

I picked up a few brothers from the hood and I drove to Yolanda's house in the middle of the afternoon when I figured that she was at work. I had the brothers break into her crib and make me a set of keys. I then decided that the kid gloves were off. It was time to put an end to this shit.

"You want us to hang around and help Kevin?" One of the brothers asked.

"Naw man, I'm straight"

"Is this her in this photo?" Another brother asked while picking up a photo off Yolanda's dresser.

"Yeah, that's her"

"Damn, well can we stay? I mean, if she is the broad that tried to kill you and shit, the least you can do is let us run a train on her or something"

"No"

"But I'm sayin…"

"No! Ya'll know how to get home from here, right?"

"Yeah" They both said.

"Well here is a hundred each. I just needed help getting in, that's all"

The brothas left, but not before raiding Yolanda's fridge.

I sat on her bed and relaxed for a while. I then went through all of her things. I found photos of me, newspaper clippings, notes that I used to write to her when we were younger, and everything from old movie tickets to other mementos from our relationship years ago. On top of all the clipping was a black diskette. I took it and booted up her computer. I was expecting the disk to have photos of us on it. Instead, I was shocked as hell to see that it was a copy of my new book.

"What the fuck?"

Now I was steaming. How dare she take a copy of my book for herself to read. Shit, in the wrong hands, this book could be a problem. I was fuming when I saw that shit. I took the diskette and placed it in my pocket. I then threw away all of the pictures, photos, and everything that could be of sentimental value to Yolanda. I then surfed the net while in her crib, made a few phone calls, and fixed myself some food.

As it got dark in the house, I let the house stay dark. I didn't turn on the TV any additional lights or anything that would give me away. It was 10:30 when Yolanda finally made it home. She walked into her house, threw her keys on the counter, and went to the bathroom to pee. I was behind the bedroom door in the dark trying to control my breathing. This was key when doing dirt when I was younger, and it was key when I was in the service. I was debating on whether or not I was going to kill her, or simply beat her ass.

"Kevin, could you hand me some tissue?"

I was stunned. I was quiet as hell. I didn't move. I was confused as hell as to how she could know that I was here.

"Kevin? Kevin. Kevin I can smell you baby. You use Oil of Olay Bar Soap. You moisturize your skin with Mary Elizabeth Lotion. Remember, I used to sell Mary Elizabeth. I got you started on that. You put on Mesmerize cologne this morning. Granted, it's thirteen hours later, but baby…I know your smell"

I was stunned. She stood up and grabbed extra tissue from the bathroom pantry. She tore open a new roll and wiped herself. She flushed and then washed her hands. She then stood smugly in the bathroom doorway trying to figure out where I was, or if I was actually still in the house.

I didn't tip my hand. I was very still. She opened the drawer with all of her mementos and had a look of shock and horror when she saw that all of our keepsakes were no longer there. She screamed.

"Kevin! Kevin where are my things!"

She stormed through the house cutting on all the lights. She began with the bedroom which is where we were. She stormed around the house turning on lights, slamming shit around the house, and cursing. When she made it back to her bedroom, I stepped from behind the door and hit her ass so hard in the face, that I took her clear up off her feet. I knocked her smooth the fuck out. I then cut off all the lights in the house. When Yolanda came too, I was sitting on the bed across from her and she was propped up in the corner of the bedroom. There were no restraints, no weapons, just the two of us. I spoke darkly to her in a Jack Nicholson sort of way.

"Yolanda, Baby, We need to talk"

She touched her face and tasted her own blood.

"Kevin, what did you do?"

"What did I do? What did you do?" You almost killed me"

"You shouldn't have been with that bitch"

"You then almost killed my wife"

"She wasn't home. I wouldn't hurt her like that. I'm not trying to hurt her. I was trying to hurt you"

"Well, you have my attention. I'm here to tell you once and for all that you have crossed a line, and this is your only pass. If you fuck with me, or my family again, I will kill you. Now you can play crazy, be crazy, hell you can even fuck crazy. But I want to make myself clear. You play this game with me, this story ends with me putting yo ass in a pine box"

"We threatening each other now?"

"Yogi, I'm ready to kill your ass"

"Well, these are the rules Kevin; family is off limits. I got that. But if you don't give us a fair chance, I'mma see that you hurt even more than you have been. I plan to bring your whole world crashing down on you"

"Whatever"

"Yeah, whatever back at you, nigga"

I walked out of Yolanda's house and jumped in the Chevy Cavalier and drove off.

BACK IN THE HOOD

I went back to the hood the next day to shoot some ball. When I got back on the court, I was happy to see that Big Slim had once again re-taken the basketball court.

"Big Kevin, what's up man? I heard that you almost died a while back over there in La-La's house"

"Yeah, that was a close call"

I looked over to La-La's place, which was only across the street from the park, and her whole crib had been re-built and re-modeled.

"Who hooked her crib up?"

"This new nigga in the hood named Darrin"

"Dope Dealer?"

"Pimp"

"Aw, naw bruh, you lyin"

"Swear to God"

"Anybody say anything to the nigga?"

"What is anybody supposed to say? He's got a product everyone wants. He has been turning out some of the finest women in the hood and putting them on display for the brothas in the hood"

"Turning them out how?"

Most pimps in the hood turned their tricks onto drugs, making them a slave to the drug and thus a slave to the pimp. It would break my heart to hear that the sweet young honey was hooked up like that.

"Is he turning women onto drugs?"

"Naw, the brother just gets in their head and talks with them. I don't know what the fuck his game is, but the nigga is smooth. His top broad is named Honey and she is Halle Berry fine. Both she and he talk to a lot of the broads here in the hood and the next thing I know, the pussy is for sale"

"Is he over there now?"

"Man, he be over there tearin that ass up every other day. He's over there"

"I think it's time that he and I had a conversation"

"What are you gonna do young Martin, Preach to him?"

"I just need to let him know whose hood this is"

"A'ight. But if you gonna go challenge that man after he put all that cash into La-La's crib, you had better take a gat"

"Big Slim handed me a nine millimeter. I told him no only because I knew if this fool pissed me off, I'd use it"

I rang the bell and a few minutes later, La-La came to the door. She had on Levi Blue Jeans, boots, and a bratop. Her abs looked incredible, and it looked like she had been working out.

"Hey Kevin, what's up?"

"You okay?"

"Yeah, why wouldn't I be?"

"I heard that you got someone sponsoring you now"

"That's right"

"Well, that's why I came over here to see if you were okay"

"That's sweet Kevin, but unnecessary"

"What do you mean?"

"I don't need saving, I'm fine"

"Can I meet this cat?"

"Who?"

"This new nigga, Darrin"

"Baby, there is someone here who wants to meet you"

"Let him in"

MEETING DARRIN

I walked in the house and it had been completely furnished with new items. There were TV's, a working phone, stereo systems, an aquarium and a computer. The place was really decked out. In the living room was a brotha on the phone that looked like Dave Hollister.

"What's up bruh?" He shook my hand.

"My name is Kevin and…"

"Hold up, Kevin? The same Kevin that gave La-La that truck? The writer?"

"Yeah, that's me"

"Can I get an autograph?"

"Are you serious?"

"Yeah I'm serious"

"Yeah, I guess, look man I came here to talk to you about what you do and how you do it. I'm not feeling your turning La-La out and pimpin her on these streets"

"Hold up player. Real pimps don't choose women, women choose them. That's the first thing. The second thing is that I really don't give a fuck what you or any of these other niggas in the hood think about me or how I handle my business. Now I don't mean any disrespect to you or your hood, but ya'll got it twisted if you think I'mma let you run script on me. Now peep this player. She called…me. I gave her a job and she is working for us both. You were gonna fuck her for free when you were last here. Well, if you wanted her now, it would cost you $350. 00. I advanced her by fixing up her crib. She is still paying me back for that. But everything in here, she bought. She did it with the money that she earned. I supply the means and the customer. All she has to do is pick and choose. Her Johns wear condoms, and every nigga in this city knows to respect my ladies otherwise they will end up catching a dirt nap. So don't hate the player, hate the game. Talk to her and ask her if she wants to leave my stable. By the way, she is free to quit at anytime, and that's not script. That's a fact. I'mma go here in the back and grab some of these ribs off the grill. I got a copy of your last book in here too. I'd really like that autograph"

This man, got up, walked pass me and went to get some food like I meant nothing to him. I looked at La-La with confusion.

"How much money do you owe him for the remodeling?"

"Why?"

"I might pay it"

"That's sweet Kevin, but I don't need it. I can make my own money"

"Turning tricks?"

"It's not what you think"

"You're fucking niggas for money, right? Then it's exactly what I think"

She leaned forward and kissed me on the cheek.

"Your money isn't welcome here. I'm okay. Thank you though, I mean that"

Darrin came walking back to the front with a fine ass woman that I didn't even know was in the back. She looked like Halle Berry, except her eyes were hazel and both her ass and titties were bigger. My mouth almost dropped open when I saw her. This sister could have played cat woman also. Damn she was fine.

"Stunning isn't she? Honey, this is Kevin Allen. Kevin this is Honey, she is the one that the autograph is for"

"Hello" I said

Honey smiled and blushed. She was breath-taking. She was so fine that I was practically speechless. My contempt for Darrin eased up a bit.

"Bo cool player. I don't want you to go on overload. Don't get any ideas about Honey either, she is $5,000"

"Five-grand for a night?", I said stunned.

"Five-grand an hour", Honey said.

I signed the autograph. I slowly left La-La's house. I looked back at Honey who waved at me innocently. There should be a book written about her and the affect that she must have on men. The book should be named Brokenhearted. Because that's how it felt to say goodbye to her.

I went back over to the Park to play ball. Big Slim was grinning at me like a damned Cheshire Cat.

"So did you straighten his ass out?"

"Yeah, I did"

"You'se a lie. I bet you saw that fine Halle Berry Motha Fucka over there and became speechless"

"How did you know?"

"I did the same thing when I found out that La-La went from hood rat to Call Girl"

"Are all the fine sisters in the hood working for this nigga now?"

"Not all, but most. Pussy around here went from free to costly to down right expensive. Some brothas have even talked about going out to get jobs!"

"Oh the horror!"

We both laughed and decided to play some ball.

"So, Slim, when you were missing, where were you?"

"Taking care of some business Kevin"

"We looked for you. Hell, even your boys didn't know where to find you"

"That's because I didn't want to be found"
"Oh, a'ight. Well, then, Check Ball!"

♦ CHAPTER EIGHT ♦
HELL HATH NO FURY

KEVIN

I shot ball with Big Slim, checked on my family, and headed back to Somerton. The insurance company was willing to re-do our home, although our premiums shot through the roof. Tamara was loving the idea of remodeling the whole house again. She took a leave of absence from teaching and spent her days making our house a home again. I loved that because we were both home at the same time ands pending quality time with one another. I was also preparing for my new book to be released. I had a tour planned, radio interviews and a heavy marketing campaign. I hadn't heard anymore from Yolanda, so I figured she got my message loud and clear.

Tamara was giving directions to the furniture people, and I was on my laptop checking my emails. I was drinking Orange Juice from the carton and almost choked when I got my first email.

It said that it was a message from the church inviting me to the celebration of the welfare to work program. When I opened it, it was a photo of me having sex with Yolanda and another photo of me having sex with Kitty. That is what happened to my cell phone that has been missing all this time. Tamara got me that damned phone. I told her when she got it that I didn't need a damned camera phone. I said that I would never use it. Now it was being used against me.

My heart started beating fast as I read and re-read the email over and over again. I read every word and every letter on the screen. The end of the email said, "I know that your wife's email is TAA@yahoo.com"

"Oh shit!"

Tamara walked by my office area and saw me on the laptop. She started giving the furniture guys directions and then spoke out to me.

"Kevin are you online? Honey leave your computer up so that I can check my email"

Oh shit, Oh shit no, not like this! Oh shit. Think Kevin, Think!

"Okay Babe" I said casually.

I logged out, went into start programs, disabled my virus protection, closed the programs menu, went to my bulk mailbox and opened every suspicious email in the box. I was sweating bullets like a mothafucka as I did it. Sure enough, a virus wiped out my brand new laptop. I casually walked away from my computer in my office, as Tamara headed toward my PC. I went upstairs to do the same thing to her computer. While she was trying to get on my PC, I was upstairs messing hers up. I then logged off, and shut the computer down that was upstairs. I casually walked downstairs to see what Tamara was doing.

"Kevin, Something is wrong with the PC"

"Really? I was just on it, let me see"

I walked over to the PC and looked at the screen like I was pissed.

"Aw Damn"

"What Kevin?"

"I think someone hit us with a virus"

"But we have firewall protection and all this expensive software"

"Honey, you know that means nothing to these damned hackers. If they want to get you, they will. It's just like having a car thief around. You can have the best alarm system in the world, but if a thief really wants your car, he's gonna get it"

"Deep. Well, I will check my email later upstairs. Hopefully that computer is unaffected"

"Maybe, but I doubt it. If one PC is down, both probably are"

Tamara went back to working and then the doorbell rang. I went to open it and there was my mother in law and my sister in law who had come over to help. There was also a strange white man walking up my sidewalk.

He looked like a damned cop. He had a buzz cut and a serious ass look on his face. I directed my in laws inside where they were anxious to help. I then walked up the walkway to meet the man.

"Excuse me sir, can I help you?"

"Kevin Allen?"

"Yes"

"It's been a pleasure serving you"

It was a damned subpoena. I slid it under my arm and went into the house, into the upstairs bathroom, and opened it. It was a lawsuit and a suit for PATERNITY. According to the paperwork, Yolanda was four months pregnant with my child. I felt weak, and passed out, hitting my head on the sink and drawing blood. I laid there in the locked bathroom for twenty minutes. I awoke to pounding on the door.

"Kevin, Kevin are you okay?"

I was stunned. My head was spinning and I needed to hurry up and shake the cobwebs out. I placed the papers back in the envelope, and spoke to my wife through the door.

"Tamara, I'm okay"

"If you are okay, then open the door"

"I need a minute"

"Kevin, what's wrong?"

"I passed out, my head hit the sink. I'm okay, I just need a minute"

"Baby, that's fine, but I want to see. Now open the door you're scaring me"

I placed the papers in the hamper and unlocked the door. Tamara cried when she saw the big ass knot on my head.

"We need to get you the hospital"

"I'm fine"

"No, You're not"

"Baby, I'm cool. Just go get me some ice in a ziplock, please"

She went to get the ice. I grabbed the papers and placed them under my arm, went to the bedroom and placed the envelope between the mattresses. I then laid down on top as Tamara brought me the ice.

"What happened?"

"I don't know"

"Well, I'm glad that your publisher called. Otherwise I wouldn't have looked for you"

"My publisher called? What did they want?"

"I don't know, they seemed anxious. They said for you to call them immediately. They said it was urgent"

"Hand me the phone"

"Kevin, I really think you should rest"

"Tamara…Stop. I'm cool"

She looked at me like she was pissed off. "Okay" She said flatly.

I dialed the number to my publisher and told the woman that answered the phone who I was. I was only on hold twenty seconds before I heard the voice of the CEO and the sound of my being put on speakerphone.

"Kevin, we would like to see you in our office tomorrow. We want to see you here in New York at 11:00 AM"

"I'm working on my house and getting ready for the book tour, what's up?"

There was a silence on the other end of the phone.

"Kevin, we need you to come here. I want to see you at 11:00 are we clear on that?"

I didn't like being talked to like a child is placed a bit more bass in my voice.

"I get that you want to see me, but you still haven't made it clear why. Like I said, I was getting ready for the book tour and I am remodeling my home. There was a fire remember? That's why I needed the advance"

"Kevin, there isn't going to be a tour, we are not promoting the new book, and we want our advance back! Now, I want to see you here at our office tomorrow at 11:00 along with your agent. Be here, on time, or I will see you in court"

There was a dial tone on the phone.

"Shit"

I got on the phone and charged a round trip ticket to New York. I would have booked it online, but I fucked my computer up. I told Tamara that I needed to leave. I decided that I needed to catch the very next flight to New York and sleep at a hotel near the publisher's office. Tamara was not pleased about my leaving.

"How long will you be gone?"

"Three days at the most, I promise"

Still Crazy

I jumped on the next flight back to New York and got maybe five hours of sleep. I had no idea what I was facing, so I prepared as best I could for the worst.

THE SUITS

At 11:00 exactly, the CEO and all of his people showed up across the table from me. They each looked at me like they were my judges and I was a man on trial. Their faces were grim and they each were waiting on the CEO to speak first.

"Where is your agent?"

"I told my agent to stay home"

"I told you to bring your agent"

"I don't need my agent"

"Where is your lawyer?"

"You didn't say that I needed my lawyer"

"Had I said that, would you have brought him?"

"Yes, I would have. Do I need him here now?"

"You will need to consult with him before it's all over"

"So what is this all about?"

"Your new book, it has come to our attention that you do not own the copyright"

"What? Are you saying that I stole this book from someone?"

"That is exactly what I am saying. The young lady that wrote the book is here and she wants to address both you and the board. She is here along with her attorney"

The CEO gave the head nod to a woman who was a junior executive. She got up from her chair and let

215

Yolanda in. Yolanda was in a Dark Maroon Suit, black stockings and heels. Her hair was down, and she sported no makeup. Even plain, she was still a very pretty woman. With no makeup on however, you could see the discoloration in her face where I clocked her. She came in, sat down across from the CEO and gave a courteous smile. Not once did she look in my direction.

"Yolanda, could you please re-count the story that you have told us thus far"

"Sure. Kevin and I used to date years ago. He came to see me a few months back and told me that he was going through writers block, and that was why he came home. He told me that he missed me and that he wanted to be with me again. I tried to explain to him that although I still care for him, some things went on in my life that scarred me against men. You see, I was molested by my father while Kevin and I were dating and…"

"…This is bullshit!" I interrupted.

"Please Kevin, you will have your say. Do not interrupt her again. Please continue"

"Well, the short of the story is this, I was not ready to get into a relationship again. In fact, I told Kevin that I was working on my own novel and I asked him could he look at it and perhaps give me some pointers. He read it, and he said that it was okay, but no one would be interested in an Urban Novel. He said that market was not ready for something like this. I thought it was no good, so it sat on my shelf all this time. Then, something in the back of my head said that I should copyright it with the Library of Congress because who knows? Maybe one day the market would like an Urban drama.

Kevin kept pursuing me. Eventually, I gave in to him. We became sexually active in spite of his having a wife at home. We have been carrying on an affair until recently. When I told Kevin that it was over, he beat me. He told me I wasn't shit, I would never be shit and he would see me dead rather than be with someone else. I presently have a restraining order against him. When it dawned on him that I might go public with news of our affair, he offered $10,000 to the charity that I work for. My boss, Reverend Turner asked Kevin for $20,000 initially, and Kevin said no. I believe he gave the $10,000 to appease me. I've even met his wife. When I did, it was to try and convince her to donate money. I could see that Kevin was uncomfortable with my talking to her, so I pretended that we had never met. When I saw his wife, it was just 24 hours after we last slept together. I just discovered recently also, that I am carrying Kevin's child"

I let out a heavy sigh. My heart sunk in my stomach.

"And you are willing to get a paternity test?" I interrupted.

"Yes Kevin, I am!"

She was so confident, her words shook me.

The CEO looked at me and asked Yolanda more questions.

"When did you discover that your book had been stolen?"

"I didn't. I just remember that Kevin had nothing on paper before he came home to Chicago. When he and I met, and right after making love, he would comment that he needed a good story because he had lost it as a writer and he needed something to trick his publisher into signing him to a lengthy deal. He said that his next few books could be bullshit books or cookbooks. He said as long as he would be able to get a contract, he would be straight financially. That seemed to be his only motivation. But to answer your question, I became suspicious when I saw all these TV ads, radio commercials and endorsements. My heart sank in my chest when I heard that the title was the same as mine. To safeguard my work, I sent your office a copy of my copyright"

"This bitch is lying!" I said.

"Kevin, did you all have an affair?"

"That's not your business"

"I'll take that as a yes"

"That's my goddamned book!"

"Kevin, you generally email your book the second you finish. You generally call me, your agent and we all celebrate. Your editor gets advanced copies. This time, your entire routine changed. Why is that?"

"I was going through some changes. Look, she stole the book from me"

"She owns the copyright. Production of the book will move forward, only it appears that the name of the author on the cover must change to the name that is on the copyright. In the meanwhile, you owe us our advance for this book, back. You also have one month before your contract expires. I am expecting our last book by then, otherwise you will be sued for breach of contract. Regardless of how things go, I'm afraid your time here at this publishing house, is over. In light of these circumstances, I'm not sure how receptive other publishing houses will be to you. That's all Kevin, I wish you well"

"That's it? No explanation from me? What about all I did for this company? What about all the money that I made you guys?"

No one even listened to me. They just walked out of the room. They escorted Yolanda out who looked at me and winked, before walking out the door.

My career, is gone.

I have a month to finish a new book.

Yolanda is about to get paid, off all my hard work.

And I'm broke.

I placed my head in my lap and I wept. I wasn't crying aloud, but I could not stop the tears from flowing. I was alone in the conference room for ten long minutes. When I looked up, there was Yolanda sitting across from me.

"I'm sorry baby, you made me go here with you"

I didn't say a word. I had a scowl on my face that was dark and clearly stated that I was ready to kill her.

"Your wife knows by now, about us I mean. You also have a baby on the way. I know you are thinking about getting up and putting your hands on me, but if you hit me and I lose the baby, that's murder now. You know that was one of the first things that George W put in place when he got into office. Your wife is gone by now, I'm sure. You are going to lose your home, no one will touch you in the publishing business, and you are broke. Face it baby, you're beaten. You might as well get back with me and be a father to your child. I'll love you, I'll fuck you, and now that I got money, I'll take care of you"

I looked up from my seat and began to tremble with anger. I was beside myself with anger and had no idea what to do next.

"Go to hell Yolanda"

She said, "You first"

She left the office and I caught the next flight home.

OUT OF THE FRYING PAN AND INTO THE MF FIRE

I took the incredibly long flight home. I got back to Somerton the next day at about noon. I walked in the door and Tamara's bags were packed and sitting by the door.

All the new furniture that she ordered, was gone. The repairs to our home, had been stopped. When I walked in, she was seated on a single love seat in the living room and in font of her sprawled out all over the table, were photos. Apparently, she accessed her yahoo account from somewhere else. I looked at my wife and her eyes were bloodshot from all the crying that she had done. She looked ill. I felt ill. I had lost my career, my money and everything that I worked hard in life to get. There was a pain in my stomach as I realized that now…I was about to lose the only thing in life that mattered.

I was frozen with fear in the doorway of our living room.

"Do you know where I was when I checked my email?

I didn't respond. I just stood there in fear.

"I was at my mother's house"

Still, I said nothing.

"You were supposed to go to Chicago to find your muse. You were supposed to be going there to create a story, to secure our financial future; those were your words"

"Baby, I'm so sorry" I said in a whisper.

" I know this isn't the first time that you stepped out on me. I knew that every now and then you slept with a fan, or had the occasional fling. I just kept on telling myself, if I just keep on lovin' him, keep on making love to him, be a good woman to him, he'll always come home to me"

"Tamara, baby I never…I mean this is the first time…the last time…baby, right now I need you"

"Why? Why do you need me Kevin? Because we're broke? The money never meant shit to me! It was nice, but I wanted us"

"We can still have us"

"There is no us! We, we are done Kevin! You did this! You did this to us!"

Just then, there was a knock at the front door. I opened it and it was the investigator from the fire department.

"Mr. Allen? Sir I need to speak with you and your wife and ask you some questions"

"Now is really not a good time"

"I'm afraid it's going to have to be sir"

"Look Chief, my wife and I are kind of in the middle of something and…"

"Sir, is this the second time that you have been in an arson fire in a matter of weeks?"

"I'm sorry, what?"

"It has been brought to our attention that this was the second fire that you were in involving a Molotov Cocktail. Apparently there is a report that you were in a house in Chicago with a woman and the two of you almost died. The home was in the name of a Miss Lolita um…hold on, I have her last name here somewhere"

Aw shit. Could any fucking thing else go wrong?

I tried to push the chief out the door.

"Look, I really can't talk right now, my wife and I…"

"Ex wife"

"What!"

"You heard me"

"T, baby you can't mean that"

"I want a divorce!"

Hearing the D word, the investigator finally got the cue and decided to move the fuck on.

"I'll come back Mr. Allen, I'm sorry"

I slammed the door.

"Don't get mad at him because of your bullshit! So who the fuck is this bitch that you were almost in the fire with? As a matter of fact, fuck that! WHO IS THIS BITCH IN THIS PHOTO?"

Tamara hadn't figured out that it was Yolanda. She just knew that the man in the photo was me. All the photos seemed to be of me and Yolanda, so I saw no need to bring up Kitty.

"Who is this bitch?"

I had a choice. I could lie, or I could tell the truth. Not knowing what else Yolanda had in store for my ass, I told the truth.

"That's my ex, Yolanda"

"Why does she look so damned familiar?"

"You met her in Chicago"

Tamara turned her head at an angle and took a step backward. She was confused but only for a second. Her mind raced to rewind her time in Chicago and the few people that she met.

"The bitch at the shelter?"

"Yes" I said in a whisper.

"Motha fucka, speak up!"

"Yes"

"The bitch that gave me the attitude and practically called me uneducated?"

"Yes"

"So she was pretending not to know you"

"Yes"

"And you went along with the shit?"

"Yes"

Tamara turned to walk away. I walked up on her to tray and hug her. She turned around and slapped the shit out of my ass.

"Don't touch me! Don't you fucking touch me!"

"Tamara, I'm sorry"

"Fuck I'm sorry! Fuck You! Do you hear me? Fuck you! I'm sorry changes nothing. I'm sorry doesn't change the fact that our marriage is over"

"Tamara you can't mean that"

"Are you fucking crazy? Kevin there is no way and I mean no way, that I can stay with you behind this shit"

Her knees buckled and she broke down crying again.

"I gave my life to you. I gave my all to you. You betrayed me"

Tamara wept. I wept, and for a long while, we sat in our empty house that was once our home, and it was then that I realized what I had done. I hadn't just lost my wife, I hurt my friend, my partner, my everything. Tamara was the sugar in my coffee, the smile that warmed my heart, and the very air I breathed. She was right there in the room with me, but the hurt I brought to our relationship, kept us miles apart. When she finally spoke to me, she seemed all cried out.

"I want to know everything. From beginning, to end. Kevin, don't leave out one detail"

"Tamara, why punish yourself like that? I don't think telling you…"

"…I didn't ask you what you thought. If you ever loved me, if you ever want a chance at salvaging a friendship between us, you will tell me everything"

I debated how much to tell her. Something in the back of my mind told me to tell her everything. I started from the beginning and I went through every detail, including my ménage a trois. That, seemed to be the straw that broke the camel's back"

"I'm not woman enough for you? Are you so much of a man that you need two women?"

"Tamara, it's not like that"

"Oh I know it's not like that. You don't have enough dick to satisfy one woman, let alone two!"

My heart sunk when she said that. That was a serious left hook to my self esteem.

"Can I continue with my story?"

"Yeah, please do. Hold up, the girl you had the ménage with, who is she?"

"Kitty"

"The young girl from the shelter?"

"She's not that young, she's of age, she's twenty"

"Okay R. Kelly"

"She was of age!"

"I said okay! Don't raise your voice to me Kevin! I didn't put us here!"

She was right. I went on to tell my story. I told her how Yolanda had all but been stalking me and begging me for another chance with her. I told her how Yolanda had even stolen my story and was now about to get paid for it. She shook her head in disbelief.

"So what about this other bitch and this fire?"

"I went to visit a sister in the hood that I knew, and while there, the house caught on fire"

"So your dick wasn't in her mouth or anything?"

She was just fishing, but just her saying so scared the shit out of me. I hate women's intuition. That shit is scary as hell.

"No baby, we were just talking"

"Yeah, right"

"Tamara, we can get through this"

"No Kevin, I don't think we can"

She got up and took her things to her truck.

"Where are you going?"

"To my mother's home"

"What about us?"

"What about us?"

"I want us. I want our marriage"

"You should have thought about that before you strayed"

"Can I call you?"

"You have work to do. You have a book to finish, and you need to get right with yourself and God. Until then, I don't want to hear from you"

"Tamara, I need you"

"And I need time. Goodbye Kevin"

She pulled off and left me there in our empty ass house.

I laid on the floor and wept.

THE NEXT MORNING

It took me all morning to get all the viruses off my laptop. I stared at it for hours waiting for inspiration to hit me. After three and a half hours of sitting there, I was in the exact same position that I was in when I first started talking about going back to Chicago.

The pressure of having 29 days left to push out a book, was too much pressure for me. Already, the publisher was calling me bugging me about giving them back the advance. I decided that they could kiss my ass. I then did what most black people do when shit gets rough. I went back to Chicago.

SWEET HOME CHICAGO

The next day I was back on the block, drinking forties and talking shit with the neighborhood guys. Once again, Big Slim was missing in action. No one knew where he was or what was up with him. One rumor had him going back to get his GED. At age forty, I thought that was unlikely.

After I shot ball, I went to my parents home and they and my sisters were wondering what was going on with me. I went on to tell them that I was broke and starting over. I also told them everything that went down between me and Yolanda. Just then, my cell phone rang, it was Tamara.

"Yeah baby, what's up?"

"Don't baby me. It just dawned on me, this bitch of yours tried to kill your ass in that fire"

"Yeah, and?"

"And…she tried to kill me. She came all the way here to Somerton to hurt me"

"She said you weren't home. I think it was just to scare you"

"Well, she did a good job. I can't believe you brought this drama to our marriage!"

Click. She hung up. I let out a sigh and went to my mother's fridge to get something to eat.

"So what are you going to do baby?" My mother asked.

"I don't know, ma. I don't know"

My sister turned on the radio and as Maxwell was going off, on came the commercial for Yolanda's new book. That stunned us all. I cut the radio off, went upstairs to change my clothes, and headed to the 9705 Bar.

BACK TO THE 9705 BAR

As soon as I walked in the bar, there was Adrienne hooking brothers up with drinks and talking shit.

"Hey baby! How are you?"

"Hey Adrienne"

"Rum and Coke?"

"Yep"

"Do you want me to just give you the bottle?"

"Do I look that bad?"

"Like eight miles of bad road. I told you about fucking with these crazy bitches out here, but no one wants to listen to me. I tried telling you, Leon, Derrick, Sean, Michael, Jamie, none of ya'll ever listen to me"

"That's because we don't want advice, we all want to tap that ass" I said while laughing.

"Yeah, ya'll want it, but ain't none of ya'll ready. You know us Creole girls, we got some shit fo yo ass!"

I laughed.

"So, I got time and a little help tonight here at the bar, what happened with you and the crazy bitch with the big bootie"

I had a few drinks and I told Adrienne the whole story all over again. She nodded as I told her all of what happened and laughed when I told her how foolish I had been. She was sorry to hear that Tamara and I had separated.

"Adrienne, what should I do?"

"Call David"

"David?"

"Yeah. He knows how crazy this bitch is, maybe he can give you some insight into what makes her tick"

"I'll think about it"

"See, ya'll niggas don't ever listen to me"

"I need a good story"

"What about telling the story about Keith, Jeff and Mark?"

"That would be too painful"

"I don't know, I think it's time that their stories were told. They were all destined for greatness. I think their legacy will be immortalized in your book"

Keith, Jeff and Mark were friends of mine that died before their time. Jeff was a hell of a running back, Keith was a hell of an athlete and the eldest of our crew, and Mark was like a mentor to me.

"I could maybe do that. Do you have a title also?"

"Yep, call the book, Pour out a little liquor"

I smiled at Adrienne. I then leaned over and kissed her firmly on the lips.

"Uh-uh Kevin, I don't know where your lips have been!"

"I'm going home to write. If this shit works out, I will put these lips on those lips" I said pointing at her crotch.

"You better be trying to get your wife back and put your lips on hers and keep that dick of yours to yourself"

"Adrienne, my dick is retired. Unless, you want a quick shot at glory"

She laughed.

"Nigga Please. I keep telling yo ass, you ain't ready. I'll have you cursing in three different languages.

"I don't know any other languages"

"My point exactly"

I tipped Adrienne a hundred dollars.

"There will be more when I get my next book deal. Aw shit…no one will give me a book deal. Even if I write a great book, I am betting that I am blacklisted"

Adrienne smiled and then shook her head in disbelief.

"Damn! Why do my black brothas have to think so small"

"What do you mean?"

"I mean, I love ya'll but sometimes you lack vision. The publisher didn't make you Kevin Allen the author, the readers did. That's who made you. That's who is keeping you afloat now. An author is nothing without his readers. Fuck these publishers. Fuck these agents and managers and editors and shit. Kevin, start your own shit. It's time"

I was stunned. I don't know if it was fear of failing or fear of succeeding. I had never thought of it before.

"Adrienne, I'll do it"

"Good. Now go on and get outta here. Bring me a hundred grand out of your first million"

"Adrienne, I will"

"I know you will. Now go and write that book!"

THE GREATEST OF ALL TIME

I like LL's new joint, Headsprung. But when I want to get hyped, I play The Greatest of All Time by LL.

I hit the crib at about 3AM. I put on some headphones, booted up my laptop, which I named Leslie, and I started hammering on the keys. My mother, and my sister started proofing pages, editing and hitting me with a variety of ideas. Joy pulled out all my old photos, journals and keepsakes from when I was younger. I talked about my friendship with each of my guys and the adventures that we had coming up on the block. Because it was our childhood, the storyline practically bled from me. There was so much to tell and it seemed, not enough paper. I knew by page five that this joint was going to be hot. I smiled as my sister joy took the headphones out of the stereo and started blasting Mama said knock you out by LL. After the first rift started, we were all singing in the living room.

"Don't call it a comeback, I been here for years!"

I stopped typing only to rest or nap. When I got up from sleeping, I was refreshed and so were my ideas. My mom hooked up some fried chicken, greens, mac and cheese and sweet potato pie. I stayed in the house around the clock to get this joint done. This book would be the last book for my publisher. The sequel, will be with my publishing house. I called my accountant and told him to liquidate everything that I had and to cut me a check. I told him that I was starting my own shit.

"It's about time Kevin, I think that's great"

"Everybody keeps saying that's it like they were expecting me to open my own years ago"

"Most of us were"

"Why didn't anyone say anything?"

"It wasn't our place. Besides, how can we see the vision if you don't?"

A *Darrin Lowery* Novel

"Good point."

♦ **CHAPTER NINE** ♦
GLASS HOUSES & THROWING STONES

TAMARA

Kevin broke my heart. All I could think about was what I had done with Keith. Even though what I did was inexcusable, it still pales in comparison to what Kevin did to me. He not only slept with other women, he let his ex destroy our lifestyle and our marriage. I told my mother and sisters what happened and although they didn't like what Kevin did, they were still hoping that we would stay together. They kept telling me what good man Kevin was, but the truth of the matter is, good men don't do things like this.

My mother insists that all men fall at one time or another. She even went on to tell me that my father stepped out on her once (while they were dating). That was the last thing that I needed to hear. I asked her, "What is it with men and infidelity? Why can't one pussy be enough? I still don't understand where I went wrong with Kevin. I cook, clean, work and fuck him practically on demand. I know I got some good pussy, but I guess it's not good enough to keep my husband"

My sister Trina said, "Girl ain't no coochie that good where a nigga won't stray"

My sister Betty (the thickest of us all) said, "I think you been spoiling Kevin with the coochie. I say put the fear of god in his ass. Maybe cut one of his balls off. This way he gets to keep his dick, but with one of them balls missing, that nigga will know you are serious"

Me, Trina and my mother all said at the same time, "What?"

Betty said, ""I'm just sayin, keep that nigga in check, that's all"

Trina said, "Girl, you abuse a man's dick. He's gonna abuse your ass"

My mother said, "That's right. Besides, I'm like the comic Monique, I don't believe in letting dick go to waste"

My mother and my sisters and I have always been able to discuss sex freely. When we did, a lot of times, my dad would just leave the house. They were trying to cheer me up and advise me at the same time.

"So what should I do ya'll?"

My mother spoke first. "You can't stop a man from cheating. You can only love that man and set good boundaries. Now, he stepped out on you. He has to be punished for that. You have to re-set the guidelines on his ass. That means no matter how much you love him, how much your body is longing for him, you make his ass crawl across desert sands and broken glass before you take him back"

"You don't think I should leave him?"

All three of them said, "Hell Naw!"

Again my mother spoke. "If he hit you, disrespected you regularly, was trifling, or just not good for you, I would be the first one to say leave him. But to leave him over some pussy? Naw sistergirl, you can do better than that. You will fuck around and let your man go just for another woman to step in and take over where you left off after all the work that you put in with that man. He fucked up. He will answer for that. But leave a marriage? No, I can't see it"

"What about the other woman?"

"Now I think you Betty and Trina need to go down to Chicago and whup her ass. That's what I think"

"But she's pregnant"

"That's some other shit" Betty Chimed in. "Has anyone confirmed that shit?"

"That she's pregnant?"

"That it's his"

"No, not yet"

"Someone needs to call that bitch's bluff"

"But we can't kick her ass"

My mother said, "But we can have a conversation with her ass"

All four of us smiled.

Trina called our father downstairs.

"Daddy, we want to go on a road trip. Could you break out the suburban?"

My father asked, "Where are we going?"

All four of us said, "Chicago!"

KEVIN (Days Later)

I was working hard to get my new joint out. I typed my ass off, placed the new manuscript in a box and gave it to my sister to take to Kinko's to get it copied. I sent the master copy via email to my agent, and cover ideas to the printer. When Joy came back with the copies, I sent the original off to the Library of Congress myself. It took me a few weeks of typing to get the rough draft of the manuscript done, but I got it done.

The whole time that I was at my mothers working on the new story, a bunch of people stopped by the house either to ask me for money or to make a guest appearance somewhere. I told everyone that I had to respectfully decline. I was working again and now, the juices were flowing.

I was surprised as hell when my mother in law, wife and her sisters showed up at my mother's house. I was on the phone with my lawyer at the time when I saw Tamara. She was looking good as hell, but in just these few weeks, she looked like she had lost some weight. She undoubtedly lost the weight worrying about our marriage and thinking about the mistake that I made.

The women came in, and my father in law parked his big ass suburban in my parent's driveway. Naturally, my mother welcomed everyone in and told them to make themselves at home. I got off the phone and walked into the living room to greet my extended family.

"Hello everyone, what's going on?"

"Hey Kevin baby, how are you?" My mother in law, Gladys gave me a hug.

"Hey babe" I said to Tamara.

"Kevin" She said rather flatly.

"So, what's up?" I said to my mother-in-law.

Gladys said, "Well baby, I am not one to get into my kid's business, but I came down here and brought my girls so that we can try and make things right. Now, I heard about this crazy, fast tailed city girl that's caused you all this drama. It seems that the reason you keep running into so many problems because this woman keeps out-thinking you. Well, I came down here to see if we can't all put our heads together and fix her ass, and then fix your marriage"

I smiled at Gladys. My mother in law was the bomb. She was a pretty and older version of Tamara. She was jazzy, she had juicy lips, and she's got a fat ass for a sister in her late fifties. That's where Tamara and her sister's got their ass from. She was fine, and cool as hell. I could tell that she was pissed about my stepping out, but she was still on my side.

Betty said, "Is it true that she stole your story and is actually trying to go to print with it?"

"Yep, she is meeting with my publisher now to put together a tour"

"How can she do that if she does not know the material?"

"She knows the material. She also knows me like the back of her hand. I'm sure when she read the story for the first time, she committed it to memory. This girl is sharp and devious. She knows what steps I'm going to take before I take them"

"How does she know you so well?"

"We dated for years. She knows all my thoughts, dreams and tendencies"

Not thinking about what I said, I looked up and there was a look of hurt all over Tamara's face.

"Excuse me", she said as she went upstairs to the bathroom.

"Shit"

"It's okay. Keep talking" Gladys said.

"But Tamara…"

"She'll be okay. Finish telling me about this Yolanda"

"Gladys, I am so sorry about the shame I have brought to our marriage and the hurt I put her through"

"It's okay. We will talk about that later. Tell me how she operates"

I went on telling Gladys and her daughters about Yolanda and the many things that we went through as a couple. I also went on to tell them about the abuse that Yolanda suffered as well as how she is fixated on being with me and me alone. As I talked, my mother and sisters served my in laws, and my mother continued to throw down in the kitchen. When I finished telling Gladys everything that there was to know about Yolanda, she gave me some directions.

"Okay Kevin, I think I understand this girl now. I think I know how her head works also. Is there somewhere that you can go and just give all us ladies some privacy?"

"Privacy? Why?"

"Because powerful things happen when black women come together. It's rare that it happens, and when it does, we hate for men to be present"

"For real?"

"No baby, I'm just joking. I do think it's a good idea that you give us a moment though"

"Okay, where is George?"

George was Tamara's father.

"He is in the suburban"

"He's not coming in?"

"He's mad at you Kevin"

I let out a long sigh. I felt bad. George was a man that I had come to respect over the years. He was a man's man. George didn't have a college education and he worked odd jobs all his life until he got in good with a construction firm in the Carolinas. From there, he learned a little bit of every trade that there was. Bricklaying, electrician, plumbing, carpentry, there were few things that George didn't know how to do. He didn't have the strongest reading and writing skills, but if you showed him something just once, he could mimic it. This man saw to it that his family never went hungry, they never went without lights and they always had a roof overhead. When it was time for his girls to go to college, they got what they could from the state via scholarships and grants, but whatever expense was left, George paid it. If there was a bill to be paid or a goal to be set, George would simply put in the overtime to make it happen. His wife and those three girls are his everything. Those are the women in his life and he has always been their protector and their provider.

I hurt one of his babies.

There is no way that he will step foot in this house and break bread with me. When I thought about the fact that I had lost this man's respect, I felt like shit.

"I'll give you ladies your time. I think my first stop needs to be an apology to George"

Gladys said, "I think that's a good idea"

FATHER OF THE BRIDE

I went out onto the side of the house and walked up to the front of the suburban, George was in the truck watching a seven inch black and white TV set. I knocked on the window and initially he ignored me. I knocked again, letting him know that I was not leaving until I spoke with him.

"Yeah?"

"I brought you a plate George. I was also wondering if I could come in and talk to you for a minute"

He looked over at me almost as if to imply that he was busy.

"Please George"

He unlocked the door. I pulled myself into the large vehicle and handed him a plate of food and a huge tumbler of Kool-Aid.

"What do you want Kevin?"

"George, I want to say that I am sorry"

"Sorry for what?"

"Cheating on Tamara"

"You should be apologizing to her, not me"

"I have been apologizing to her. I have also apologized to your wife. Now, I'm apologizing to you"

"Why are you apologizing to me?" He said while still engrossed in his TV program.

"I'm apologizing for hurting your daughter, letting you down, and losing your respect as a man. I still love Tamara George. I love her with all my heart. I love your family as well. Man, I love you to George. You have been like a father to me since I moved to the Carolinas. Not too many men would take me in like you did. Not too many men would give their daughter away to a man that they didn't know for a long period of time. I remember when we first met. You laid the ground rules out to me and I listened attentively and gave you the respect that you deserve"

"You couldn't have been listening to well, because one of the first things that I told you when I met you was that you had better not hurt my baby girl. I said if you hurt her or ever put your hands on her, I would bust a cap in yo ass. Didn't I tell you that?"

"Yes sir, you did. All I can say is that I'm sorry. I was wrong and given a second chance, it will never happen again. I have a lot of things that I need to work on. I need to work on myself, I need to work on my marriage, and I need to work on re-gaining your respect"

We both sat there in silence for a while. After a minute or so, George turned the TV off.

"Kevin, you haven't lost my respect. You have lost some major points with me though"

"Yes sir"

"You hurt my baby"

"Yes sir"

"You brought shame to your house, and you may have lost your wife"

"I know…I know"

"As long as you know. Listen, I don't mean to lecture, but I just don't get you young people anymore. Kevin, I thought you were different. I was so happy when I met you and Tamara told me that she was no longer seeing that damn boy, Keith. She introduced you to me and I was blown away at the fact that you had on slacks and not some damned baggy jeans hanging off your ass. Then when you spoke? Shiiit, I thought you were a damned teacher or something. The point is, when I met you, I thought to myself, this is the type of man that I can release one of my girls to. This is the type of man that will love them like I love them; someone that will respect them like I respect them. That's what I saw in you. Now? I don't know what it is that I see anymore. In my day, you dated and you had sex. Back then, when you dated a woman, you dated a woman. You courted her, you spent quality time with her, you got to know her and you spent your hard earned money on her. Don't get me wrong, I have slept with many other women. Your generation ain't the only generation to do a whole lotta fuckin. In the seventies, we had ya'll's ass beat. Only now with AIDS and Herpes and all this other shit, free love is gone. Sex now comes at a very high price. Sometimes that price is a life. Anyway, when a man decided that he was going to take a wife? That meant that there was something so special about that woman, that there was no need to search further. Bottom line? Marriage means no more outside pussy. I can't understand why you young niggas can't keep your dick to yourselves. I have never stepped out on my wife. Don't think I ain't thought about it or had my opportunities. I love that woman in there. I would give my life for that woman in there. If that woman said we were going to take up in a shack in the woods, create a new language and re-populate the world, the only thing I would say is okay baby, grab a rifle, pen and paper to take notes and plenty of Viagra"

I smiled at his joke.

"Marriage means not giving up. Marriage means I love you in spite of. Marriage means that you love the other person, stand by the other person, and respect the other person. You got that son?"

"Yes sir. I swear…it will never happen again"

"It had better not. I already owe your ass a bullet"

We laughed a little bit together.

"If you ever see the need to cheat on your wife remember this. A real man will not cheat. A real man, will be man enough to leave and go be with that other woman"

"Yes Sir"

George started eating my mother's cooking and that softened his stance a bit more. I sat with him as he ate and we watched a re-run of Sanford and Son on that seven inch TV. By the end of the episode, we were drinking Kool-Aid and talking about sports.

"So what do you think the women are talking about in there?"

"Oh shit, that shit ain't about to be nothing nice"

"You think?"

"My wife, my daughters, your mother and your sisters? Shit. I feel sorry as hell for that girl you slept with. Her ass is about to catch it"

Just then, my father pulled up in his car. He went in, fixed himself a plate, and came outside.

"What's going on?"

I told him what was up and he told me and George to kick it with him downstairs in the basement. We took the rest of the food downstairs, grabbed a few beers, some sweet potato pie, and man...we got down while we were there and had a little meeting of our own—listening to JB's, Al Green, and Richard Pryor Records.

MEETING IN THE LADIES ROOM
TAMARA

I was hurt by Kevin's words about his ex. My mother sent his sister Joy upstairs to get his photo album and gave us each pictures of Yolanda. She was a pretty sister with better curves than my own. Looking at her and Kevin in the photos hurt the hell out of my heart. My mother told me to get over it though because she had a plan.

"Joy, what kind of work do you do dear?" Gladys asked.

"I'm into publishing, just like Kevin"

"Then, I am placing you in charge of going to New York, meeting with Kevin's publisher, and stopping this book that Ms. Thang stole from Kevin"

"How am I supposed to do that?"

"I don't know baby, but that is your job. Take your time and pray, something will come to you"

"Meka, what do you do dear?"

"I'm a student and a DJ"

"Well, I can't see too much need for a DJ right now. Let me get back to you"

"Mrs. Allen, this baby this girl is carrying. Do you really think its Kevin's? I mean this girl Yolanda, was she loose? Is she fixed on Kevin alone? Could there be another man in her life?"

Mrs. Allen said, "Another man, no. But I bet that little bitch is conniving enough to get pregnant by someone else and blame the shit on my Kevin"

Gladys said, "Betty, your job is to watch this Yolanda all day for the next couple of days"

"Got it mom"

"Trina, your job will be to act like Kevin's other woman"

"Kevin's other woman?"

"Yeah, she has tried to hurt anyone else taking Kevin's attention. I think it's time that we gave her something else to look at"

Mrs. Allen said, "Damn that's devious"

Gladys said, "If she wants to play this game, she needs to play it hard. I got a trick or two for her ass"

"What about me momma?" I asked.

"Oh baby, I have a huge role for you to play"

"What's that?"

"You and Kevin have to play like you are madly in love and giving your relationship a second chance"

I was stunned.

"But momma…"

"…Do you want your man back? Do you want your marriage back? Do you want this other woman out of your way?"

"I don't know what I want anymore"

There was a silence that overtook the room.

Mrs. Allen spoke first.

"Tamara, I know my son hurt you, but baby, he loves you. I'm not advocating for any man stepping out on a woman, not even my own son. He was raised better than that. You deserve better than that, but you all both deserve another shot at being happy"

Joy spoke next.

"My brother is an asshole for what he did to you. You need to know though, he is miserable without you. You are going to be a sister to me whether you all stay together or not. All I'm gonna say is think about it"

Meka said, "And listen to your heart"

Trina said, "He's a good man"

My mother took her hands in mine and then spoke, "Just play along for now. Let anything else that happens, take its natural course"

"Okay momma"

Gladys said, "All right then. We are all set and everyone knows what their role is, right?"

Everyone nodded.

"Then that's all I have for tonight. We need to get a hotel room"

Mrs. Allen said, "You all are more than welcome to stay here"

Gladys said, "Are you sure?"

Mrs. Allen said, "Yeah, we can make this headquarters, or home base"

Gladys said, "I like that"

Trina said, "Okay, let's fill Kevin in"

KEVIN

I was kicking it with my father and father in law as they both were trying to teach me how to step. I was just starting to learn how to step properly as my father in law called it, when I got called upstairs. Gladys filled me in on everything that they had been talking about, and told me what everyone's assignment was, including mine and Tamara's.

"Act like I am in love with my wife? Yeah I can do that" I said.

"Can you?" Tamara said.

"Watch me" I responded.

"So..." Gladys interrupted, "When will you see Yolanda again?"

"I hadn't planned on seeing her again"

"Has she tried to make contact with you?"

"She's tried. But I haven't been answering the phone. The only thing that I have been working on was my next book and meeting with my lawyer"

Tamara asked almost anxiously, "Why were you meeting with our attorney?"

I said, "I plan to start my own publishing company. I'm going to need his input"

"Oh"

Gladys asked, "So, she hasn't asked you to meet her so she can beg for you back?"

"Naw, she knows that I am still pissed about her stealing my book. Let her tell it, she has beaten me so I just need to give in to her"

"It's that type of conceit that is going to do her in"

"I hope so. She did put an invitation in the mail though, for the Welfare-to-Work program and the ball / fundraiser to kick off the opening"

"That might just be the opening that we need" Gladys said. "Meka, I just might need your DJ skills after all"

Trina and Betty began whispering among themselves. A few minutes passed and they kept nudging each other to ask their mother something. Finally, Trina said, "Betty and I want to see more of Chicago before we put in all this work. What is there to do on a Thursday night here?"

I said, "You two want to go out?"

They both nodded yes.

"Baby, will you kick it with us too? Please?"

Tamara nodded.

"A'ight. We can kick it. Let's go out to Secrets"

♦ CHAPTER TEN ♦
A NIGHT ON THE TOWN

KEVIN

My wife and her two sisters all put on Phat Farm sweatsuits that they got from my sister Joy. I was looking like I was the motha fuckin man, as they each came downstairs with their suits on. Trina was in baby blue, Betty was in Royal Blue and Tamara was in Pink. All three had their belly's out, all three had just hella ass, and each one had on flawless makeup. Tamara's hair was short and cropped nice. It was wavy and looking curly and almost wet. Her sisters both had long free-flowing hair. The three of them looked like a set of black Charlie's Angels.

"Damn! Oh my God, you all are stunning! God bless ya'll daddy, damn!"

"I had a little help in that too!" Gladys said.

Looking back at my mother in law's ass, I was like, "Yes ma'am. Yes you did!"

"A'ight, don't make me kick yo ass!" George chimed in.

I laughed and grabbed the keys to the minivan out back. I took Tamara's arm and led she and her sisters to the car.

SECRETS

I jumped onto the Bishop Ford Freeway and sped out south to Dolton Illinois. Secrets is this hot spot in the south burbs where some of the finest sisters in the city hang out. Thursday nights, Secrets is the place to be. I took the Bishop Ford to Sibley West, got off the expressway and took Sibley to Chicago Road. I banked a right heading north again, and bumped music in the van all the way there. Power 92 was jamming some old house music and I was bumping my head and rocking the whole way as I listened to the music from my youth.

Within minutes, we were pulling up in front of Secrets Nightclub. I know I must have looked corny as hell to a lot of brothers as I pulled up in that white minivan, but when brothas saw Tamara, Trina and Betty in those Baby Phat sweatsuits, I was an even bigger celebrity!

"Damn man, where did you get those fine ass women from?" One guy said.

"Look at the asses on those sisters" Another one said.

"Damn baby, can I get a minute to talk to you?"

"Can I buy you a drink?"

"Fuck that, will you marry me?"

Brothers went on and on with all types of crazy comments. I told my wife and sisters not to mind them and to move in the club. A bouncer walked up to me to frisk me and ask me for cash.

"It's a $20.00 cover tonight bruh. That's $80.00 for you and the girls"

"Here you go"

I gave the brotha the cash and let him pat me down and let the girls get wanded. Tamara had a look of alarm on her face. They don't do this in Somerton.

"It's cool baby. Young niggas in the Chi don't know how to act sometimes, so everyone has to get checked"

We all got checked for weapons and were then allowed to go in the club.

The bass from the speakers was booming. The music was so loud that you could hardly hear one another speak. My wife and her sisters walked in the club looking good as hell. They were stunned however when they saw how fine the other women in the club were.

The sisters that roll up in Secrets on a Thursday night are some of the finest women that God put on this planet. Sisters are generally in there with low riding jeans, their asses are out, their breasts are sitting up, and its one hell of a fashion show. Sisters be in the club with flawless makeup, long hair, short hair, no hair or dreads, and their shit is tight. Most of the women that come in the club are young, fit and any one of them could model in a magazine or on TV. Secrets was the best kept secret in the south burbs. If you come to Secrets nightclub in Dolton Illinois, your shit had better be on point.

The bouncers at Secrets didn't take any shit. When you were in that club, you brought you're "A Game" and zero drama. For the brothas that like to act up, Secrets has some big no-neck MF's that will bounce your ass right out of that club. They aren't the biggest problem though. The smaller security guards? Those brothas will whup the dogshit out of anyone getting out of order. Them short MF's will beat that ass and explain to you why they are beating your ass.

The music in the club was jumpin. Women were in there looking good as hell. I bought my wife and sisters a round of drinks and was stopped by a crowd of women that wanted me to sign an autograph. I began signing napkins, papers and this one sister wanted me to sign her breast. I started to sign it, then I looked up at Tamara and gave a half smile. I told the woman that I would sign my autograph, but no body parts.

"Why not?" She asked.

"One, my wife is here with me tonight, two, I need to respect my wife"

"Is she that insecure?" The woman said loudly.

"You know what? You have a nice evening sweetheart"

I walked off and grabbed Tamara by the hand to dance.

"Did that bitch want you to sign her breast?"

"Something like that"

"And I bet if I wasn't here, you would have, wouldn't you?"

"The old Kevin, might have"

"Oh, but you are the new Kevin, huh?"

"Yes I am. And the new Kevin would never do such a thing"

I grabbed my wife and pulled her close to me. I kissed her on the lips.

"I miss you" I said.

"I miss you too, but I am still mad you"

"I know baby, I know"

"So why did you bring us here?"

"Because it's safe. Because it's fun. I like it out here"

The Rhythmic Sounds in the club had everyone hyped. Multicolored lights were spinning above. A smoke machine started slowly spitting out it's mist and the beats from the tracks just kept getting hotter and hotter. I looked over at Betty and Trina and Brothas had them surrounded. They quickly caught on to many of the dances and started "juking" to the music. Brothas were watching those asses move back and forth and were hypnotized by the dance movements (and those big juicy asses). Men started begging and making promises to Trina and Betty and started telling them all the things that they would do for them. I could tell that Betty and Trina liked the attention. They started dancing more seductively and even I was a little moved by the way they were putting it down.

"Damn baby, you and your sisters missed your calling"

"Is that right?"

"Yeah, ya'll should have been exotic dancers. Are you sure George didn't meet Gladys in a strip club?"

Tamara playfully hit me in the chest.

"Those are my parents!"

"I'm just sayin. I mean your moms got this big ole ass, and your sisters are out there straight up throwin that ass around like mad mules or some shit"

"Kevin I will kick yo ass if I catch you lookin at my sisters that way. You aren't supposed to look at them like that" She said laughingly.

"Shiiit, the only man that wouldn't look at you and your sisters like that is a blind man"

We laughed together. It had been awhile since we shared smiles. It felt good.

"Damn, I miss you", I said.

Just then, the DJ played a joint that threw both Trina and Betty off. The DJ played this hot beat that had a house vocal over it that chimed, I want to fuck you in the ass. That was the name of the song and that was the chorus of the song. Sisters heard that beat and those lyrics and a lot of then got up in place, no matter where they were, and a lot of them began to dance sexually and move their asses around and around and gyrating like they were having sex. Most of the women in the club knew all the words to the song, and they were dancing and singing to the joint at the same time. One sister with a fat ass, rocked side to side, but made her big juicy ass roll around and around as she danced. Her ass was so big, this MF needed it's own time zone.

Betty and Trina, being from the south, stopped dancing the second that they realized what the record was saying. Hell, in the Carolinas, sodomy is illegal (for real).

Trina and Betty walked over to me and Tamara.

Betty said, "What kind of damned song is that?"

Trina said, "You Chicagoans are nasty as hell"

Tamara said, "Ain't they? Look at how these women are up in here dancing"

Trina said, "Kevin, you like this?"

I said, "Shit yeah. I love this shit. This is home. This is how nightlife in the Chi is supposed to be"

The three of them looked at me like they were crazy.

"A'ight. I know, ya'll ain't feeling me. It's cool. Let's just dance"

All night I danced with my sisters and my wife. We found a little corner of the club where we drank, ate, and partied until the early hours of the morning. I danced until I got tired. I then just sat in the corner, in my wife's arms as she rubbed my head. My sisters found guys to dance with nearby and they danced until they got tired.

"So what is it about the black women here that are so amazing?" Tamara asked.

"Chicago women? I guess if anything, it's the style that they have. A lot of the women here are confident, beautiful and they know how to have a good time and relax"

"Is that where I failed you? Am I too uptight?"

"What?"

"Kevin, I...I'm just trying to understand. How did we get here?"

"Baby you could never fail me. I failed you. I fucked up, that's all. Given the chance, it will never happen again"

Tamara took my chin in her hand. She looked in my eyes for sincerity. When she saw that it was there, she gave me a gentle peck on the lips. She them laid back in my arms.

"So what is it with the nasty dancing?" She asked.

"I don't see it as nasty dancing, I just see women dancing. They are expressing themselves"

"They are expressing themselves sexually"

"Okay, true. But we are all sexual beings. Plus, I think that you are not seeing the club with your natural eyes"

"Natural eyes? Kevin, what the hell are you talking about?"

"Get up for a minute"

I sat on the couch in the club and I had my wife sit back and lean in my arms. I then kissed her on her neck a little and then I moved my head where I was right in her ear so she could hear me. I hugged her tight as I talked.

"Okay, look at all the women around the club. Watch their movements. Whether they are sexual, rhythmic, or full of energy. Watch those women as they dance, and then lose yourself in the beat"

Tamara began to watch the women in the club, I mean really watch them. She then started dancing in place a little herself, almost mimicking the movements that she saw.

"Okay, now look at each woman dancing. Are they all dancing the same?"

"Well, no. Some of the dances are similar, but no two are the same"

"So the music could have different meanings for each one of them"

"I guess"

"Don't guess. Feel the music, and then feel the women"

Tamara watched the various women in the club and tried to make sense of the dancing.

"I don't know what you want from me Kevin. I mean, the whole thing looks like a mating ritual"

"It could be that. What else could it be?"

"It could be a party. Hell, this is a party"

"You're the teacher, what's another word for party?"

"Celebration"

"Okay, good. What could everyone here be celebrating?"

"I don't know, being black?"

I smiled. Tamara could see that I was on to something.

I told her, "They could be celebrating being black, being free, being off work, getting a raise, or simply escaping everyday stress and adversity. Music means something to everyone. When women dance, at least this is my opinion; when they dance, they are releasing energy. They are expressing themselves. The movements to me, aren't sexual, they are dynamic. I want you to do one more thing as you watch these women. Look past the makeup, past the clothes and past the aesthetics. Then, listen to the music, but ignore the words, and just listen to the beats.

Tamara looked around the room. She looked past the women and concentrated on the movements. She then tuned out the lyrics and listened to the beat.

"Now, picture all the women in here, and picture that they are each, African. Then tell me what you see"

Tamara looked and watched, and began to lose herself in the music.

"What do you see?"

"Black people"

"Doing what?"

"Celebrating being black, and fellowshipping with one another"

"There ya go"

Tamara was seeing things differently in the club. She leaned back and kissed me.

"Okay Kevin, I'm feeling you. But you can't tell me that a lot if these women aren't dancing to seduce and entice these men"

"They probably are babe, but music is also seductive. What's wrong with women dancing and enticing men?"

"They might entice someone else's man…my man"

I let out a sigh. She was right. I kissed her on the forehead and held her tight until Trina and Betty were ready to go. They each collected about twenty phone numbers. We then called it a night about 4:00 A. M. We went back to my mother's place and went to sleep.

♦ CHAPTER ELEVEN ♦
BACK TO BUSINESS

KEVIN

I awoke the next morning to my mother shaking the shit out of me. At first I thought something was wrong.

"Kevin? Kevin, get up!"

"Wha…What is it ma?"

"Someone keeps calling my damned phone every five minutes and then hanging up when either me or your sisters answer the phone. The caller ID says UNAVAILABLE. I bet it's that little fast tail girl. The next time that the phone rings I want you to answer it"

"Okay, when the phone rings, I'll get it"

I felt like I was in high school all over again. Shit, I might as well have been in high school with all the games that Yolanda had been playing. Sure enough, the phone rang about five minutes later. I answered the phone in a groggy ass voice. Gladys had come upstairs to coach me on what to say. When the phone rang I knew the role that I was supposed to play.

"Hello" I said.

"Get up sleepy head"

"Yolanda, what the fuck do you want?"

"I'd like to see you"

"No. Hell No, I'm hanging up now"

"Don't hang up. Where have you been?"

"Not that it's your business, but I have been here"

"I know that you are at your mom's. What I mean is you haven't really left the house much"

"I was finishing my last book. I was also taking care of business"

"So are you back home because your wife kicked you out?"

"Actually, Yolanda, My wife and I have been to counseling and we are working things out. I may not have much money, but I have her and for me, that's enough"

"Have you thought more about giving our relationship another chance?"

"Actually I have"

"And?"

"Fuck...You"

I hung up the phone. It continued to ring for a while, and then it stopped completely.

Gladys said, "Good Job. Let's see what the day brings"

BETTY, TAMARA'S SISTER.

I waited outside of this woman's apartment complex. I had my cell phone with me so that I could call my mother when this woman made a move. I followed her to the local donut shop in the morning where she had a bagel and then I followed her to work at some shelter. I parked outside where I noticed a young light skinned woman that met Ms. Yolanda at her car. The two women had a long discussion and both of their voices became louder and louder. The next thing that I knew, Yolanda slapped the younger woman. She then grabbed the young lady by her arm and pushed her into her car. I followed the two women as they pulled off. I called my mother and told her what was happening.

"Stay with them Betty" My mother said.

I followed the two women to a restaurant where the two of them argued the entire time. They argued so much that they didn't hardly eat. When the two of them left, the light skinned woman looked hurt. I followed Yolanda's car to a train station where the younger woman got out. She said something else to Yolanda who got out of the car like she was ready to fight the young light skinned woman. Afterward, the young woman went into the train station. Yolanda followed. I waited there almost two hours. Yolanda was on her cell phone yelling when she finally appeared again and was getting behind the wheel of her car. I followed her again back to the shelter.

This time she was met by the Reverend outside of the building. The two of them had words and the Reverend escorted Yolanda into the building. If I didn't know any better, I swear I thought I saw the reverend checking out Yolanda's ass. I parked the car outside the shelter and waited. I called my mother and asked her what should I do next.

Gladys said, "Just watch her and let's see what develops"

I thought that I might be in the car for the next eight hours or so, but as it turned out, Yolanda only stayed in the shelter another two hours. She then got back in her car and took off again. I followed her to the mall where she bought some lingerie, and the grocery store where she picked up a number of items including wine. I thought her next stop might be home, but her next stop was right back at the shelter. She stayed in the shelter for another three hours or so and I waited patiently outside as I ate food that I packed earlier.

Yolanda left the shelter again around 4:30. Her next stop was parked about 100 yards from Kevin's mother's house. She picked up her cell phone and looked as if she made a number of phone calls and could not get who she was trying to get on the other end. I called my mother and told her what was up. That was when she put the next phase of her plan into play.

KEVIN

My mother in law is slick as hell. She told me today to take Tamara out for a night on the town. I thought this was cool, this plan of hers. She was trying desperately to piss Yolanda off, but at the same time, she was trying to help me mend my marriage. When she suggested that I take Tamara out, I smiled an award winning smile.

I took Tamara out to Houstons to eat. Afterward I took her on a carriage ride down Michigan Avenue in downtown Chicago. From there we went and saw the new movie with Denzel Washington, and afterward we had ice cream. I took her to a south side park where I pushed her in a swing and we talked as we did when we first got together.

"Do you remember the first time we met?"

"Of course I do, with your arrogant ass" She said while smiling.

"Arrogant? Me?"

"Yeah, Nigga, you remember how brash you were. You just knew that you had me"

"Actually, I thought you were digging John"

"He was tearing it up on that saxophone. But naw, I knew you were watching me"

"No fucking way"

"Oh yeah my brother, way"

"Are you serious?"

"Yeah, I'm serious. I bet you think that you seduced me also on our first date with all your smooth talk and shit"

"Now Tamara, don't front. I know that you were impressed with how I came at you"

"Men, you all are so predictable"

"So you're saying that our meeting was all your doing?"

"Maybe not all, but I knew that you were going to approach me from the first moment we saw one another"

"But you played so hard to get in the beginning"

"That's how the game is played — playa"

She smiled as she swung in the swing. My head was all fucked up.

"I bet you think the first time that we slept together was your idea too, and that you seduced me into bed that first night"

"Okay now baby, I know your ass is going too far with that one. I remember that night well. I took you to see some corny ass movie at the show that had women crying in it, I also took you to dinner at the most expensive place in town, I brought you a dozen yellow roses that night, and I also took you dancing. I was looking good as hell and I know that I was so smooth that I seduced you. Come on baby, you have to admit, that first night was all me"

Tamara started laughing and my ego was bruised like a MF. I was smiling, but I was confused as hell.

"Do you remember what outfit I had on that night?"

"Oh hell yeah! It was a canary yellow laced joint. The panties were really pretty, the bra was matching, and the garter, stockings and heels were the bomb!"

"Now Kevin, think really hard. Is that the type of shit a woman wears on just any night?"

"Isn't it?"

"No Kevin. I knew the day and the exact time that I was going to give you some. I had planned on possibly giving you some that day anyway. When you showed up with the flowers and looking good as hell in your suit, I knew before we left my house that I was going to give you some. We women know how the day is going before we get out the door. The thing is, whether or not you men are going to say or do something to fuck it all up. There are many days that men do stupid shit, say stupid shit, end up fighting or just look at another woman too long and we women decide, damn, I was going to give him some, but he fucked up"

"For real?"

"For real"

"Ain't that a bitch?"

We talked and talked there in the park and Tamara educated my ass on women. We talked about the first time that we made love. The first time we made love in our home, and the many trips that we have taken together.

"When all this shit is over with, I'm going to take you to the Cayman Islands"

"Damn, we haven't been there in a while"

"I'm hoping that we can get a new start there"

"Well, I don't know how long it's going to take for me to forgive you, but I think a trip to the Islands is a damn good start"

"Baby?"

"Yeah Kevin?"

"I'm sorry"

"Yeah, you said that"

"And I am going to keep on saying it"

We kissed for an eternity there in the park.

"Do we have to go back to your mother's house?"

"Where would you like to go?"

"I'd like to maybe go and get a room somewhere"

"Yeah?"

"Yeah"

Tamara and I got a room at the Essence Suites. We got a room with a Jacuzzi, King size bed and all the extras. Yolanda followed us, Betty followed Yolanda, and We all let the night unfold the way that it was meant to.

BETTY

As Tamara and Kevin headed into the Essence Suites, I could see Yolanda going apeshit in her car. I called my mother and told her what was going on play by play. My mother told me to hang up with her and call the police and let them know that there was a woman outside the Essence Suites damaging a man's vehicle and to give the police the plates.

"But momma, she hasn't done anything like that"

"Wait on it. Now Betty, you do like I told you"

I called the police told them what I saw, and sure enough, Yolanda got out and started fucking up Kevin's ride. I called my mother telling her everything that went on.

"Mama, I'mma kick this bitch's ass"

"You will do no such thing"

"But momma…"

"No I said. Let the police do their job"

The police arrived on the seen when Yolanda produced a bat out of her trunk. They apprehended her and then knocked on Kevin and Tamara's door. Kevin showed the police a copy of the order of protection that he had against Yolanda. He then retreated back inside and turned up the music in his room as he and my sister got their groove on.

"Damn, I hope if I ever get a man and get into trouble with my man, my sisters look out for me like I am looking out for Tamara. Shit, I hope I can get a man as nice looking and with as much money as Kevin has"

The police took Yolanda off to jail after Kevin signed a complaint.

I called my mother back again when the police took Yolanda away.

"Good, now we are creating a paper trail"

JOY

I loved New York. I have been here on many occasions. If there is one place in the world I would like to live, it's here. I am thinking of becoming a literary agent, and I hear that this is the place to do it. The only problem that I have with New York is that it's so damned expensive. Anyway, I came here to meet with my brother's publisher, and meet with the CEO of the company, Mr. Harrison.

"Ms. Allen, I admire you for coming all this way to advocate for your brother, but the truth of the matter is, Kevin Doesn't own the copyright"

"Aren't you worried that if what Kevin is saying is true, and this is not Yolanda's book, that she will not be able to produce a second book for you?"

"If that happens, we will sue her for breach of contract"

"But then you will re-coup nothing"

Mr. Harrison thought about my words.

"Do you have any proof that this book is really Kevin's?"

"Yes actually, I do. Did you all read Kevin's new book yet?"

"I haven't but one of my people have"

"And?"

"Well, to be honest with you, my people say that it's brilliant. They say it will be an Essence Bestseller"

"Well ask your staff member to look at the book that Yolanda allegedly wrote, compared to the story Kevin just gave you. Yolanda's alleged book is called The Homecoming. That book is about our old neighborhood. I know all of those stories like the back of my hand and all the characters because those characters are inspired by the people that my brother used to hang around when I was little. Kevin's new book, Pour Out a Little Liquor, is the perfect sequel to the book that Yolanda allegedly wrote. Now let's say that Yolanda did write the book. It's impossible for Kevin to write such a perfect sequel that flows so well. Ask the editors here to review both stories and to look at the language and continuity of the stories. Then tell me whose story this really is"

Mr. Harrison thought about my words and sunk in his chair. It was obvious that he didn't care very much for my brother. I think he let his dislike for Kevin, cloud his judgment.

"What about this baby mess? What about these allegations of abuse against your brother?"

"Well, for starters, they are untrue. And also, it's not your business. Your business, is these books"

"What about the copyright? I can't just ignore that"

"What if I brought you an earlier copyright?"

"Do you have one?"

"You know what? I do"

A POOR MAN'S COPYRIGHT

I left the publishers in New York and told him that I would be back. I took one of the copies of Kevin's book, The Homecoming, and I went to the nearest post office. I put the Manuscript into a large envelope and addressed the envelope from Kevin to Kevin. I then went to the post office and found the ugliest brother that I could find and told him that I needed a favor.

Kevin owes me big time. I had this big Kunta Kinte looking brother backdate the postmark on the envelope. I then had the envelope sealed with stamps of a date that was four months before Yolanda sent her application to the copyright office. I then returned to the publisher's office with the envelope in hand.

"There it is"

"What's that?" Mr. Harrison said.

"It's a copy of the original manuscript. Only, it can't be opened here. It has to be opened in court in the event that Yolanda tries to challenge it"

"And you think this is sufficient?"

"It will hold up in court"

Mr. Harrison smiled.

"This envelope looks awfully knew to me"

"What can I say? I take really good care of shit"

Mr. Harrison could see through my bullshit, but that didn't matter. I was creative enough to get this shit done under pressure and in a matter of an hour.

"You know what Ms. Allen, I like your initiative. I also asked my editors was there any way that two different authors could have written these two books and they said that whomever wrote one, wrote both. I'm convinced that these are your brother's books. You must really love him"

"I do, he has been my mentor all my life"

"And did he teach you how to take initiative like you did with this copyright?"

"Well, I think that is something that I learned to pick up since I have been in the publishing industry"

"That's right. You work for a small publisher in Chicago, right?"

"That's right"

"I tell you what, I'll put the book back in the name that it belongs in. I will also get my lawyers here to side with your brother against Ms. Carter, on one condition"

"What's that?"

"You take a job here in New York"

"For how much?"

"Well, let's negotiate"

I really celebrated with the brotha from the post office. I saved my brothers book, got a job in a city that I love, and negotiated a low six figure salary. I called my mother and screamed in the phone with Joy. I was getting out from under Kevin's shadow and coming into my own. I was due to be in my office in New York in thirty days.

♦ CHAPTER TWELVE ♦
PHASE TWO

KEVIN

My wife and I made love over and over again through the night. She wept and I wept as we tried to get back what was once a powerful bond between the two of us. The next day, we went back to my mother's house and had breakfast. As we walked into the house and everyone there was silent about our being out all night, but happy that we were trying to get back on the road to being together again. The elephant was in the room and no one said anything about the fact that we spent the night out last night. Tamara was a little embarrassed, but I was like for what? We're still married.

Everyone was at the table having breakfast. I leaned in and kissed my mother on the cheek good morning, and I also kissed Gladys on the cheek.

"What was that for?" Gladys asked.

"Being you. Thanks Mom"

I pulled a chair out for my wife and sat beside her.

"So what's next?" I asked.

"What's next is you meet your sister in law Trina, and you take her out on a date"

"What?"

"I want you to take Trina out to a movie, and make sure that you stop at a jewelry store"

"And then what?"

"I'll tell you when you get there"

Everyone else had a puzzled look on their face, except George, my father in law.

I said to Gladys, "I hope I never get on your bad side"

"I hope not either. My bad side is the last place that you ever want to be"

"Amen" George said.

We all laughed.

I waited until the house phone rang and the caller started hanging up again before I left the house to go on my date with Trina. This whole thing seemed to be getting more and more weird as it progressed.

THE DATE WITH TRINA

After Betty had a really long nap, I left the house by myself and headed to Evergreen Plaza, where I met my sister in law. Trina looked like a thick Alicia Keyes.

She had long black hair, which was down and she had on some skin tight Levi Jeans. Trina was my boy John's wife. She was who John was playing the sax like a madman for when I first met Tamara. With as nice as her ass was looking in these Levi Jeans, I can see why my boy John never came back to Chicago. The ass on my wife's older sister is off the chain! I hugged Trina as we met in the plaza, and we walked over to The Original Cookie Factory, to have hot chocolate chip cookies.

"So what does John think about you doing all this?"

"He says that you and he have been friends forever. He talks all the time about how you all came up on 92nd and Sangamon and how you all are practically brothers. He says that he will do anything for you"

"I will have to remember to call him and thank him for loaning me his wife. Does he know that you are dressed like this? No disrespect sis, but you are looking good as hell!"

"Well, I figured I would try to look my best to make this other hoe jealous"

We laughed together and ate our cookies. A few minutes later, Betty called us to let us know that Yolanda had been following me from the moment that I left the house. Yolanda was watching Trina and I from one of the upper levels of the mall.

"Show time" I said.

"Okay" Trina said.

I led Trina by the hand and we walked through the plaza and started shopping for clothes. I told Trina to buy anything that caught her eye. That was a mistake. She and I did some power shopping from the moment I let that shit walk out of my mouth. I thought my wife was a power shopper. She ain't got shit on her sister.

Trina tried on Baby Phat, FUBU, Sean John, DKNY and a host of other designer clothing. She pulled some of the nicest stuff off the rack, and she tried on a number of sexy outfits. Some of the outfits and jeans that she put on, couldn't even accommodate her ass. That's how big and round it was. My mouth practically watered as she tried on a bunch of different outfits. Just then, almost as if on cue, my cell phone rang.

"What are ya'll doin?" It was Tamara.

"Oh hey babe, we are just shopping"

"Shopping where?"

"Right now we are in Fresh Wear, why?"

"I just thought of something. I know that you are an ass man, and I know that my older sister has the biggest bootie. Don't get hypnotized by that motha fucka"

I laughed.

"You know what? As a matter of fact, I was just checking your sister's rack out. My boy John is a lucky man"

"Kevin, don't make me kick yo ass"

"I'm straight babe. Is that the only reason that you called?"

"No, my mother wants to talk to you"

"Put her on"

"Kevin?"

"Yeah Gladys, what's up?"

"Take Trina to look at jewelry, let her try a few rings on, and then take her to a motel and stay there at least an hour"

I damn near choked at the prospect of my taking Trina to a motel. She was definitely the prettiest of the three sisters and again, she had the biggest ass. I let out a deep breath as I thought about this role play. I had to keep telling myself that this was all an act.

"Okay Gladys. Got it"

I hung up the phone.

"What did my mother say?" Trina asked while trying on a pair of J-Lo jeans. She was looking so good that other brothers stopped doing what they were doing to watch her model the jeans for me"

"She says we are to look at Jewelry, you are to try on a ring or two, and we are to hang out in a motel for an hour or two"

"Let's go"

We headed to the nearest jewelry store walking hand in hand.

"Put your hand on my ass"

"I'm sorry…what?"

"Do it. That will make this girl Yolanda jealous"

Without hesitation, I palmed my sister in law's ass as I leaned at the counter and she tried on jewelry. That motha fucka felt so good. I enjoyed that shit so much, I was sweating. Now Trina's cell phone was ringing as she was trying on rings.

"Hello?"

"I'm telling!"

"Betty, girl be cool. What is Ms. Yolanda doing?"

"Hold on, let me see. Aw man, she is going ape shit. She is crying and she looks angrier than a trapped bear"

"Good"

Trina hung up the phone.

"I can't do the ass thing, Trina, I feel guilty"

"You should, but this is all an act remember? It's okay. I am glad that you are nervous about it though, that means my sister has a good man"

I was thinking to myself, Good man, right. Damn I felt guilty.

I took Trina by the hand, she kissed me on the cheek, and we took her bags of clothes back to the car. From there, we went to a small motel right off of Halsted. I parked the car, got a room, and Trina and I turned on the radio and started acting goofy. The idea was to lead Yolanda to think that we were in there having sex. Trina and I were in there doing old dances like the running man, the Robin Hood, the Robot, the Bump and any other old dance that we could think of. I told her how her man once sported a fro, how he once wore wrangler jeans, and how crazy he used to act back in the day. She told me some embarrassing stories that John had told her about me. She told me that John told her that I had the nappiest hair in grade school, I used to dress in the poorest clothes, and how I used to listen to a lot of white music back in the day. I felt embarrassed as hell to admit that Boy George, Wham, Tears for Fears, Sting and Genesis were some of my favorite groups. I mean, I loved my house music, but I had a unique love for all music.

Trina laughed her ass off as we talked about old times. I told her what it was like to grow up with John

Gandy and what a great musician he was. I told her how ever since we were little, he knew he wanted to grow up and be in the Marine Corps. I also told her that her husband was one hell of a cook.

"Cook? John can't cook. That's why he is in cooking school"

"Shiit. Your man can cook his ass off. He just doesn't"

"Kevin you are lying"

"Ask him"

"I will, the second I get back home"

We continued to talk. Trina's phone rang again.

"Hello?"

"Get out of the room!" Betty said.

"Why?"

"I followed her to the nearest liquor store. This bitch bought a bottle of brandy a pack of cigarettes and some matches. We are headed back your way!"

Trina said, "We have to get out of here!"

Once again, Betty called 911 and reported the crime before it actually happened. By the time that Yolanda got back to the Hotel, Trina and I were in the office of the Motel Manager. We all sat in the window and watched the drama unfold.

Yolanda got out of her car, stuffed napkins in the bottle, lit the bottle and threw it hard into the window of the Hotel room.

"Kevin! Kevin I will see you dead for doing this to me! This time, you will die!"

There was only one door to the Motel room. The room went up in flames quick as hell. I had flashbacks of the fire that I was almost caught up in at La-La's house. Trina and I did not leave the manager's office. The manager however, ran out to confront Yolanda. I don't know what got into Betty, but as Yolanda sat there yelling at the door waiting for me to make some attempt to come out of the fire, Betty caught Yolanda on the side of her head and started whipping Yolanda's ass.

"You crazy bitch! What the fuck is wrong with you?"

Betty tackled Yolanda. She then slapped Yolanda and started punching her like crazy in her face. Yolanda was surprised as hell at the onslaught. Yolanda curled up into a ball as Betty whipped her ass for old and new. By then, the police pulled up and pulled Betty off of Yolanda.

One officer said, "What the hell is going on here?"

The manager explained that he eye-witnessed Yolanda throwing a Molotov Cocktail into the window of the hotel room.

Yolanda was arrested.

"And her, what's her story?" The officer asked.

"I don't know" The manager responded.

"Ma'am, how do you fit into all this?" The officer asked Betty.

Thinking quick on her feet, Betty said, "I saw this woman throw that Molotov Cocktail into the window. I didn't know if there were people in there or not. I don't know what came over me officer, I just lost it. I tried to hold her for you all, but she swung on me and I just started whipping her ass"

"Good Samaritan, huh"

"Yeah"

"Well, what you did borderlines on vigilantism. We appreciate your helping, but next time, just step aside. Was there anyone in the room?"

"I don't know"

The officer turned to the manager, "Was there anyone in the room?"

"No, the couple was in my office getting snacks and then they asked me what was that woman doing to their room"

Another officer came in to question me and Trina. Once again, I pulled out a copy of my restraining order. Yolanda was arrested.

"Will she stay in jail this time?" I asked.

"She will unless someone pays her bail, which I would imagine would be too high for anyone to pay"

I signed a complaint against Yolanda and now I had two incidents in two days on her. My paper trail just got bigger. We called Gladys and told her everything that happened. Yolanda went to jail. Trina and I went home and that night we all celebrated Yolanda's small defeat, Joy's new job, and my getting my book back in my name. When I got back to my mother's house, I asked my mother in law the magical question.

"So, what's next?"

YOLANDA

I can't believe that Kevin would have the nerve to cheat on his wife. I can't believe that he can be with other women, but can't be with me. Doesn't he understand that I love him? Doesn't he get it? How can he not know how much I love him? I can't live without him. I need him. He will see it my way. He will see it my way or I will have to kill him. I won't live without him. I won't be denied. I won't let anyone come between us. Kevin can't have his cake and eat it too. He's mine—all mine! I'll kill that bitch that he was with today. Then, I'll kill his wife. Then he'll come back to me. Then he will understand. He has to. I just have to make things clear for him. He can't see me because of all the obstacles in our way. I just have to clear the obstacles, that's all, then we can be together.

"I'm coming baby! As soon as I get out of here, your woman will be home!"

This is what Yolanda said aloud in her cell as she waited to be transferred to Cook County Jail. Yolanda started praying in her cell. She asked God for a way out of her cage. She prayed for a way for her and Kevin to be together again. She was in jail four hours when she heard the footsteps against the concrete floor.

"Open up on seven!" A guard yelled.

"Yolanda Carter?"

"Yes?"

"You are being transferred to Johnson Park Hospital"

Yolanda smiled. She allowed herself to be handcuffed and transferred to the Hospital. She kept praying to God to help her escape her restraints. Four hours later, the door to her room was opened.

"Yolanda Carter?" An orderly asked.

"Yes?"

"You have been released into the custody of your clergy"

Yolanda looked to the heavens and said, "Thank You God"

She smiled as she exited the hospital.

KEVIN

"What do you mean she was released from prison?"

I was on the phone with Officer Sean Harrington, best friend of my childhood friend, Derrick Boyd. Sean was a cop with a lot of connections. He explained to me that Yolanda was released to Johnson Park Hospital.

"Well, can you confirm whether or not she is still at the hospital?"

Sean said, "She's not there either Kevin. She was released into the custody of her clergy. Apparently, she was hospitalized before and she was released into the custody of a Reverend Turner"

"Turner? What the hell is that about?"

"I don't know man, you want me to dig into him too?"

"Naw, thanks Sean. You have been a tremendous help. Thank you man"

"No problem"

I told Gladys that Yolanda was no longer in jail. Gladys seemed cool, calm and collected.

"Whose custody was she released into?"

"Reverend Turner, her boss and our so-called pastor"

"Why don't you and I pay him a visit?"

"Okay"

Gladys seemed to be like the chessmaster and we all seemed to be like pieces on a playing board.

"Kevin, how many times now has your paternity test been pushed back?"

"Twice, why?"

"Neither time you were the one to cancel the test, right?"

"That's right. Each time, Yolanda came up with some excuse not to make it"

"It's time that you called that bitch's bluff. Let's stop at your lawyer's office,"

"Yes ma'am"

We headed to my lawyer's office to compel Yolanda to take the paternity test today. We went from my lawyer's office, to see a judge, and then to the sheriff's office. From there we headed to the church and I was amazed at my mother in law's thinking process. As we drove to the church, I asked Gladys a question that was burning in my head.

"Gladys, how do you know Yolanda so well? I mean, how is it that you think just as devious as she thinks?"

"I was just like Yolanda when I was younger. I wasn't as mental as she is, but I did use the hell out of men and play a lot of games with men when I was younger. This bullshit that you are going through is just that, bullshit. There is also an old saying that comes to mind…"

"…Don't bullshit a bullshitter?" I interrupted.

"That's right. You can't outslick a can of oil. Baby, once upon a time, I was as slippery as they come"

We stopped at the church first to see Reverend Turner to get an explanation. Our next stop would be Yolanda's house. As we pulled up in front of the shelter, I saw Ruben, the homeless man that I had met earlier. He was raking leaves out front along with a number of the shelter's participants. They were making the lawn look nice and the children of the women were playing in the backyard of the shelter in the playground.

"Hey Ruben, how have things been going?"

He hugged me like we were old friends.

"They have been great my friend. Where is your lovely wife?"

"She's at home. This is her mother, Gladys"

"And she is every bit as stunning as her daughter"

Gladys blushed. She also smiled from ear to ear. Ruben cleaned up well. He looked good with his hair cut, nice crisp clothing and well trimmed beard. He looked like a new man.

"So what is it like living here?" I asked.

"Living here has been very rewarding for me Kevin. I have been helping the young ladies get their GED's, helped some to get into college, and I have been able to help others with life skills and employment skills. It's a trade off. They make me feel like a man should feel, and I make them feel how women should feel—respected"

"I'm glad everything is working out for you. Where is the Reverend?"

"He's in his office. He's not to be disturbed"

"Well, we are going to have to disturb his ass today. We have some questions that need to be answered. Is that his office?" I said as we walked quickly toward the building on the left, which was obviously the convent sleeping quarters.

"Kevin, really...he doesn't want to be disturbed right now. In fact, he told me to keep the women here busy for the next hour or so that way he could get some peace and quiet..."

"The hell with that Ruben. The good Reverend always seems to bug the shit out of me when I'm trying to relax. With as much money as I have given his ass over the years his ass needs to be on call"

"But Kevin..."

I walked up the stairs, Gladys was right behind me, as was my lawyer, a sheriff and a Chicago cop.

As I walked up to the door, it sounded like someone was trying to move furniture in the office. Initially, I thought that the Reverend was re-arranging his office. Then I heard heavy breathing like he was maybe having an asthma attack. It wasn't until I pushed the door open that I heard a woman's breathing.

"What the fuck!"

There was the good Reverend, in his collar, pants around his ankles, sweating his ass off and pounding away inside Yolanda on the desk. She was on her back, legs spread into a "V" and head leaning back over the edge of the desk.

"Oh my God, Kevin!"

"Kevin?" The Reverend said.

"What the fuck is going on here?" I said in a rather odd tone that surprised even me. There was a stunned feeling that came over me and for a second, I was jealous. I don't know if it was because I was seeing my ex sleep with another man, or if it was my hate for Reverend Turner.

Yolanda quickly got up off the table and started getting dressed. The good Reverend ducked behind his desk.

"Close the door!" He yelled.

Smiling, I slowly pulled the door up so that the two of them could get dressed.

"That's most likely the father of her child" Gladys said.

"Better him than me. Let's get this done to be sure"

The sheriff decided that the two of them had enough time to get dressed. He pushed the door open.

The sheriff said, "Yolanda Carter?"

"Yes?"

"Ma'am you will need to accompany us to Saint Mary's hospital. This is a court order compelling you to test for paternity"

Reverend Turner said, "Paternity?"

"Yeah, she's pregnant" I said.

"Or at least she said that she was pregnant" Gladys added.

"Ma'am, come with us. Mr. Allen, we will meet you at Saint Mary's"

Before they could get out of the door good, another sheriff arrived with a certified letter from my publisher.

"Yolanda Carter?"

"Yes. What the fuck is it now?"

"You have just been served"

"What?"

I said, "That letter is probably a letter from my publisher informing you that I copyrighted my book before you stole that copy from me. Your book deal…is off. You are also being sued for defamation of character, perjury, and falsifying documentation. There is also a charge of theft coming as well as criminal trespass"

"That's impossible. You had just finished the damned book when I made a copy!"

"You all heard that, right?" I said to the Sheriff and the officer.

"We will see you at the hospital"

They left and took Yolanda with them. Gladys and I turned around and that left us to deal with Reverend Turner. I turned around to face him.

"Kevin, I…"

SLAP!

I backhanded him like the bitch that he was.

"So here I am giving you money [SLAP] while you are bleeding my parents out of their retirement money [SLAP] always bugging the fuck out of me for money [SLAP] and here I am trying to be civil about my crazy ass bitch of an ex-girlfriend [SLAP] who stole my book [SLAP] burned down my fucking house [SLAP] ruined my marriage [SLAP] and has been trying to kill me, and not only are you fucking her, but you bailed her crazy ass out of jail?"

I pushed the good Reverend to the floor. His mouth was bloody and his face was swollen. I had wanted to kick his ass for some years now.

"You can't keep Yolanda locked up Kevin, she's sick"

"She's so sick, that she needs dick to make her all better?" Gladys said.

"I'm a pastor, not a priest. I haven't taken any vow of celibacy. Yolanda and I are in a relationship. We are two consenting adults"

"The bitch has been trying to kill me. If you are fucking her, that means that you are in on the shit too"

"I didn't know that she was pregnant. How could I know that she was trying to hurt you?"

"Save that shit! That bitch is going to jail. If I find out that you had anything to do with any of this shit, you are going with her ass!"

"I think he planned all this from the very beginning. I think that he planned it all, but didn't plan on Yolanda falling back in love with you" Gladys said.

"Let's go!" I said.

"Where?" Reverend Turner asked.

"We are going to see if I am this baby's father. If I am, I have some planning to do. If not, your ass will be getting tested next!"

"I'm not submitting to a paternity test! I…"

"…You will do it or I will round up every nigga that I know in the hood, and we will burn this motha fuckin church down tonight with your ass in it! Let's go!"

THE HOSPITAL

We got to Saint Mary's and out front was the Sherriff, the Cop, a Doctor, and a Nurse. They were all laughing and joking and as I pulled up with Gladys and the Reverend, the four of them seemed to be amused by the confused look on our faces.

"You guys did the paternity test that fast?"

"There was no need for a paternity test. She isn't pregnant"

"Are you sure?" I asked.

The doctor said, "I'm pretty sure"

"But I have an X-ray or a photo of the baby. She sent that shit along with the legal papers that came in the mail"

I went into the back of my car and pulled out the legal document and handed it to the doctor who looked up at it in the sun and laughed a little to himself. He handed the sheer photo the nurse who smiled also.

"This is someone else's photo. If you look at the canal here, whomever this photo belongs to, this person had three or four children. I don't think Ms. Carter had any. I'm sorry sir, you have been duped"

Stunned, I sat there with my mouth open. Gladys walked by and closed it for me.

"So where is Yolanda at now?" I asked.

"She left", the cop said.

"Left? How could you let her leave?"

"We just had orders to establish paternity. We had no right to detain her"

"So she's gone again, shit. She needs to be in either jail or a hospital" I said.

"Can't you just leave her alone?" Reverend Turner said.

"I'll leave her alone when the bitch leaves me and my family the fuck alone!"

I sat on my car frustrated as hell that Yolanda was getting away. I knew her. She was going to probably move from her apartment and disappear for a while. My biggest fear would be the minute that I relax, she will pop up and hurt someone that I love. I thought about the fact that Tamara could have been in the house when she set it on fire. She could have actually killed me when I was in La-La's house. Unchecked, Yolanda could bring my whole life crashing around my ears again. She was exposed now. This means that her shit is out there in the open now. She might feel vulnerable enough to strike us hard.

I looked at my mother in law with a look of defeat on my face.

"What do we do now?"

"Relax baby, the final phase of my plan hasn't even started yet"

YOLANDA

So I wasn't pregnant. So I faked a pregnancy. What woman hasn't done that before? There are a lot of women that would do what I did if they thought it could get them their man back. I was hoping that the Reverend would get me pregnant, but that little dicked MF could barely get it up, getting me pregnant seemed to be out of the question. He thought he was using me by helping to mastermind getting the twenty grand out of Kevin. I used him to get everything else that I needed, including that high ass bail to get me out of jail. I can still use the Reverend, and I intend to keep using him.

If I didn't know any better, I would say that Kevin was jealous to see me sleeping with another man. I know he still loves me. I know he wants me back. I just need to get that bitch Tamara out of my way. I'll get her out of the way, and I will tell Kevin that I forgive him for being with that tramp. Then, he will forgive me for sleeping with the pastor.

♦ CHAPTER THIRTEEN ♦
FINAL PHASE

KEVIN

Two weeks later I was putting on my tuxedo. I hated the idea of going to this fundraiser, but Gladys insisted that we go. My sister Meka was the DJ and I knew that she would be spinning some deep house after she finished spinning old Motown joints. That made me a little happy. What made me even happier was how stunning my wife looked in her black DKNY dress. It was all black, it had spaghetti straps, and it hugged the hell out of her hips and ass. The end of the dress was tapered with rhinestones. They ran all across the bottom of the dress and up and down the split. The dress showed off

Tamara's gorgeous legs. She had on some high heels that were black and suede. Her outfit was off the chain. Around her neck was a diamond necklace that I bought her for our first year wedding anniversary. In her ears were simple half carat round diamonds that sparkled beautifully as the light hit them. Her short wavy hair was cute as hell and her perfume got my manhood hard.

"Look at you. Damn I'm a lucky man. Baby, you look—stunning!"

Tamara smiled from ear to ear. Her pearly white teeth and dimples made me feel so special. Damn my woman is pretty. She looked so good that I wanted to take her somewhere and make love to her over and over again. I hugged Tamara and moved in to cuff her round ass. I kissed her on the neck and collarbone and began to nuzzle a little in her ear. I heard someone behind me clear their throat.

"Excuse us, don't you two get started" Gladys said.

"But look at her!" I replied"

Tamara was still smiling.

"Do you all remember the plan?" Gladys said.

"Yep" We said.

"Then let's get to it! I need to make a phone call and have a conversation with someone"

"Aren't you coming?" I asked Gladys.

"Yes, but your mother and I need to handle something first"

"Where are you two going?"

My mother said, "We're going to have a conversation with Claudette"

"Oh"

I took Tamara by the hand, and led her to the car so we could go to the event.

"Whose Claudette?" Tamara asked.

I pulled off and said, "Yolanda's mother"

YOLANDA

I could not believe that I was here at this damned fundraiser. My role as director was just a front so I could get close to Kevin. I could give less than a damn about these welfare bitches. If you asked me, they should have kept their legs closed, took their asses to school and stopped fucking around with trifling ass men. The only reason that I am here tonight is to see how much money gets raised tonight and try and figure out how I can use some of it to relocate. Shit is too hot right now in Chicago. I think I need to get some money and move out to the Carolinas. That way, I can deal with this bitch Tamara, on my own terms.

The fundraiser was being held in the gym of the shelter. The gym was large enough to accommodate a lot of people and at the same time put on quite a show. We had a number of things lined up for the night entertainment wise. We had Sean G, singing R & B hits. We had a number of comics, radio personalities, local celebrities, and a dynamic speaker, Darrin Lowery Smith acting as the host for the evening. We gave all of our benefactors awards for their contributions, gave awards to the radio personalities for giving back to the community, and we gave checks and awards to all of the women in the program so they could buy clothes to go on job interviews. After we finished with the formal part of the evening and a fabulous dinner, the music started and people began to dance. I don't know why we had to have Kevin's sister be the DJ. She didn't like me and I most certainly didn't care for her.

I was having a drink and almost choked on my wine as I saw Kevin walk into the gym. He looked so handsome in his black Pierre Cardin tuxedo. I saw him and almost ran to him and begged his forgiveness. Then I saw — her. Kevin had the nerve to bring his tramp ass bitch with him. I looked at her with contempt. I took a few steps backward near the refreshments so she could not see me. I looked her up and down checking her out with that ugly ass dress that she had on. That bitch thinks she's cute. I think I'm gonna have to just handle this shit woman to woman and beat her MF ass!

Kevin and Tamara slow danced one song right after the other. Damn that bitch of a sister of his. Does she have to keep playing slow cuts all fucking night? That's too close for the two of them to be dancing. I looked at Kevin and his whore and pictured that it wasn't Tamara in his arms, but it was me. I imagined that it was me that he was smiling to. I imagined that it was me that he was holding so close. I pictured that it was me that he was laughing with, and whispering sweet nothings to.

Always and Forever finally went off and I thought that Kevin and Tamara were going to take a break. Meka, his sister, then began playing steppers cuts. Chicago is serious about stepping, so instead of taking a break, Kevin grabbed Tamara by the hand as R. Kelly's Step In the Name of Love came on. I was mad as hell to see that Tamara didn't know how to step. Kevin was out on the dance floor teaching her. When he and I used to date, we used to step all the time.

"See, that bitch don't need to be with him, with her uncoordinated ass!" I said aloud.

Kevin kept trying to teach her, and pretty soon, she and he were out there stepping to cuts like Mindblowin, Who wants to be like the Joneses, and a shitload of JB's. Kevin's sister Meka started playing Papa Don't Take No Mess, Pass the Peas, JB Monorail, and The Big Payback. Kevin and Tamara worked up a sweat, but they never took a break. They just kept holding one another and kissing one another. What the fuck did they have to be happy about? If they think I ain't fin to burn they shit down in the Carolinas, they are mistaken.

Just then, Meka finally gave the audience a break and played some Al Green. Kevin and Tamara sat down for a minute to rest. My heart raced fast as I looked across the room in the gym and saw Kevin's other woman! She just walked in wearing a Navy Blue dress with pearls. She was on the other side of the room talking with a few people. When men saw her come in, they automatically intercepted her and tried to get her phone number. She declined them all and sat in the rear of the gym as a few men offered to get her something to drink.

God truly does love me. This is perfect! Kevin will get caught up in his own bullshit with these two bitches, and then Tamara will leave him. When she does, I will be free to pursue him!

I stood there glued to my spot on the wall watching the other woman as she talked with men that approached her.

Look, over there you stupid bitch! Look over there at Kevin. Damn! Why can't you see him? Why can't you see that he is here with another bitch? This is what I thought to myself as I stood there fuming. I then scanned the room for Kevin and Tamara, but Kevin was alone. I quickly looked for Tamara and a few seconds later, I noticed that she was walking into the ladies room.

"Perfect"

I saw this as an opportunity to finally confront this ho about my man!

MEETING IN THE LADIES ROOM (PART II)

I walked into the ladies room and there was Tamara in the mirror (figures) looking at her goddamned reflection with her conceited ass. She looked up at me and was shocked to see me. I looked at her with contempt at first, but then I ignored her. I stood beside her and looked at my own reflection in the mirror. I began to check my makeup.

Tamara's ass was just as big as mine, but mine was more round. My breasts were bigger than hers also. I had long free flowing hair, and this bitch had a short cropped cut. She was cute, but she wasn't fine. Niggas are willing to give me anything that I ask for. All the ballers, corporate brothas, playas and even other women beg me for a taste of this. Tamara was cute. Me? I'm music video beautiful, and baby, this bitch needs to recognize that shit.

"Let's just cut the shit. I don't know what the fuck it is that Kevin sees in your ass"

"You don't need to see it. As long as he does, that's all that counts"

"Yeah, well you ain't won this shit yet. As far as I can see, I still have the advantage" I said.

"Really? And just how do you figure that?"

"I know that not a day goes by that you don't think about him fucking me. That shit is going to be with your ass forever"

"Maybe for an insecure woman it might be, but that's not me. Besides, you all had your one night or two, but I'm his WIFE, and bitch—that means forever"

"Yeah, well that means that I will be fuckin with ya'll forever, cause I ain't goin no where!"

"Is that so?"

"Yeah, bitch that's right. I ought to kick yo country ass right here in this bathroom"

"Don't talk about it Yolanda, be about it!"

I took a step backward. I was expecting Tamara to back down, but she looked like she was ready to give her all to fight for her man. I didn't want to be the cause of the drama this time, so I backed down some and decided to play my trump card.

"I would fight your little country ass, but I got something better in mind"

"Yeah, well bitch what do you plan on pulling next? Whatever it is, I'm ready for your ignorant ass!"

"Kevin's other bitch is here!"

"Kevin doesn't have another bitch"

"Oh yeah he does. He has you and me and then there is this other bitch in the gym that just walked in. She's got long hair and she has a body that's better than yours and mine put together. I saw him with that bitch the other day. He bought her clothes, he bought her jewelry, and he took her to a Motel and fucked her for about two hours. I know, because I tried to set his ass ablaze when I found out about that shit!"

"You are a lying bitch!"

"Fuck You! I don't have to lie to you. Take your ass out there and ask her"

"What does she look like?"

"Bitch, I just told you. She is in a Navy Blue dress, she got long hair, a big ass and she is a little lighter than me"

Just then, the woman that I was talking about walked into the ladies room. I was shocked.

"That's her! This is the woman that I am talking about! This is Kevin's Other Woman!"

"Hello, you don't know me, but my name is Yolanda. This is Kevin Allen's wife. I bet you didn't know that he had a wife. I know this is kind of messed up to ask, but weren't you with Kevin the other day at a Motel?"

"Yes...Yes I was"

I turned around to face Tamara.

"See bitch! I told you!"

I then heard the bathroom door lock. I turned around, and the woman in the navy blue dress had took off her shoes. I turned around and Tamara had stepped out of her shoes. One of the bathroom stalls opened up and the woman that jumped me at the hotel that day stepped out and smiled at me. Overhead, I could hear house music blaring loud. I tried to yell for help, but the music was so loud that no one could hear me.

"Yolanda, these are my sisters. Now what was that shit that you were talking about a few minutes ago?"

"Oh shit"

"That's right bitch, Oh shit"

KEVIN

Before the house music started playing, my sister Joy put a sign across the ladies bathroom that said out of order. Meka then played house music really loud over the speakers. The joints that she played, all had hard beats to them and a lot of bass. Women that had to go to the bathroom were directed to go to the building next door. I felt sorry for Yolanda and what was obviously happening in the bathroom, but she brought that shit on herself. About 10:30, Gladys came in with my mother, Yolanda's mother, my childhood friend, Dr. David Allen, and some paramedics. The music stopped as they walked into the gym.

"Where are they?" Gladys asked.

I pointed to the ladies room.

Gladys walked in and screamed, "That's enough!"

Trina, Tamara, Betty and Gladys asked the paramedics to come into the bathroom. Yolanda needed medical attention. My wife and her sisters, whipped Yolanda's ass for old and new like the old folks used to say.

I asked David, "What are you doing here?"

He said, "Having Yolanda committed"

"Good, that bitch is crazy"

"Kevin, she's sick. Her father molesting her, truly did a number on her psychologically"

"Will she ever be normal again?"

"Who knows?"

"What set her off?"

"Probably your dumbass. You slept with her?"

"She pursued me"

"Didn't she hit your ass with a car back in the day?"

"Yeah, that was a long time ago"

"So the fact that she hit you with a car didn't send any bells and whistles blowing off in your head while she was pursuing you?"

"Not at the time"

"It sounds like your ass needs some therapy too"

"Naw, I just need some marriage counseling"

"I do that also"

"Really? How much do you charge?"

" 300. 00 an hour"

"Damn!"

We both smiled at David's success.

"So what will happen to her now?"

"Now, we put the pieces back together again, one day at a time. Like I said, she's sick"

"Sick my ass. That bitch is still crazy!"

"Did you hear what happened to Big Slim?"

"No, what?"

"That brother is in County Hospital. He has cancer"

"Damn. For real?"

"Yeah. In the morning, we should go over and see him"

"Let's do that. Come scoop me in the morning"

Yolanda's wounds were tended to and she was strapped onto the gurney. She was then taken to Johnson Park Hospital where her mother signed paperwork to have her institutionalized. I sat down in a chair as Yolanda kept screaming my name over and over again. Emotionally and psychologically she was a wreck.

THE NEXT DAY

The next day I went to the hospital with David to see Big Slim. Apparently, when he was missing from the hood, he was getting treatment from the Cancer. When he was drinking heavily, it was to help medicate the pain. The money that he hustled playing basketball, was to help support his girlfriend and child on the west side of town that no one knew about. He was happy to see David and I when we went to the hospital. He was also embarrassed at our having to see him in such a weakened state.

"Hey, Kevin, David how are ya'll players doin?"

"We're okay man, how are you?"

"Man, I'm fine. I've beaten this shit before, I'mma beat it again"

"That's cool. In no time you will be back on the basketball court"

"Naw, not this time Kevin. My days of playin ball are over. When I get out of the hospital this time, I'mma just spend time with my girl and my son. Ain't no telling how much longer I got. I need to spend that time wisely"

A silence fell over the room. It was hard seeing Big Slim like this, but he was right.

"Anyway, I didn't know that you wrote books man. Why didn't you say something?"

"That's not the type of information that you share in the hood Slim"

"I guess you're right. The hood has always been proud of you Sangamon boys. You all really did your parents proud"

"Slim whatever happened to your parents?" David asked.

"My dad got killed trying to rob a liquor store, and my moms is out there on drugs"

"Do you have any family?" I asked.

"Just this boy that I have, and my son's mother"

"I'm sorry to hear that Slim" I said.

"Don't be. I made the mess that I call my life, and I can live with the consequences of my actions, which is a lot more than most people can say. So listen, I heard you had some drama with that woman you used to mess with. I heard she tried to kill your ass on quite a few occasions"

"Yeah, she did"

"Here's my question, how come you slept with her in the first place? Didn't she try to run your ass over with a car or something when we were all younger?"

"Everybody keeps bringing that up"

"Motha fucka, it's a relevant point!"

We all laughed.

"Why would you sleep with a crazy bitch?" Slim asked.

"She was fine"

"Okay, so why would you sleep with a fine crazy bitch?"

We all laughed again there in the hospital bed. We talked shit, told jokes and tripped hard with one another.

A month later, Big Slim, my friend, was dead.

I started writing a book in his honor. I'm calling it, The Life of Big Slim. 50% of the proceeds will go to cancer research. The other 50% will go to his baby's mother and his son.

HELL AND BRIMSTONE

It was a humid August Sunday and my wife and I were back in Chicago listening to the Good Reverend Turner's sermon. He preached that day about faith, infidelity and giving in to life's temptations. He talked about the sins of man. He talked about the sins of today's celebrities and then he talked about the sins in his congregation. He yelled, pounded his fist, screamed and told the entire congregation that they must be—born again. After his very moving sermon, he told people to dig deep into their pockets. He told them to give from the heart, not from the head. He told them to be wary of being cheap because they might be able to cheat him—but they can't cheat God.

I told him earlier that Sunday that I had an announcement to make in regard to the welfare to work program and I had one other announcement that I wanted to make. As they passed around the collection plate, Reverend Turner asked me to take the microphone to make my announcement. I took the microphone and I addressed the audience.

"Givin honor to God, the Pastor, and the church. You all know me as Kevin Allen the writer and the son of Sister and Brother Allen. I came here because many of you all have asked me to make an announcement that has been long coming. This message is for you Reverend Turner. I have met with the board, the members and the benefactors of the welfare to work program. By the bi-laws and the majority vote of the members, deacons and mothers of the church, we respectfully have decided that you are no longer what we are looking for to shepherd this flock. Your services are no longer needed, today's collection has been cancelled, and that sermon that you just preached, is your last. Taking over the duties as pastor is the assistant pastor, Reverend Jenkins. Taking over as Director of the welfare to work Program is our good friend, Brother Ruben"

The church erupted with applause. Reverend Turner was stunned.

"He's a homeless man! He's not qualified to create that program! I created that program!"

"He's more than qualified, which is more than I can say for you. Reverend Turner, your things have already been packed. Please leave before I forget I'm a Christian and get that ass in front of the congregation" The good reverend saw that I was serious, and scornfully left the church that day. He left in his $ 58,000 truck and God knows how much money that he scammed the parishioners out of. He will no doubt take his act on the road and take the reigns of another church somewhere else.

EPILOGUE

Yolanda got the help that she needed and remained hospitalized. Her mother visits with her regularly. Kevin and Tamara went back to their home in Somerton. Kevin got a four book-twelve million dollar deal. He and Tamara began re-decorating their house and working hard on their marriage. If Kevin needed to go to

Still Crazy

Chicago to get inspiration to write, he took Tamara with him. The sisters went back to their lives, as did Gladys and George. Joy took the job In New York. Kevin was going to start his own publishing company, but he decided it could wait. He cut Adrienne the bartender a check for $100,000. David Allen went back to his private practice, and Kitty—had Kevin's baby. She moved to Indiana to have his baby and told no one. We may see her again. Tamara never told Kevin of her almost fling with her ex-Keith. She felt that was something that she needed to keep to herself. La-La became a prostitute and her pimp, Darrin and his top girl, Honey will be spoken of again…very soon.

A FEW MONTHS LATER
KEVIN

So here I am again in bed, and I am having another sleepless night. I look over at Tamara who is somehow sleeping fine. I am walking around my house and wondering how is it that I managed to get and keep such a wonderful woman. I walked downstairs, started cutting on lights and turned on ESPN. I watched Sports Center and popped some popcorn. I started to write, but I wasn't feeling it right now. I stayed up watching TV all night and by the time that Tamara was ready to go to work, I was ready to go back to sleep. Tamara decided to quit her job. She told me that she wanted to go to cooking school and I told her that I thought it was wonderful that she was switching careers. Today, was her last day and it was the day that her co-workers decided to throw her the mother of all parties with teachers and students alike. I promised her I would be there about 3:45 to help her celebrate. Because I had been up all night, I hurried up and took my ass to bed the minute she was out the door. For whatever reason, I could sleep during the day, but I had challenges sleeping at night.

I went back to bed and was awaked a few hours later by our front doorbell. I got up feeling groggy and I walked down to the door, opened it, and was fully awake when I saw what was left at my doorstep. There was a baby almost a full year old. A pretty little boy about a month or two old.

"What the fuck?"

I rushed out into the yard to see if I could find out who left the baby at my doorstep. About a half block away, I swear that I thought I saw a woman run off. I left the baby where it was and ran toward the woman in my robe. One of my neighbors was watering his grass and I asked him to watch my house to make sure no one broke in. I didn't even pick up the baby who to my surprise, was not crying at all.

"Hey! Hey you, come here!"

The woman ran down the street and I gave chase in barefeet. Granted, I live in a rich area, but a black man chasing a black woman in his robe in a very affluent neighborhood, doesn't go over well.

A block and a half later, SPD stopped the woman that I was chasing and they stopped me too. She was placed in one squad car, I was placed in another.

"What is going on here?" A white cop asked.

"That woman left a baby on my doorstep"

"A baby? You mean like an infant?"

"No, like a fucking bearcub, of course an infant!"

The officer didn't appreciate my sarcasm.

"And you just left the baby there?"

"I didn't want the baby. What the hell am I going to do with a baby?"

"Leaving it on the porch is neglect"

"It's not neglect if it's not mine" I said. The one cop asked me to sit peacefully in his car. I was not under arrest, or held against my will. The cop told the man that caught the woman what I said and the two officers stopped to confer with one another. A few minutes later, the cop whose car I was in came back and started up the squad car that I was sitting in.

"You're Kevin Allen, right? The author?"

"Yeah, that's me"

"Mr. Allen, we are going to drive back to your house to sort all this out. By the way, the woman in the other car, the mother, she says that the baby is yours"

"I'm sorry, what?"

We got back to my place where my white neighbors (who I never spoke to before today) were caring for the infant that was left on my porch.

"Damned irresponsible for you to run off like that", my neighbor said.

"I'm sorry. I didn't know what else to do"

"You should have maybe called the police"

"Right. Whatever. Anyway, thank you for your help"

The other squad car pulled up and the woman pulled out of the car had on a navy blue hoodie. The closer and closer she got to my home, the more I began to recognize her. It was Kitty, from the shelter.

"Aw shit"

"Mr. Allen, do you know this woman?"

"I do"

"Is that your baby?"

"No sir. This woman, like another woman in Chicago that I had an order of protection from, is most likely trying to extort money from me"

"Extort money? I have never asked you for a thing, not one fucking thing!"

Now our situation was looking like domestic violence.

"Kitty, what are you doing here and why are you leaving a child of all things at my doorstep?"

"I was hoping that you would take care of him. By the way, the child's name is Noah. He's your son!"

"Let's just say for one second that I believe you, which I don't because Yolanda tried to pull this exact same bullshit, why leave the child with me rather than try and hit me up nasty for child support?"

"I don't need your fucking support! I don't need any handouts! I can take care of myself, but babies need pampers, formula and a whole lot of shit that I can't afford, but you can!"

"This is not the Bank of Allen and I am not a goddamned ATM machine! If you can't handle a baby, why didn't you abort? If this is my son, why haven't you said anything to me about it?"

"Yolanda threatened to kill me, that's why!"

"So you do know this woman intimately?" A cop asked.

"I did"

"Would you mind explaining to me what happened?"

I retold the entire story about Yolanda. I even told the cops that Kitty and I and Yolanda had an affair. The cops seemed to get off on hearing that shit. Kitty was now 21, and ready to move on with her life and she was ready to do it minus the baby. She told the cops that the baby was mine and she was hoping that I would do the right thing and take care of the child and give it the life that she could not give it. As she went on with her story, I was pissed off to see that Tamara's ex, Keith was driving up in a moving van, and moving in across the street from us.

"There goes the neighborhood" I said as he smiled at me, gave me the universal head nod, and started moving his things in.

"I know that nigga can't afford to live here, what the hell is he doing across the street from us?"

I seemed preoccupied with Keith, and the white cops didn't appreciate that shit one bit. In fact they seemed put out by lack of empathy for the child or Kitty. What they didn't understand was that I was tired of drama, tired of bullshit, and ready to move forward with my life.

"Mr. Allen, there is one way that we can dispel all this chaos. If all parties are willing, we can go to Saint John's, up the street and get a paternity test done"

"It's cool with me"

"It's fine by me also"

We went to Saint John's Hospital.

Two hours later, I was a confirmed father.

Tamara was having her goodbye party and wondering where the hell I was.

Kitty didn't want the baby, I didn't know what I wanted, but I knew that I didn't want to subject my wife to any more drama. I was in a bad place. It also looked like things were about to get worse for me. I was in a daze and confused. I didn't know what my next move would be. I just stood there in the hospital stunned and the news of my being a new father.

"Mr. Allen? Mr. Allen? Sir, what would you like for us to do?"

"She tried to abandon her baby on my step, that's neglect on her part. In reference to the baby, I don't know. What are my options?"

"Sir, I think we should call children's services"

Someone in the sheriff's department called Children's Services and the child was placed into the temporary custody of the state until I could figure out what it was that I was going to do. The caseworker asked was I giving up my rights, putting the baby up for adoption, or asking the state to keep the baby until I was able to complete the relative adoption papers. I asked that they keep the baby until I met with my lawyer to begin the adoption proceedings. That bought me some time. When I left the hospital, Tamara's party had been underway over an hour. I am sure that she was fuming that I was not there.

When I exited the hospital, I was met by six or seven local newspaper reporters. One of the cops called the press. I was pissed. The press had already talked with my neighbor who I asked to watch my house as I chased Kitty down the street. The neighbors had already given an exaggerated account of what happened earlier. Let them tell it, there was a domestic violence situation with my "baby's momma" she left, and I gave chase down the street leaving our child crying on the porch. Reportedly, I was so distraught that I looked disheveled as I chased her in my bathrobe and bare feet.

Then came the news that I was putting my baby in the state, which made me the most cruel person in the world and yet another black man shirking his responsibility. I kept screaming no comment to the reporters as they hassled the shit out of me. I jumped in my car and went home.

TAMARA

I was trying to enjoy my last day at work and I was wondering where the hell my husband was once the party had started. I hated the fact that my answer came via, one of my co-workers turning on the TV and local media was at a hospital questioning my husband about a baby. I couldn't even enjoy my party when I saw that shit. A silence fell over the room as we all listened to the press' accounts of what happened at my home in my absence.

When the reporters referred to Kevin's "baby's mother" I thought this was some more bullshit with Yolanda. When they showed the woman, I put two and two together and assumed that this was the other woman that Kevin slept with. I gathered my things at the office, said my goodbyes and headed home. At least I will not have to face any questions at work tomorrow, because today is my last day.

I got home around 5:30. When I got there, Kevin was just sitting there in the living room of our newly designed house. He sat there in silence. I know he was at a loss for words. I told myself that he and I had come too far to end our relationship. I told myself that this was just one more hurdle that I needed to get over in my marriage. Once again though, Kevin brought shame to our home. I love my man, but I am so tired of the bullshit, ya know?

I was just about to sit across from my husband and talk with him. I was ready to listen to him and later comfort him and together, try and figure out our next step in this whole mess. Just as I walked into the living room to speak, the doorbell rang. I stopped, turned around, and looked through the doorway thinking that it was a reporter. To my surprise, it was Keith.

My heart sank as I waved him off hoping, praying that he would leave. He wouldn't. He kept ringing the bell and kept knocking until I thought Kevin was going to get up any minute and see what all the commotion was about. I was furious. I opened the door.

"Can I help you? What do you want?"

"Did you tell Mr. Chicago about us?"

"There is no us! Please leave!"

"Did you tell him what happened between us!" He said loudly.

By now, Kevin was standing. Kevin was headed toward the door. I stepped toward Kevin to intercept him, and Keith walked all the way in the house. The three of us stood there for a minute in silence.

"What are you doing here?" Kevin asked.

"I came back for my lady" Keith said.

"Motha fucka what?"

I thought to myself, Now I have brought shame to our house. What do I do?

Keith said, "Tell him or I will"

Still Crazy

"Tell me what Tamara?"

"Kevin, have a seat. Baby, I have something to tell you"

I took in a deep breath, closed my eyes, and began to speak.

To be continued……………..The End.

"Wild Thangz"
DESCRIPTION

Jazmyn, Trina and Brea are young & fine with bangin' bodies and are in the midst of their sexual peak.

As they explore different paths towards their own individual goals in life, these drama-magnets learn invaluable lessons from experience and each other.

Lust, temptation and greed test the limits of their friendship bond.

It is what they have in common that leads the trio repeatedly into all kinds of trouble.

Wild Parties, Wild Situations & Wild Nights are always present for these Wild Thangz!

"Wild Thangz is HOT! Winstson Chapman shonuff brings the HEAT!" -- Mysterious Luva, Essence Magazine Best-Selling Author of "Sex A Baller"

BRAND NEW!
From **BLACK PEARL BOOKS**

ISBN: 0-9728005-1-4
www.BlackPearlBooks.com

"Sex A Baller"
DESCRIPTION

Mysterious Luva has sexed them all! Ball players, CEO's, Music Stars -- You name the baller, she's had them. And more importantly, she's made them all pay......

Sex A Baller is a poignant mix of a sexy tale of how Mysterious Luva has become one of the World's Best Baller Catchers and an Instructional Guide for the wanna-be Baller Catcher!

No details or secrets are spared, as she delivers her personal story along with the winning tips & secrets for daring women interested in catching a baller!

PLUS, A SPECIAL BONUS SECTION INCLUDED!

Baller Catching 101

- Top-20 Baller SEX POSITIONS (Photos!)
- Where To FIND A Baller
- Which Ballers Have The BIGGEST Penis
- SEDUCING A Baller
- Making A Baller Fall In Love
- Getting MONEY From A Baller
- What Kind Of SEX A Baller Likes
- The EASIEST Type of Baller To Catch
- Turning A Baller Out In Bed
- GAMES To Play On A Baller
- Getting Your Rent Paid & A Free Car
- Learn All The SECRETS!

BY THE END OF THIS BOOK, YOU'LL HAVE YOUR CERTIFIED BALLER-CATCHER'S DEGREE!

"CAUGHT UP!" DESCRIPTION

When Raven Klein, a bi-racial woman from Iowa moves to Atlanta in hopes of finding a life she's secretly dreamed about, she finds more than she ever imagined.

Quickly lured and lost in a world of sex, money, power-struggles, betrayal & deceit, Raven doesn't know who she can really trust!

A chance meeting at a bus terminal leads to her delving into the seedy world of strip-clubs, big-ballers and shot-callers.

Now, Raven's shuffling through more men than a Vegas blackjack dealer does a deck of cards. And sex has even become mundane -- little more than a tool to get what she wants.

After a famous acquaintance winds-up dead -- On which shoulder will Raven lean? A wrong choice could cost her life!

There's a reason they call it HOTATLANTA!

BRAND NEW!
From **BLACK PEARL BOOKS**

ISBN: 0-9728005-5-7
www.BlackPearlBooks.com

"Slick"
DESCRIPTION

Dana & Sylvia have been girlfriends for what seems like forever. They've never been afraid to share everything about their lives and definitely keep each other's secrets ... including hiding Dana's On-The-DL affair from her husband, Jonathan.

Though Sylvia is uncomfortable with her participation in the cover-up and despises the man Dana's creepin' with, she remains a loyal friend. That is, until she finds herself attracted to the very man her friend is deceiving.

As the lines of friendship and matrimonial territory erodes, all hell is about to break loose! Choices have to be made with serious repercussions at stake.

If loving you is wrong, I don't wanna be right!

"SLICK!!! .... Ain't That The Truth! Brenda Hampton's Tale Sizzles With Sensuality, Deception, Greed and So Much Drama – My Gurrll!"

- MYSTERIOUS LUVA, BEST-SELLING AUTHOR OF *SEX A BALLER*

"HYPED" DESCRIPTION

Maurice LaSalle is a player – of women and the saxophone. A gifted musician, he's the driving force behind MoJazz, a neo-soul group on the verge of their big break. Along with his partner in rhyme and crime, Jamal Grover, Maurice has more women than he can count. Though guided by his mentor Simon, Maurice knows Right but constantly does Wrong.

Then Ebony Stanford enters Maurice's world and he begins to play a new tune. Ebony, still reeling from a nasty divorce, has just about given up on men, but when Maurice hits the right notes (everywhere) she can't help but fall for his charms.

While Maurice and Ebony get closer, Jamal is busy putting so many notches on his headboard post after each female conquest, that the post looks more like a tooth-pick. When a stalker threatens his life, Maurices warns him to slow his roll, but Jamal's hyped behavior prevails over good sense.

Just as Maurice is contemplating turning in his player card for good, stupidity overrules his judgment and throws his harmonious relationship with Ebony into a tale-spin. When it appears that things couldn't get any worse, tragedy strikes and his life is changed forever!

A Powerfully-Written Sexy-Tale, *HYPED* is a unique blend of Mystery, Suspense, Intrigue and Glowing-Sensuality.

"Buckle Up! HYPED Will Test All Of Your Senses and Emotions! LUKE Is A Force To Be Reckoned With For Years To Come!" -- WINSTON CHAPMAN, ESSENCE MAGAZINE BEST-SELLING AUTHOR OF "CAUGHT UP!" AND "WILD THANGZ"

"TWISTED" DESCRIPTION

Nadine, a sultry, ghetto-fine conniving gold-digger, will do whatever it takes to make sure that she is financially set for life -- even at the cost of breaking-up a family.

When Wayne, Nadine's man since high-school, is sentenced to two years in prison for a crime he did not commit, he's betrayed by the two people he trusted the most—his woman (Nadine) and his cousin (Bobo).

Asia, a curvaceous diva and designer-clothing boutique owner with a wilder-side sexual-preference becomes an unlikely confidant to her best-friend Nadine's man (Wayne) during his incarceration.

Meanwhile Bobo, one of VA's most notorious and most successful Street-Entreprenuers, manages to hustle his way into staring down a possible life sentence.

Now that the roles are reversed, it's Bobo who's now facing some serious prison time, as Nadine tries to do whatever it takes to keep her hands on the secret stash of cash hidden in a suitcase that Bobo left behind.

Money, greed and sex always have as a way of gettin' things **Twisted!**

"Daaaaayummmmmm! Holland Jones brings it! A hood-licious story that combines deceit, murder, freaky sex and mysterious-twists! You gotta get this one!"

-- Winston Chapman, Best-Selling Author of *Caught Up!* and *Wild Thangz*

Black Pearl Books

Get In The Mood!

www.BlackPearlBooks.com

Your Best Source For HOT & SEXY URBAN STORIES!

JOIN THE E-MAIL LIST!
New Releases, Specials & Free Giveaways

On-Line Ordering:
www.Amazon.com

AUTHORS:
Interested In Being Published By Black Pearl Books Inc.?

Send Synopsis Cover Letter
& (Non-Returnable) Full-Manuscript To:
Black Pearl Books
3653-F Flakes Mill Road ■ PMB 306
Atlanta, Georgia 30034

* Review Process Takes About 3-4 weeks *

BLACK PEARL BOOKS PUBLISHING

Your Best Source For
Hot & Sexy Urban Stories

LOOK FOR THIS LOGO – For Quality Urban Books!

WWW.BLACKPEARLBOOKS.COM

JOIN OUR E-MAIL LIST
FOR NEW RELEASES,
SPECIALS & FREE
GIVEAWAYS!!

Black Pearl Books Publishing

Get In The Mood!

www.BlackPearlBooks.com

Visit Darrin's Website

www.DarrinLoweryBooks.com

To Order Additional Copies Of Black Pearl Books Titles:

On-Line Ordering:
www.Amazon.com

Authors:
Interested In Being Published By Black Pearl Books Inc.?

Send Synopsis Cover Letter
& (Non-Returnable) Manuscripts To:

Black Pearl Books, Inc.
Attention: Editor
3653-F Flakes Mill Rd ▪ PMB 306
Atlanta, Georgia 30034

Review Process Takes About 3-4 weeks

BLACK PEARL BOOKS INC.

ORDER FORM

Black Pearl Books Inc.
3653-F Flakes Mill Road- PMB 306
Atlanta, Georgia 30034
www. BlackPearlBooks. com

YES, We Ship Directly To Prisons & Correctional Facilities
INSTITUTIONAL CHECKS & MONEY ORDERS ONLY!

TITLE	Price	Quantity	TOTAL
"Caught Up!" by Winston Chapman	$ 14. 95		
"Sex A Baller" by Mysterious Luva	$ 12. 95		
"Wild Thangz" by Winston Chapman	$ 14. 95		
"Crunk" by Bad Boyz	$ 14. 95		
"Hustlin Backwards" by Mike Sanders	$ 14. 95		
"Still Crazy" by Darrin Lowery	$ 14. 95		
"Twisted" by Holland Jones	$ 14. 95		
Sub-Total		$	
SHIPPING: ___ # books x $ 3. 50 ea. (Via US Priority Mail)		$	
GRAND TOTAL		$	

SHIP TO:

Name: _____

Address: _____

Apt or Box #: _____

City: _____   State: _____   Zip: _____

Phone: _____   E-mail: _____